About the

As an academic in the field of English Literature, Matt worked in both the UK and the US, authoring a monograph, *Milton and Modernity: Politics, Masculinity and 'Paradise Lost'* (Basingstoke: Macmillan, 2000). He has been a member of the Labour Party since he was 18, and his politics belong to the mainstream of British social democracy. He has demonstrated against a lot of things, including the Iraq War.

Remarks concerning Matt Jordan:

'The most frightening person I have ever known.' – Liam Byrne, MP

'You're never going to write for *The Sun,* are you, Matt?' – Peter Mandelson

'Like Morrissey, a man, but funnier.' – Margaret Kean, St Hilda's College, Oxford

NEW TIMES

NEW TIMES

MATT JORDAN

Unbound Digital

This edition first published in 2018

Unbound

6th Floor Mutual House, 70 Conduit Street, London W1S 2GF

www.unbound.com

All rights reserved

© Matt Jordan, 2018

The right of Matt Jordan to be identified as the author of this work has been asserted in accordance with Section 77 of the Copyright, Designs and Patents Act 1988. No part of this publication may be copied, reproduced, stored in a retrieval system, or transmitted, in any form or by any means without the prior permission of the publisher, nor be otherwise circulated in any form of binding or cover other than that in which it is published and without a similar condition being imposed on the subsequent purchaser.

This book is a work of fiction and, except in the case of historical fact, any resemblance to actual persons, living or dead, is purely coincidental.

ISBN (eBook): 978-1-912618-77-4

ISBN (Paperback): 978-1-912618-76-7

Printed and bound in Great Britain by Clays Ltd, Elcograf S.p.A.

Dear Reader,

The book you are holding came about in a rather different way to most others. It was funded directly by readers through a new website: Unbound.

Unbound is the creation of three writers. We started the company because we believed there had to be a better deal for both writers and readers. On the Unbound website, authors share the ideas for the books they want to write directly with readers. If enough of you support the book by pledging for it in advance, we produce a beautifully bound special subscribers' edition and distribute a regular edition and e-book wherever books are sold, in shops and online.

This new way of publishing is actually a very old idea (Samuel Johnson funded his dictionary this way). We're just using the internet to build each writer a network of patrons. Here, at the back of this book, you'll find the names of all the people who made it happen.

Publishing in this way means readers are no longer just passive consumers of the books they buy, and authors are free to write the books they really want. They get a much fairer return too – half the profits their books generate, rather than a tiny percentage of the cover price.

If you're not yet a subscriber, we hope that you'll want to join our publishing revolution and have your name listed in one of our books in the future. To get you started, here is a £5 discount on your first pledge. Just visit unbound.com, make your pledge and type NEWTIMES18 in the promo code box when you check out.

Thank you for your support,

Dan, Justin and John
Founders, Unbound

With grateful thanks to Vera Baird for helping to make this book happen.

Super Patrons

Timothy Bewes
Duncan Chapple
Ian Cropper
Derek Draper
S Godden
Elspeth Graham
David Llewellyn
Susan McCafferty
Edward Porter
Ed Ryland
Tom Sheahan
Barry Stuart
Nadia Tuercke
Joseph Wittreich
Jo Wood

Son: And must they all be hanged that swear and lie?
Lady Macduff: Every one.
Son: Who must hang them?
Lady Macduff: Why, the honest men.
– William Shakespeare, *Macbeth*

Contents

Chapter 1	1
'It's alright, I told him I was a lesbian'	
Chapter 2	11
'I plan to romp and stomp like a horse'	
Chapter 3	23
'Are you serious?'	
Chapter 4	31
'Feminism and your ego are not coterminous'	
Chapter 5	39
'New Labour New Coffee'	
Chapter 6	49
'Opium is the opium of the people'	
Chapter 7	59
'She wants me to put up shelves!'	
Chapter 8	71
'That's differently interesting'	
Chapter 9	83
'First Iraq and now this!'	
Chapter 10	95
'Informed choices without explicit thought'	
Chapter 11	103
'The face of a malevolent hamster'	
Chapter 12	113
'Hysterical people who aren't very good at reasoning'	
Chapter 13	125
'A vast conspiracy of death'	
Chapter 14	135
'Women are so difficult to work'	

Chapter 15   143
'People, you may find,
are not universal sockets!'
Chapter 16   151
'A sort of dismally failing Son
in the wilderness'
Chapter 17   159
'A lower deep still threatens'
Chapter 18   169
'A name to put on flyers'
Chapter 19   177
'The vast herd of independent minds'
Chapter 20   187
'A quiet inglorious Milton'
Chapter 21   191
'The futility of all human endeavour, especially his'

New Thanks   201
Patrons   203

Chapter 1
'It's alright, I told him I was a lesbian'

March 1988

When John Somerville Beaumont built Manchester University Students' Union, he wasn't mucking about, and he didn't mind if you knew it. A free-standing rectangular block of red brick with a facade of grey concrete, it was the kind of place that might have served one of the more routine divisions of a secret police force as a headquarters. It was much in this spirit that, a few decades later, a leather-jacketed Marxist–Leninist was engaged in ad-hoc enforcement of ideological discipline with the help of one of the building's second-floor windows. From it, he was dangling a scrawny youth who, with considerable presence of mind, was threatening legal action in urgent Lancashire tones.

Bewildered, but at least on the correct side of the glass, sat Brian Harper, over whose left shoulder most of the young man had left the building: first a gaping, whitened, soundless face, then saggy light-blue polo shirt and jeans. Whether greying trainers, some eighteen inches north-west of Brian's nose, would follow seemed an open question. He had chosen to sit right at the back of the room in order to get a better look at things, but things, it seemed, had sought him out just the same. He had previously sounded impressive to himself as he expressed doubts about whether student politics were serious enough to bother with, but all of a sudden at this, his first meeting of the Manchester University Labour Club, it was looking as though they might be a matter of life and death.

Not before time, a female voice cut through the confusion.

'Sean!! Put Alan down!!'

Started from his befuddlement, Brian rose and turned and wrestled himself a bit more than a half share of Alan, and pulled him in to safety.

'Alan! What do you expect if you *will* be so *silly*?'

Brian allowed himself a full glance at the source of the voice at the front of the room, conscious of all the faces turned toward the back of it. A statuesque woman with golden blonde hair and large dark eyes, she had her arm round the shoulders of a shorter girl.

'And you shouldn't go around scaring young women. Look at poor Colleen!' – the young woman whose long dark hair she was now stroking – '...and in any case, what on earth do *you* know about Ireland?'

Pausing for a moment to accept a proffered can of Diet Coke, take a sip and hand it back with a 'Thanks, hon,' she proceeded to restore order.

'Alan, you sit down there' – she pointed at a seat in the corner next to Brian – 'and Sean, you come and sit here, next to me.'

Sean needed no second asking, but Alan replied, in a voice of complaint, 'Maria!'

His resistance lasted no longer than it took him to register the admonitory look that was its reward. He slumped into the chair next to Brian. Brian had received one piece of paternal advice about university – as he and his father drove through the streets of East Manchester and his father remarked, in a tone that suggested he was reassuring himself as much as his son, 'Well, you can still tell it's England, can't you?' – and that had been: 'Don't get into arguments about Ireland, whatever anyone says to you.' Now he was further discomfited.

''Ere mate' – the fellow called Alan had leant slightly toward him – 'what do you reckon to the girl at the front? Do you think she's horny?'

Brian, who blushed easily, supposed that he was doing so as he spoke, but managed an 'I suppose' before his new companion made a musing sound and remarked, 'I suppose I just haven't objectified her enough yet. She might keep me off the boys, though.'

Brian was all at once mustering the courage to point out that you shouldn't objectify women, trying to square this with the fact that his interlocutor seemed to be homosexual and taking in the commanding countenance – aquiline nose, haughty cheekbones – of the woman his

new friend informed him was 'Maria Rafferty. Big lesbian. The one woman I want 'ere I don't reckon I can 'ave.'
Finally Brian managed to remonstrate: 'You can't call someone a lesbian just because they don't want to have sex with you!'
Alan was amused. 'I bloody well can! And anyway, she *is* a big lesbian. Lesbian and Gay Rights Officer on the Students' Union Executive, in fact.'
All at once Brian felt wistful. It may be some consolation how poetic stymied lust can feel.

The chief business, amid the grey curtains and grey-green institutional paint of MR (Meeting Room) 7, was a motion to condemn the recent shootings of IRA suspects in Gibraltar. Brian shrank into his chair, sank further yet into himself, tried to pay no mind to the new friend sitting next to him. Maria Rafferty, meantime, chaired proceedings like a queen attending her own Privy Council, which is to say she seemed to call on and dismiss speakers, register mild assent or severe disapproval and generally exercise discipline by means of lolling in various attitudes, now apparently fainting with boredom, now crumpling in disgust or despair, occasionally waggling a leg and from time to time seeming to fix a pointily booted toe in some definite yet strangely indeterminable direction. She said nothing. Then she swiftly but sufficiently gave Brian a look that he would have understood if he hadn't thought he knew her proclivities. As it was, all he registered was the aspect of appraisal in her eyes, an assessment he only dimly realised he was determined to pass.

When it was all over, Alan made straight for a woman across the room. Contemplating this pigeonishly purposeful pursuit, Brian realised Maria Rafferty too, was moving – and moving was the word – in his direction, dressed in black that was exactly tight enough. He made up his mind to leave, but took so long about it that he was still sitting down when she reached him.

'Friend of Alan's, are you?' In her voice were challenge and amusement and something Brian no longer dared detect.

'Er, no; he was just sent to sit next to me. Remember?'

'So who are you, then?'

'Oh, I'm no one. That is to say, I'm Brian,' he said, with a slight apologetic nod.

'Brian! That's not a name for these times, is it?'

'I suppose not, no,' he acceded.

'I'm Maria Rafferty,' declared Maria Rafferty, shifting her weight from one hip to the other, tilting one foot back on its heel as if to inspect her boot. 'So why'd they call you that then?' she inquired, and Brian tried to stop himself from trying to determine whether her eyes really were purple.

'Oh, I don't know. It's quite funny really.' Brian felt the desire to impress and its futility, as well as a pang for the parental wonderment that had shown so little regard for or awareness of what would have made for a good name in England in the late '60s. 'It means 'high', or 'noble'. It was the name of a great king of Ireland.'

'Oh, I wouldn't know about that,' said Rafferty.

Brian was suddenly aware she was poking her breasts at him and almost, despite himself, took exception to it, but before he could she asked. 'Anyway, what brought you here?'

'Oh,' shrugged Brian, 'just thought I'd see what was going on, you know.'

In fact, he suspected, Historical Forces had brought him there, just like anyone. But to allow ourselves no more latitude, though rather franker and less modest content, than he would allow himself when he began telling Rafferty his life story a few minutes later in the Serpent Bar, we might say that having graduated, during a long holiday in France to celebrate his 'O' Levels, from a generalised, Paul Weller-idolising moddish radicalism, to the workerist rigours of *Lutte Ouvrière* ('Workers' Struggle') – due to the intercession of an elfin provocatrice by the name of Aurelle – he had nonetheless balked at the Trotskyist group's insistence that he move to Bolton, get a job in a bleach factory and help build a revolutionary cell there: his intelligence had won him considerable esteem already, and he was fond of reading besides, and he wanted to go to university to study English. Inoculated against the charms of Oxbridge by trailers, in the early 1980s, for *Brideshead Revisited* and, moreover, smarting from *Lutte Ouvrière*'s firm judgement that he was 'not a cadre', the most likely place to find him just then was right where he was, in Manchester, the spiritual home of the English-born radical. The strictures of *Lutte Ouvrière* had weighed sufficiently on his youthful conscience to deter him from halls of residence and student politics but, not tempted by the intellectual mediocrity and crypto-adolescent ire of the Socialist Workers' Party, he had discovered to his dismay that, wherever the revolution was, it wasn't in Cheetham Hill Labour Party. Disappointed politically though not sexually, he had taken to reading Marcuse's *Eros and Civilization* while having his cock and balls sucked by a gamine hairdresser's assistant named Sam, in an attempt to justify the punctiliousness of his attendance at the Haçienda. But however gleefully he thrilled to the posturing affirmation that 'The Haçienda Must Be Built!' he nonetheless felt that there should be more to political commitment than his fledgling attempts to 'theorise' whether the scenes in the club reminded him more of the liberation of desire or of the enslavement to the machine in Fritz Lang's *Metropolis*.

'Well, something else is going on now,' affirmed Rafferty. It was an end to their conversation and the start of something else.

Over half a dozen drinks in the Serpent (Brian trying Sapporo, Rafferty insisting on drinking Sol with a twist of lime in the neck in a way that made him feel leaden-footed), Brian told her a version of this life story and she warned him off Socialist Organiser, the main Trotskyist group operative within the Labour Club ('very dodgy on the Soviet Union and, despite what the mainstream says, there's *no* drugs and while there may be sex, there's *nobody attractive at all*'). Brian told her that, despite the lack of action in the North Manchester Labour Party, he wasn't sure that student politics were for him.

'God no!' was Rafferty's response. 'I wouldn't call them wankers exactly; it's more that I'm not sure they're even doing that properly. I'm only in it as a way of educating the young and inexperienced in the course of my official duties, naturally in a manner as far removed as possible from that approved by Clause 28. You want to come in with my lot in Moss Side, Socialist Campaigner. *Very* sound on Yugoslavia.'

'But I don't live in Moss Side! And I've already paid my rent up to the summer,' Brian lamented. Rafferty's hand had offered to rest on Brian's thigh a number of times in the course of their little tête-à-tête, but only now did it alight. In the half-light of the Serpent, with its grey–blue airport-lounge banquettes, she was ever more a lady of flashing eyes.

'Darling, neither do I! I live in Whitworth Park. It's *much* more sanitary. And besides, Engels used to live there when he made the English working class. Now *there's* history and a sense of tradition for you.'

Brian was pretty sure it wasn't just this invocation of tradition that stirred him. 'So how do I go about moving into Moss Side?'

'You don't. You just register round my mate's. Matt. Only comes into the Union for parties and gigs. 446 Moss Lane East. Big place. Servants' quarters and all that.'

'They've got *servants?*' Brian asked, incredulous.

'No, of course not; but the Victorian upper-middle class did. Middle class, come to that too, probably.' Rafferty's eyes seemed to mist a little. 'I'd have been good at having servants... Still, I have my kittens.'

'*Kittens?*'

'My girls. They do like to look after me. Didn't you notice them either side of me – one red, one dark brown, to set me off; both rather petite, but then I tend toward the imposing.' Brian blushed, annoyed with himself, both for his ignorance of the ways of lesbians – though he was pretty sure Rafferty was not a typical lesbian – and at exposing himself to sexual disappointment again. Was she doing it deliberately? Consciously? Were they different? The same?

'Right then; we should go out properly... Now, I can't be doing with the Hass: I've always prided myself on being counter-cyclical. We can go to the Playpen.' Brian looked puzzled, which Rafferty took for dissent, and hastily clarified. 'Don't worry – we can still neck some Es.'

'Oh, it's not that – though I'm definitely up for some. Just never heard of the Playpen, that's all.'

'Ah, the Playpen, my dear, is Manchester at its finest, because least pure. We should stop drinking, get there early, get stoned, then drop a couple about ten, see us through to right about when it's time to get stoned again to work up an appetite for breakfast.'

Brian was impressed: 'Sounds like a plan.' Rafferty looked shocked. 'Oh, it's not a plan! That's far too a prioristic, far too rationalist for our times; it's a probabilistic prediction based on extensive, not to say intensive, prior research.'

'Is that bollocks, philosophy girl?'

'It is tonight. Anyway, I'll just get the girls up. We'll look like we're on a date if just us two go.' She touched his knee firmly and briefly with the tips of her fingers, a gesture that might have been more discursive than flirtatious. 'Not that we're *not* on a date. I'll just get the barman to call down.'

'Well, I'm just going to the loo then,' said Brian, politely.

Rafferty smiled. 'If you hurry up I'll wait for you.'

With its repetition over the years, Brian would have ample occasion to ponder this apparently throwaway phrase.

The Playpen was quite light for a club, and so far just full enough for a sociable atmosphere. Brian got some water and they all sat on the ground near the dancefloor. Suddenly there was a sharp electronic intake of breath and 'Voodoo Ray' at once established what it was going to do with the diaphragm of every last person in the room. It had compelled Brian from the first, seeming to speak of a new age. There had been electro before, but this seemed to come from a strange and alien dimension that was also grounded in the body; the familiar strange that one forgets, making one feel both at sea and newly at home.

It was not yet Brian's place to urge his new friends to dance, so he simply went over and leant back against the speakers. He always lamented, before it happened, the passing of the time when what he thought of as electronic tom-toms would cease to occupy his abdomen, and he didn't want to waste it. Simultaneously he contemplated the arrangement of sounds, sparse enough for each strand to gain attention to boggling effect, fades up and down drawing his mind into the mix. Female voices, archaic yet thrillingly present, sensual and dreamy, calling to the listener while singing to themselves, were almost a vision of eternity. Then the proclamation, 'Voodoo Ray', stark and enigmatic, but emphatically assertive: enjoining and resisting interpretation.

When Brian got back Rafferty had cadged a giant spliff, the product of a rolling mat, off one of the hippies sitting near them ('It's alright, I *told* him I was a lesbian.') For some unknown reason, there was an unofficial amnesty on getting stoned. 'So you like "Voodoo Ray", then?' Rafferty deadpanned.

'Oh yes. It's like electronic tom-toms,' Brian enthused.

Rafferty was both amused and in agreement. 'Electronic tom-toms from outer space.'

Brian expanded: 'Like pulses emanating from a dark star.'

Rafferty pounced with her hands: 'A black star. A voodoo ray of black light.'

Brian, floundering, grabbed for scholarly knowledge: 'Like the song says, "back to modern times".'

Rafferty looked over Brian's shoulder: 'And to think it was made in a bedroom not half a mile from where I live.'

They settled back, watching hippy chicks dancing to 'Sweet Home Alabama', then 'Transmission'. It was quite a mix. Rafferty nudged him to look at a girl with a smiley face on each of her buttocks: 'I'd like to take that one home with the girls and bite my way through those grins.'

Brian responded gravely: 'Don't bite her, darling; leave her be. And anyway, what about me?' Rafferty's expression made it clear he was going to have to let the night take its course, and equally evident that this would be Rafferty's. Still, they were on Ecstasy which, as everyone knew, makes people who are attracted to each other much more likely to have sex (indeed, it makes everyone *more* likely to have sex, which is by no means to say it makes it likely).

Brian had felt himself becoming less dense for some time before his comrade rose to her feet, flashed her eyes in an arc that took in all of them and announced, 'Going up!' before starting to move. They joined her, and soon the cry had gone up of 'Acieeed! Acieeed!' – the sign that from here on in it would be bass and 4/4 beats – and she was already striding for the filling dancefloor.

Many have waxed lyrical about Ecstasy for effecting a collectivisation of consciousness that is an enhancement not an abnegation of self. Brian was as yet at the speedier end of the experience – their pills contained some amphetamine, as well as some LSD – but as he danced the rhythm caught him, and for a while his sense of the others was diffuse as he became aware of the synchronisation of his impulses with the movement of the small, intense crowd. Then he caught the eye of an acolyte and smiled without thinking. She smiled back. He smiled at the others. They smiled back. They danced, from time to time picking out a rhythm with their hands and smiling. Rafferty was shouting something, and he noticed he was getting some visual distortion as he moved over to find out what. He didn't have to get too close to hear her roaring 'Dance it up! Dance it up!' They exchanged smiles and got on with doing exactly that.

What you breathe is lighter yet stronger than air. You dance until it runs your veins and will not be resisted. It may take you through the top of your head, dragging you till your lungs collapse with the speed of ascent and the rarefied stuff at its peak. Or its rhythms may drown you briefly for joy, coursing peacefully. Sometimes you flow more easily than breathing, your limbs the shapes of the surging inside, each movement an eddy in a larger tide that creeps over your skin like an infinite caress. Dispersed, you contain multitudes. A haven in a world from which the heart had been retracting, contracting, in the middle of the economically frozen North.

Rafferty raised her arms, free, a wild angel, dripping drops of coloured light, and Brian's last coalescent thought for some time was 'birdgirl'. She was light like dust, an excitation of molecules as she wheeled and turned. Hanging about her was the promise of a softness, yet at moments she was lone as a piece of stone. As they danced, gazing, Brian felt close to Rafferty, and scarcely less so to her friends, and solicitous of them, and felt sure without quite realising it that these feelings would be the saving of humanity; and so they danced, and dissolved into embraces, and danced, and dissolved, though all he would remember for some time was a man with bulging eyes grabbing and hugging him, shouting 'I'm a hyper-sybaritic fuck-face, that's me!', and the collective joy of 'We are Family', and people fetching water from the bar to throw over the grateful crowd.

Clubs in those days closed at two, so they had not yet entered that condition where you cannot remember anything but dancing, see nothing but dancing before you, when they had to clear out. They careened back to Rafferty's small room and all sat on the bed, legs outstretched, and talked and embraced and nodded to Rafferty's tunes, and got stoned and had breakfast and went to the pub and had first a couple of sharpeners, and then a couple 'to take the edge off'. It was early afternoon before the group separated to sleep in the small beds of Whitworth Hall and, though they held each other and kissed as they dozed, it was evening before Rafferty turned to Brian and said, 'just think, you're on the same spot as Engels wrote *The Condition of the Working Class in England*, and there's a fair bet he didn't get what you're about to, at least not for free, and certainly not as good.'

Chapter 2
'I plan to romp and stomp like a horse'

August 1989

FAC 201 Dry Bar was space, light, definition: steel, dark-blue slate, blond wood. From their seats in the corner, the bar receded thrillingly. On the sound system, Shaun Ryder was affirming his indifference to saving yer. Having glanced at the publicity material in the office of the student newspaper, *Mancunion,* some days earlier (while dropping off a letter seeking support for the ambulance workers in their growing pay dispute with the Health Secretary, Ken Clarke), Brian was trying to construe the Dry style in terms of the principles of minimalist artist Donald Judd. Rafferty was not impressed.

'It's not the bar, it's what they call the "drinking ledges" that they say are inspired by Judd.' In truth, she was as thrilled as Brian at the idea of an intervention that intermixed high art and low life.

'I'll tell you what it is a bit like, though; it's like the lines in that Ed Ruscha painting, "Standard Station",' said Martin. A fellow English student of Brian's whose Situationist sympathies had impelled him to Manchester, Martin was regarded as a 'contact' – a potential recruit – who had been picked up during the postal workers' strike. He loved the feel of the bass so much that the last time they had been out he had only been prevailed upon to desist from trying, entirely implausibly, actually to enter the bass bins by the promise of more Es.

'I've never been anywhere like this before,' said Michelle, a tiny, intense, dark-haired medical student in NHS glasses who had joined Socialist Campaigner a few weeks previously. 'Not to drink, anyhow. It's like a gallery.'

'I don't think there is anywhere else like this. Not to drink, anyhow. Not in England,' said Matt, big-framed but somehow louche of physique, who had emerged from his Moss Side lair to familiarise himself with the latest defamiliarisation.

'There was certainly nothing like this in Oxford,' remarked Martin.

'What was it like there?' asked Brian, desirous that the reality accord with his own image.

'Oh, appalling; for me at least. Apart from Eagleton's crowd at Wadham, who were all just trying to be rhetoricians, there was *nothing* theoretical happening at all, apart from some deconstructive tossers who wanted to show how clever they were by being nihilists. Dressed-up sixth-form stuff, really. And then there's the whole appalling Oxford nonsense, and the whole appalling public school nonsense. So, all in all, appalling, really.'

'What are public school people like?' asked Michelle. 'Are they really obnoxious?'

'Well, they *seemed* alright, most of them, most of the time. You know, they try to be nice. But they have these drinking clubs. Some of them.'

'Sounds alright to me,' chirped Rafferty.

'Well, maybe; but these are *appalling* drinking clubs. The worst of them is this thing called the Bullingdon Club, which is for the real toffs, the most *appalling* people you can imagine.' The rest of the table leant in eagerly. 'It's not very interesting, really. They just get drunk and trash places while dressed in blue tailcoats they have to get made specially. Then they pay for the damage in cash, to show how rich they are.'

'Oh,' said Rafferty, expressing the general disappointment. 'So they're just yobs then. That's a bit boring.'

'In blue tailcoats, yes. With obscene amounts of money. Then they run the country. On much the same principles, it would appear.' Martin half lifted a few pages of *The Guardian* with a finger.

'Appalling.'

'We could have a drinking club,' ventured Brian.

'Why?' demanded Rafferty. 'We drink anyway.'

'We could elaborate principles diametrically opposed to those of the Bullingdon.'

'Why would we bother?'

'It might be a laugh. For instance, instead of asinine traditions we could have a practice of rational discipline that consisted in breaking with traditions. Like always going to the newest bar in town.'

'That would be a tradition,' objected Martin. He had a face like a modified Modigliani, angular but softened, as if, with his finger and thumb, he had pulled it into shape for your amusement.

'There's a difference between a practice, which is at least in part consciously motivated and continued or discontinued insofar as it meets the ends of those engaged in it, and a tradition, which is mere convention.'

'Don't you suppose the Bullingdon meets the ends of its members? Which would be strengthening class solidarity through ritual affirmations of exclusiveness and superiority? One man's convention is another, richer man's, practice.'

'Alright then, so it's our tradition against theirs. But ours is better because it's newer.'

'Don't traditions enhance with age?'

'No. New traditions are closer to their original purpose. Purer.' This seemed an appropriate sentiment amid the newly introduced clean fresh lines of internationalist minimalism, and they set about thinking up some rules.

Rafferty assumed control. 'What do we call ourselves, then?' She looked around.

'The Silly Bastards,' suggested Michelle.

'No,' said Martin. 'The Dry Bastards. We should be named after where we were formed.'

Suddenly Rafferty sprang up, stamped her elegantly booted left foot, spread her manicured hands and exclaimed 'The Dry CUNTS!' Her rich throaty laugh bubbled and flowed like boiling treacle. Around her there was a shocked silence. This was 1989, and derogation of the female genitals was a live issue. But Rafferty was Rafferty.

'Alright then,' said Michelle. 'The Dry Cunts it is. And the first rule is that, rather than dressing like a wanker, you must on no account dress like a wanker.'

'Agreed,' agreed Brian, hurrying to make what he thought was the rather clever point he had in mind. 'And the second rule is, rather than pay money for trashing the joint, we're so nice and cool with our friends behind the bar that they serve us drinks for free.'

'Of course,' said Rafferty, who had already made friends with the one person behind the bar with whom she had not had sexual relations. There was silence. 'Can anybody think of any other rules?' she asked. They looked at one another. No one could think of anything it was sensible to propose that they did not already do. Even the name 'Dry Cunts', after an attempt to raise a second toast in its name was cried down as boring, lapsed into instant desuetude, supplanted by the question of what they wanted to do that night. Martin, who had only been in Manchester since Christmas, wanted to go to the Haçienda: 'To refuse the Haçienda experience on the grounds that it is repetitive would be dogmatic and sublimely miss the point.'

'I'm sick of hanging out with the Flare Bear Bunch,' objected Rafferty.

'It *is* Nude tonight. Mike Pickering,' Martin persisted.

'It's been going for years. I've 'ad enoof,' said Rafferty, adamantine.

'Dancing to house transcends the monotony of labour by citing it, performing it in a mode which both indicts the culture and produces a surplus yield of pleasure,' Martin experimented. 'Martin, that's bollocks,' said Brian, though in truth he was rather impressed.

'And,' Martin persisted, 'to go there is to inhabit a space which enhances our love of the buildings which surround us, the warehouses, the disused cotton mills, the red brick, because it is itself a warehouse. Its decor, the iron girders and pillars, mimics the principle which informs them: functionality. The black-and-yellow diagonal stripes are incomprehensible except as representing the meaning "industriality". Functionality becomes an aesthetic quite as frivolous as the most curlicued Oxbridge outhouse. I could happily die in there.'

'Yes, but have you been to the Ritz?' challenged Rafferty. 'No,' conceded Martin.

'Well,' said Rafferty, 'I know a girl who's going to the Ritz tonight who has a lot of speed, and I fancy some of that. The Es are no good these days anyway. I plan to romp and stomp like a horse.'

'Me too,' agreed Brian. 'I think I'm going soft, what with all this oceanic oneness. Something a bit sharper is in order.' And it was settled.

The nature of relations between Brian and Rafferty was, from Brian's point of view, less securely established. If it had been suggested to him, Brian might have agreed that he was not unwilling to comply with Rafferty's able leadership – particularly since she was willing to let him do much as he pleased in respect of other women: the principal sign he wanted someone for a girlfriend had always been that he fantasised about being unfaithful to her. But if, as in Milton's Bower, Love lit his lamp in Rafferty's chamber and revelled, in the guise of the fairy lights that draped her disused fireplace, there were certainly harlots to be found there, even if their smiles were not bought: Rafferty continued to seduce girls, despite spending most of her time in Brian's company, and this could cause him considerable disquiet. For a long time he thought this was just feeling left out combined with frustrated lust; later he would wonder if he recognised in it possessiveness, the smarting of his self-esteem, perhaps even wounded love. He asked Rafferty why she needed quite so many lovers, but she confessed to having any number of theories and yet no real idea. 'But then I think that's the way with sexual fantasy, and its realisation; it's all at such a tangent, it could be anything. Is it my father's relation to me? Mine to my father? My relation to my mother? My father's relation to her relation to him? My relation to that? My relation to my mother's relation to me? I'm exhausted and I'm not halfway through the permutations. And then there's how I got on with all the people at school!' This seemed intuitively right to Brian, even though it made his head hurt. Besides, he reflected, maybe he was one of those, like the protagonist of *The Golden Notebook*, who find that they require to live on a knife-edge of placation, without which they are bored. Certainly, almost a year and a half had passed in which he had been quite absorbed in Rafferty without anything much happening in the way of dramatic incident or crisis: perhaps it had all been, in a way, one long peak experience for the subtle masochist in him.

Now Rafferty budged up over to him. 'Juliet has got a bit of a thing about you.'

'Is this the usual bit of a thing?' asked Brian, who all but rolled his eyes.

'Yes. She fantasises about having sex with you, at the moment quite insistently,' said Rafferty, flashing hers.

'With you there?' Brian almost sighed.

'Well naturally with me there. Who would want me anywhere else?' asked Rafferty.

'You know I think this whole thing is to do with me being yours?' said Brian, serious.

'Well yes,' conceded Rafferty. She squeezed one of his buttocks. 'But also because you're very cute.'

On their way to the Ritz they passed the New Union pub and there, standing outside it, chatting to a couple of friends, was Tony Wilson. They all regarded him with silent awe as they passed him – all, that is, apart from Rafferty, who slowed and turned and, unbelievably, advanced upon him.

'Alright Tony, is it true that you're a wanker?'

Unruffled as a swan, Wilson turned, all equanimity and benevolence: 'That is a position which has been maintained by some very great artists. And some wankers. By whom do I have the privilege of being addressed?'

'I'm Rafferty,' said Rafferty, as she tended to at such moments.

'Irish. Very good. And what are you planning on doing with yourself?'

'What, tonight?'

'No. If you're not going to the Haçienda it's a civic misdemeanour and I don't want to know about it. With your life, I mean.'

'Have a bloody good laugh!'

'That's the spirit. Never be a careerist. Richard Branson once said to me, "You're very good at selling bands and you're very good at making television programmes, but you'll never be great at either until you decide which one you want to do." Bollocks to that. I'm a butterfly and ordinary greatness would be too heavy a burden. I like the irony of two lives, multiple selves, extravagance, waste. Dispersal throughout the multitude. That's why you should always take the legend over the few mere facts whose sole virtue lies in the fact they can be corroborated. Alternatively, you want to gather your wits into a singular soul, best make for the Charterhouse of Parma and disappear.'

'The where?'

'*The Charterhouse of Parma*. A novel by Stendahl. There was a man.' From then on it became a totemic book among those present to witness Wilson's edict. 'Anyway, I'd best stop boring my friends. Nice to meet you, Rafferty.'

'Nice to meet *you*, Tony. Cheers!'

If they'd been shocked and dazzled into silence at first view of Wilson, their lack of words now was profounder, meditative. Then Martin muttered, 'It's like seeing the face of God. It's a sign! We should follow the path to the Hass.'

'No, the Hass will be here forever; the Ritz might disappear tomorrow,' said Rafferty. But they passed the queue to the Hass a little guiltily, until Brian broke the mood in excited tones.

'That man *is* the nearest thing to God I've seen. He's a genius. A genius of life. The man who knew that what Manchester needed was not just a bard of the streets or the realistic self-expression of the salt of the earth but a radical *intervention*, something transformatively daring and imaginative: to be defiantly frivolous and pretentious in the middle of the North. He was a man, like Morrissey, with the vision and guts and classic Mancunian self-flaunting self-immolation for the culture. "Manchester, North of England": modernist, collectivist, changing the world. "What Manchester does today, the world does tomorrow." Now is the time of the "Prole Art Threat".'

'Amen,' said Rafferty, and the rest followed suit.

The Ritz was a cavernous old ballroom, of a kind you could imagine full of dust and cobwebs, full of music that roared. Barely had they sat at a table on the balcony than the hundreds beneath were forcefully raising their arms at 'Chien' in The Pixies' 'Debaser', bouncing up and down on the sprung dancefloor in a manner Brian could scarcely believe was safe or, indeed, legal. His mind turned briefly to a story he'd recently heard in a lecture on Marlowe's *Doctor Faustus* of the collapse of the upper gallery at a performance of the play, with loss of life, that had been blamed on God's displeasure. But Rafferty had already found Juliet, or rather been found by her, and had brought her over.

By the standards of 1989, she was provocatively dressed. Knee-length white boots and hot pants were like two flaps from the daring end of a page offering you the chance to dress a club girl in a range of styles; but the white shirt she wore was diaphanous and barely fastened. Rafferty got Brian to shift up while thrusting something into his hand. 'What we've got's a bit different to the others.' Brian was intrigued.

'What is it?'

'Cocaine!' Rafferty flashed her eyes. Brian looked at Juliet with added respect.

'Where did she get *that*?'

Rafferty made a gesture toward shaking her head. 'I don't know. London somewhere, I suppose.'

'How much does it *cost*?'

'I don't know. She wants us to have it, anyway. Don't sniff it up all at once. It wears off quickly, not like speed. It's got to last all night, though I think she's got some more.'

Just then the spare, rocking sax riff of The Fall's 'Hit the North' started up, and they both scrambled to dance, Rafferty grabbing Juliet by the hand on the way.

The floor moved less than it seemed to from above. As they nodded steadily along with it, lifting their heads to shout the refrain, it seemed to Brian, correctly despite his inability to decipher any of the other lyrics, an incantation that invited anyone, but particularly the government, to come and have a go, again, if they thought they were hard enough to quiet the defiance of, for instance, those who came to the Ritz, and millions upon millions beyond.

She danced a bit to the left and he took in her face, childlike in its lack of edges. There was a smile in her eyes and on her closed but slightly curving lips. It seemed guileless, but no one who smiles like that and looks into your eyes does so vacantly. Her eyes were round, two shallow pools of a paleness he knew was blue. Rafferty had dispelled some of his anxiety about objectification – 'Darling, it's context that counts, or if there's nothing *but* objectification' – and so Brian allowed himself, when he followed Juliet back up the stairs, to verify that her backside was as curved as the rest of her. Only her blonde hair was entirely straight.

Brian was surprised by how quickly the cocaine took effect; it seemed almost instantaneous. Certainly within ten minutes he was shouting volubly into Juliet's ear, and she into his. It was surprisingly mellow; whenever he stopped talking, he felt almost stoned. And the effect was surprisingly short-lived. Brian had established only that she studied Management Science at UMIST, and that she felt she would be fulfilled by running something really big, without exploring further what that something might be, before he felt the urge to return to the toilets. It was thus perhaps cocaine depletion that was responsible for him and Rafferty having a shock when they got her back to their place.

The surprise was not that she turned to Brian and said 'Brian, did you know that cocaine has significantly less impact than speed on sexual responsiveness?' He'd already noticed that. Nor was it that she was prepared thoroughly to prove her point. It was that, when they had come to rest, it became clear that she was not at all the same kind of anti-authoritarian that they were.

'I'm a libertarian,' she said simply. 'There's quite a few of us on the party scene around London. Have you heard of Sunrise? We're setting up a thing called Freedom to Party, to campaign against all this 'music characterised by a succession of repetitive beats' nonsense. We're launching at Conference in mid-October.' Brian frowned.

'Conference isn't in mid-October. It's the first week of October.'

'Well now, Brian, that would depend which conference we were talking about, wouldn't it?' smiled Juliet.

'You mean... you're a... *Liberal Democrat?*' said Brian, shaking his head and squinting at her as though in pain. Juliet began to laugh.

'Don't be silly: do I *fuck* like a Liberal Democrat? Was there any yes/no, ooh maybe if you insist nonsense? Even my backside, I just said no, right?'

'Yes, well I only tried it because some women like to be asked,' said Brian, apologetically.

'It's perfectly fine. But come on. Nymphomania. Cocaine. Management Science. Put it together.'

Rafferty intervened: 'You fuck like the little bitch–whore Tory you are, posh girl.'

'I thought you approved of class-consciousness,' Juliet giggled. 'Anyway, I don't reckon you'll throw me out straightaway after that performance. Have some more coke.' Rafferty cackled, accepted the rolled-up note from Juliet and despatched a line. Brian, after a few moments of incredulous pondering about whether there was no end to wonders, or whether he was just naive, followed suit.

Rafferty and Brian, who had never knowingly known a Conservative voter, let alone an activist, learnt many things about Tories in the hours that followed, besides how game they could be. For them, the Tories were more or less evil incarnate, although they would not consciously have put it in religious terms; and Trotskyism was simply the most uncompromising form of opposition to it. Capitalism and conservatism had never struck them as things you could believe in, but seemed rather a conspiracy of evil or an expression of ignorance, prejudice, pettiness, spite: no more than the theory and practice of human limitation. But Juliet didn't fit their image of a Tory. She seemed reasonable, if wrong-headed. She explained that she abhorred the idea of stifling individual initiative in the serfdom of subordination to bureaucracy; that she considered the market the most sophisticated and subtle means of coordinating multiple individual preferences and distributing resources; that the competition thus engendered was the surest means to excellence. In short, that the lot of everyone was improved by everyone doing what they want. 'I don't altogether understand why you aren't Tories,' she said. 'I mean I understand, but there are shit things associated with any political alliance, and you're just the kind of strong, self-determining individuals we attract. Aren't you just seeking power in your own way? Shouldn't you do it a bit more honestly, on your own account? You should read some Nietzsche.'

'I don't trust anyone who reads Nietzsche after the age of sixteen, except for academic purposes, and sometimes even then. Anyway, the Tories are for a police state, the destruction of working-class communities, rape within marriage, deportation of ethnic minorities, the recriminalisation of homosexuality,' protested Brian.

'We're for the social fabric as it is currently constituted, as a counterbalance to the operation of particular merit through the market,' returned Juliet. 'Regardless of the views of specific empirical individuals, we don't in essence care – we strictly take no view – on whose might the market makes right – or rather, whose dynamic, creative efforts, productive of wealth for all, are rewarded. And what we care about, socially, is cohesion: a society strong enough to bear the strains and stresses of competition without breaking apart. Look at the 1970s.'

Brian didn't care to discuss the 1970s, especially since he had found that cocaine offered him a new, sharper perspective on feminine physical charms. He could really *see* that the other two people in the room were 'exact of taste'.

'Juliet, put those boots back on. Nothing else, just the boots.'

Chapter 3
'Are you serious?'

May 1992

Life had got complicated, although for Brian this was a sufficiently novel phenomenon that he hadn't yet thought of it in these terms. Things had not reached a pitch where he was caught up in ethical contradictions, which he might still have sought to resolve in some apparently clear-sighted Marxist way. Rather, his life didn't quite fit at the seams, its various aspects wouldn't quite settle into place. Brian felt ill at ease without quite knowing why, without there being an obvious cause, such as exams. Something is happening here but you don't know what it is, he would find himself reciting.

From the outside, all might well have appeared busy success as, for instance, he stood up in the MDH (Main Debating Hall) to intervene in a GM (General Meeting) by denouncing the fact that unemployment had now risen for a full twenty-four months in succession: two years! Peals of applause accompanied each subclause of mounting indignation and a wave of it, much of it from people standing to cheer, carried him, Chair of the Labour Club, back to his seat. Things were going with quite a swing.

Brian sat down heavily, in the way speakers sometimes do when their sentiments have been vindicated and deemed generally significant, the meeting of backside and chair a kind of exclamation mark. But Brian, who had at first revelled in the applause he garnered in such contexts, had soon come to feel it was gained too easily. All he ever seemed to be was indignant that more money was not being spent and, while this was not a sentiment with which he disagreed, he was nagged by a feeling that there must be more varied, more sophisticated and perhaps even more realistic things to say. He felt this ever more keenly now, after the disappointment of the General Election in April: what good had all the protesting and shouting been in the end? This is perhaps to put things a little more clearly than Brian understood them, for now: his principal feeling was one of inadequacy, and of being unworthy of the acclaim he had once again won with such facility. Indeed, insofar as Brian felt pleased at all it was with a job efficiently done – after all, Labour could not go without prominent and articulate representation in meetings such as this just because he didn't feel like it.

Not that it was all bad. Chair of the Labour Club, in those days, retained a certain radical chic and seemed to come with a supply of posh girls for whom sleeping with a student leftist represented the exact quotient of exoticism and rebelliousness they'd come to university expecting to get under their belt and, usually, out of the way, before marriage to a complaisant instance of the male of their own species. Just the night before, he had been invited, by a willowy brunette called Olivia who was given to sporting thigh-high patent-leather boots, to dinner with her TV producer mother and a few friends. In truth, Brian had been a little intimidated, especially because he didn't really know who the 'chattering class' that kept being disparaged were, but the effect had been to make him rather calmly stick to his socialist guns and, when mother et al. had departed, he had been deemed to have 'failed gloriously'. Invited up to Olivia's room as a reward, he had found that her way of getting past the first few moments of awkwardness endemic to such transactions was to brandish a copy of *How To Please Men In Bed* and point out that it had a full index.

Tonight, however, it was – for Christ's sake! – the SWP quiz. Quite why Rafferty was so insistent on going, he didn't know. The SWP would have a number of contacts there and Rafferty would like the thought of looking glamorous and enticing in front of them, just as she liked the idea of shining intellectually, however dim the surrounding lights. Still, there were no *political* reasons for impressing SWP-type no-marks. Maybe she was set on winning herself a piece of the Berlin Wall, the top prize on offer. Brian felt he ought to be excited at such a prospect, especially since he was much exercised by the intellectual implications of the fall of the Wall. Maybe his lack of desire for the material object was a symptom of some deep flaw in him, he wondered to himself, as he directed his steps toward the English Department Office to check his mail.

There he found his supervisor, Dr Patrick Deegan, humping armfuls of essays from one pile to another.

'Ah, Brian! How's Foocourt?' Foocourt was Deegan's determined anglicisation of the name of the French thinker Foucault, more usually pronounced something like 'Foocoe'.

'Oh yes, Foocourt's fine, Pat, despite the pastings I keep giving him,' replied Brian, turning to go but interrupted by a thought of Deegan's: 'Brian, I was having a think and I wondered if you'd thought about going to any conferences? I know only dreadful careerists do, but the way things are going it's becoming a bit of a thing, you know?'

'Ah yes, Pat, I'll keep it in mind.'

Brian kept it in mind, with furrowed brow, as long as it took him to walk the few yards from the English Department to the Students' Union, to be replaced in his thoughts, as he mounted the several flights to the Solent Bar, by a resolution that, if he encountered, yet again, a beardy type with a Sociology degree making weak jokes about how their alarm had not got the memo about 'the End of History' and had gone off that morning altogether as if history was continuing, he was going to clock him one. Once in the door, his eyes were drawn immediately to the figures of Rafferty and, next to her, Terry Gallagher. His twinge of annoyance or foreboding at seeing Gallagher quickly morphed into something like acceptance: the pair of them fairly shone from the general dreariness.

The encounter with Gallagher had been in the offing for some time. The Manchester District Executive Committee of Socialist Campaigner had decided that Rafferty should become Chair of Moss Side Ward Branch Labour Party. (She had learnt of this at the Moss Side Fraction Meeting of Socialist Campaigner, at which preparations were made to advance her candidacy at the next meeting of the constituency Broad Left, with the securing of which her accession was guaranteed.) As a result, she gained a place on the Executive Committee of Gorton Constituency Labour Party, where she met

Terry Gallagher, the member for the Trades Union section and, more impressively, the Political Officer of the GMB, North-West Region, at the age of thirty-two.

Terry Gallagher was a consummate political bruiser at this level, who had seen the likes of Rafferty before. For both personal and professional reasons he showed little mercy in ridiculing and belittling such proposals and contributions as Rafferty had been instructed to make; and, combined with a few blunt expressions of sexual interest, this had been enough for her to consent to meet him for lunch from time to time, on which occasions he was much more patient and really quite charming. Rafferty was still far from giving up the core of her beliefs, but Gallagher was able to convince her that his own essence was sufficiently similar, as well as more suffused with proletarian realism, for her to confide, over a lunch that was part of another ongoing little campaign of her own, 'I feel randy as hell. I want him to take me, ravish me, tear my mind to pieces, leave me in a heap of nothing. But at the same time I don't want some old bastard just sticking his cock in me.'

With this in mind, Rafferty did her best. She got hold of the hardest black male homosexual porn she could bear and, on pain of immediate and utter banishment from her presence if she blabbed, got one of her girls to be as stringent with her as she could manage. She bought a leash, and told Brian that not only did she need to let the reins of power fall slack from time to time, she actively felt a call to explore the submissive dimensions of her being. But it was no good. Gallagher's size, manner and political weight would not leave her.

When Brian observed that she had been away more than usual of late, he had been unable to tell whether her attempt to lie was halfhearted; it had certainly been unsuccessful.

'Have I? I suppose I have.' The lightness in Rafferty's voice was fake.

'Just making an observation, that's all,' Brian lied, in a similar tone.
'Oh yes?'
'Well, no, not really.'
'Well, I suppose I've been seeing a bit more of Beth.'
'You're not interested in her any more!... What have you been up

to?' Brian sought to insinuate a teasing tone, but his words sounded starkly interrogative.

'You're so sharp you'll cut yourself,' said Rafferty, initiating an old one-two of theirs.

'Too sharp,' responded Brian. 'My wit works at a sub-molecular level.'

The time Rafferty was spending with Gallagher was, in truth, a burden on her conscience. It was an unusual feeling, and she wasn't sure why it was importuning her. He was a bit lumpen; enough for her to think of herself as just working something out of her system, something she had to undergo on her own, something that had nothing to do with her and Brian.

'I've got a new friend for you,' Rafferty conceded after a while.

'Oh yes? A new secret friend?'

'It's not a secret. I'm telling you, aren't I?'

'Only because I asked.'

'Well, since you ask, it's a friend with a difference.'

'What kind of a difference?'

'Well, he's the same as you.'

'Ah.'

'Well, not quite the same as you, obviously. He likes boys.'

'Maria, I'm not homosexual.'

'No, but you're not exactly a stickler for detail, are you?'

And now here he was, a biggish, bluff, blond bloke in a dark-blue suit and red tie, set off to proper advantage in the context of the SWP at play. They were, as ever, grey and shrunken, sullen and muttering when not angry and shouting, personalities diffused in a General Resentment. A casual eye might have supposed them all to have the same haircut. Brian was overcome with anger at the thought that none of these bastards really cared that the Tories had just won: it was just more grist to the revolutionary mill. Although Socialist Campaigner was in the Labour Party, it would later seem to Brian that he was being presented with a stark choice in life between the compression of boredom into grim anger and something that was at least buoyant. He couldn't even be bothered to pick a fight.

A couple of postgrads versed in the history of Marxism, plus a Political Officer steeped in Labour history, were more than enough to win the quiz, but not enough to secure a piece of the Berlin Wall: they were told it was too valuable to bring to the quiz and, utterly unconvinced, decided to depart with good grace. Over a drink, the three of them agreed their rules of engagement and repaired to Rafferty's chamber. Sexually, it was not an unmitigated success, Brian finding it difficult to get hard in the presence of another man, although Terry reassured him that he'd had the same trouble at first. But once all three were sated for the while, the talk turned to politics and Gallagher stressed the fundamental egalitarianism that united them without diminishing the radicalism of his thinking:

'I don't think even One Member One Vote goes far enough; because then you're still talking about the views of the few hundred thousand most left-wing people in the country. We need to be reaching out to the mainstream, to the people who decide elections in this country. That's what went wrong in the election. We thought we just needed to be clear about our tax plans and that the money was going to fund care for the elderly and things like that. But that Shadow Budget was a gift to the Tories. An absolute Birthday Gift. What the people who decide elections in this country heard was one, conforming to type, we're going to raise their taxes and two, conforming to type, we're for the *poor*, i.e. *not them*. Result? We barely get beyond our core vote. *Again*. It's no good. The question you have to answer is: are you in politics to feel good about yourself or are you in it to win the power to change things? Are you *serious*?'

For all their spontaneous hedonism, indeed perhaps as a function of it, both Rafferty and Brian were suspicious of self-deceiving motives for action, and Gallagher's words found their mark. For the first time, the ground in which the vaulting structure of their opinions was embedded knew unsettlement. This was compounded by what was, from their perspective, the sheer extremity of Gallagher's beliefs. He was arguing, not for the mainstream positions they were habituated to countering, but for things that were quite outside their universe of discourse, which thus took on the aspect of enigmas to be puzzled over and rendered meaningful, rather than contested and withstood: for law and order as a working-class issue; against the determination of education policy by teachers (Brian and Rafferty, who had always been against the determinations of teachers, were fertile ground here); the punitive and hence unacceptable nature of Labour's former policies on taxation: 'most of the people we need to vote for us are aspirational, even if in a modest way. They want a slightly bigger car, a slightly better job, an extension to their home; and they shrink from policies that define us as hostile to aspiration. That is to say, as far as they're concerned, hostile to *them*.'

Brian, who had spent the first six years of his life in his grandmother's council flat overlooking the approach road to the Dartford Tunnel, felt that he was coming to understand her and his father's politics for the first time. He had been working his way through Laclau and Mouffe's *Hegemony and Socialist Strategy* and its intellectual hinterland, and it was those aspects that undermined his faith in traditional class politics that now struck him most forcefully – that absolute truth was unreachable, and thus that the description of the prevailing relations of production as contradictory was not a scientific truth, but a political gambit whose efficacy was dependent on its acceptance by a majority, for instance – and which he found himself offering up to Gallagher.

When Brian finally surfaced the next day, Gallagher's departure that morning was a faint after-image of shirt tails and socks, like a Frenchman in a brothel when the police call round in some farce.

Chapter 4
'Feminism and your ego are not coterminous'

1994

'Come here.'

Brian yanked on the leash Rafferty had bought herself, taking care not to do so *too* gently. Rafferty's response was a little drama of punctiliousness. This wasn't really Brian's kind of scene. He was alive to the attractions, in fantasy, of dominating one's partner; but translation into reality seemed to render them unreal, silly indeed. He wondered whether it bespoke a rather abstract and cerebral approach to carnality; and perhaps a higher form of it. When Rafferty had first instructed him to tell her what to do he had found it hard to think of anything beyond changing the cassette to a compilation of what Martin had dubbed 'Emotionally Implicit Dance Music'. He had signally failed to embody the tolling impulsion of Jaydee's 'Plastic Dreams'. And today he was definitely in a 'Little Fluffy Clouds' frame of mind after a typically cocaine-fuelled London all-nighter that had ended by depressing him, as they so often did, after he had found himself in conversation with a pupil barrister named Fraser who was sporting a red bandana with white spots, arranged over his head like the first mate on a pirate ship.

'Did you see The Shamen on *Top of the Pops* this week?' Fraser had asked. Feeling rather snobbish at the juvenility and straightness of his interlocutor's cultural reference points, honesty had nonetheless forced him to concede that, indeed, he had.

'Seminal, man; seminal,' his legal friend had opined. Everything about this conversation had seemed wrong, and he had suddenly felt in need of a drink; but there was none to be had under a railway bridge in Vauxhall at four in the morning, only bottled water at £1 a pop. How he now wanted innocence, no matter how saccharine: little fluffy clouds seen from somewhere in the Midwest.

He was not really in any position to lay down the law. His feelings in relation to Rafferty had clarified from an easy acceptance of her orienting vibrancy to a keen desire to attune himself to her frequency. Brian was increasingly under a compulsion to alleviate in Rafferty a tendency to boredom and scorn he knew keenly from his own emotional dynamics. His self-esteem had dipped, which he wondered whether to blame on expending libido on an object other than his ego. That's what he supposed Freud had recognised in the masculine poetry of love, although he suspected it knew no gender. In Brian's case this was magnified by his almost religious belief in feminism: he was in awe of the fact that he, a mere man, should seem to be worth so much of Rafferty's time and erotic energy that he should have secured some kind of exemption. Accordingly, he was coming to realise that his self-worth was increasingly a function of the amount of attention it sometimes seemed she was doling out to him, though he was unresentful, indeed at times self-abasingly grateful, at feeling himself the object of such largesse. As he had once said, quoting Milton while gesturing jokingly and adoringly at her breasts (although the lines would just as well have applied to the forehead, as originally intended), her 'fair large front and eye sublime declar'd absolute rule'. Rafferty had called him a masochist, and in response to his protests had simply pointed out that his favourite Madonna track was 'Borderline'. Perhaps she had got his number. Brian only hoped the equation by which she had arrived at it was elegant enough. Indeed, Brian was increasingly aware that he hoped it was enough, at some point, for Rafferty to feel it was worth her sole attention. For her part she affirmed, apparently in jest, 'You're not fit to breathe the air I walk on.'

Brian had his distractions. Rafferty may have failed to exert any sway over Sarah Hattenstone of *Socialist Organiser*, but whether because he was safely in another faction, or because it could to some extent be legitimised as a bid to convert him, or whether it was rivalry with Rafferty, or the aura with which Rafferty imbued him, or whether it was just because, as most all the girls agreed, he was cute, Sarah had tilted her cap at Brian. He, taken with her good looks, the size of the pale-blue eyes with which she sauced him, the neatness and brunetteness of her bob, her exciting maturity in years (she was twenty-four) and her motherhood of a son, had readily tilted back. Furthermore, when not detumescing at Sarah's licensing whisper 'You can come now,' or trying and failing to get excited by the effort to dominate Rafferty, he was trying and failing to understand, as part of his research toward what was now a PhD, Francis Barker's opinion that, in Milton's *Areopagitica*, generally held to be an early argument for freedom of the press, the liberty of the political subject is restricted to the private sphere.

Although the nearest he had ever had to a personal ambition had been to be an academic, inasmuch as this seemed, from a distance, to be all about reading and discussing books and ideas, he was beginning to fear that research was not for him. As an undergraduate, literary theory had possessed the same promise of a higher knowledge, arcane to the uninitiated yet universally operative, as Marxist–Leninism. Although he could not acknowledge it, Brian felt, like Althusser, the call of the clerisy, though in secular guise. Now, called upon to adjudicate between rival constructions of similar ideas, rather than invoke them to make a clever point in an essay, he feared he was finding the limits of his capacity for abstraction. Martin, whose thesis was on 'The Representation of Thought in American Popular Culture', urged him to recast his project so that he was primarily engaged in interpreting texts, rather than seeking to rethink the terms of political modernity. 'I don't have to be an expert on Hume or Berkeley or Kant. I just have to know about them, and transport that knowledge into the domain of my texts.' Somehow, though, this was not enough for Brian, and despite some desultory hours trying to sketch alternative approaches, nothing had taken wing. He confessed to Rafferty that he could not make head or tail of Bataille. 'I rather think that not distinguishing head from tail is more or less the point of Bataille,' she replied.

In the end, these preoccupations did not distract him from Rafferty's increasing absence. His god had moved in mysterious ways; now those ways seemed merely underhand. For all this – indeed, it would seem to him later, *because* of this, since a sense of the prelapsarian is an effect of being fallen – their time together in her room took on a new value. (It was always her room: Brian's was bestrewn with work, unlike Rafferty's, despite her own research on second-wave feminism; and besides, it had always delighted him keenly to be an alien element accepted, on sufferance, in feminine space.) It took on an aspect for him of Adam and Eve's bower in *Paradise Lost*, sheltering them even from a cosmos with which they were almost one. He felt there a sense of timelessness all the more dilatory for being snatched from epochs of Rafferty's other concerns: they were moments when he was right with his god. 'With thee conversing I forget all time,' he quoted, and invented for her what he called 'Neo-neo-platonism': 'through the object of our adoration we achieve salivation.' Rafferty's eyes shone black in the fairy lights, and a peace reigned that he could not bring himself to disturb for some weeks.

Sexually, however, their relations were proving less fruitfully disturbing. Brian was keen to show willing, especially once warned by Rafferty that any objection to her relations with Gallagher would be regarded by her as sexist and possibly homophobic, given his complaisance when it came to women. And yet, the more Gallagher and Rafferty paraded dramas of dominance and subjection, each dispelled with an expiatory kiss, the less Brian continued to desire Rafferty. Was this the secret heart of her yearning? If so, it was a depressing thought, especially for him. He was coming to wonder whether he respected her desire; whether, in light of this, the secret sources of his own were drying. When he and Rafferty were alone together, which was increasingly rare, he felt himself an inadequate competitor to Gallagher. It got to the point at which, assured by Rafferty of her desire to do anything he wanted, he firmly espoused tradition: 'How about a good old-fashioned fuck?' He was yearning for a more decent drapery about the lineaments of desire, for a girl who knew when too much was enough; at least, this is what he thought he had discovered when he fell in with Tommy – Thomasina, if you please – a be-jodhpured blonde with finely developed buttocks and thighs whose unproblematised enthusiasms for both horses and the sexual act seemed for a time a compelling alternative. Rafferty professed herself 'riven with displeasure' at this turn of events, but Brian retorted: 'Feminism and your ego are not coterminous. In any case, for all one's tastes to be unconventional would be doctrinaire.'

And yet the thought of what might be should he prove himself worthy of Rafferty's sole attention strengthened its hold on him all the more for that it was barely conscious. Her enthusiasm for the concretely minded Gallagher was diminishing his enthusiasm for the more abstract speculations in which he was engaged, especially as they seemed negligible in yield. Martin, by contrast, seemed a model of productive and happy endeavour, pioneering a new academic professionalism whereby he not only attended conferences but, without even finishing his thesis, submitted – and had accepted – articles for publication. Brian began to feel that such a life was not for him, pondering Raphael's admonition to be 'lowly wise', and thought of himself as becoming more worldly, after what, it seemed, his unworldliness had brought him. The first outward show of this was his decision to follow Rafferty out of Socialist Campaigner – 'the husk of a misspent youth', as she described it to him, perhaps taking a subjective view – and into the Fabian Society. It came to seem that the appeal to him of Socialist Campaigner had been its policy of 'entryism' – the tactic of joining the Labour Party in order to connect with and coordinate the more left-wing elements within it – which had allowed him temporarily to reconcile his radical instincts with his emotional, familial connection – descendant of a plethora of Labour councillors of the 1945 generation that he was – to the Labour Party.

He and Rafferty were not alone in their apostasy. It was not uncommon for those on the Left, at their perhaps impressionable age, to experience Labour's defeat in the General Election of 1992 as a spur to a demoralised determination: by the next election, the hated Tories would have been in power for almost two decades, and something, *anything* had to be done to get them out. Emboldened by their assimilation of Gallagher's world view, and possessed in any case of a sufficiency of charisma, Brian and Rafferty were able, with a minimum of recriminations, to wrest Moss Side Labour Party from the grip of Socialist Campaigner and render it firmly loyalist. 'We can't just wait for the millennium!' exhorted Brian.

Indeed, they were almost on the disloyal side of loyalism. Gallagher, who owed his living to a trades union, urged Rafferty and Brian to be as discreet about it as he was himself; but he shared in the impatience felt in some influential quarters at John Smith's belief that, as they put it, 'one more heave' would do the trick, that it was Labour's turn next time and all that was required was not to scare the horses. His impatience, for young minds newly unmoored, was infectious. Labour needed far more fundamentally to come to terms with the modern world: there could be no going back to the 1970s. 'We must lay the ghost of Bevan to rest. If the Labour Party is a crusade, it is nothing; mere tilting at windmills. We've got to be *serious*, and our serious task is to orientate ourselves to the mainstream and nudge it in a progressive direction. People don't want a return to overmighty unions, beer and sandwiches at Number 10. They want the unions to be responsible in ensuring that people have decent rights at work, not seeking to be partners in running private enterprise. They know nationalised industries were inefficient: renationalisation is a losing hand. They think business is the business of business, but they want security and decent public services and an end to all this Tory sleaze. They want *fairness*. That's what we stand for.' When John Smith's heart gave out at last, they knew their time had come early.

And when a by-election had come up in the north-west marginal of Illeshall, and feelers were put out for a suitable and available candidate for an informal position as 'researcher', during the campaign, to the up-and-coming Peter Middleton, it seemed to Terry Gallagher that, Rafferty having departed for an internship on the *Sunday Mirror*, there was nobody more suitable than Brian, who had shown himself an articulate and able organiser for Tony Blair on the Gorton Executive Committee. He had put the offer to Brian in The Welcome, gripping his thigh rather longer than was comfortable for anyone but the most manly of men's men in that establishment. Nonetheless, the offer promised a blessed release from his academic labours. 'And if he wins, which he will, I think we can sort out a nice little number for you, making sure he holds it, that kind of thing. Ideal for you. You're not the London type, not one of those ponces rising through the ranks of

Labour Students.' Brian's desire to be a cadre now had concrete and remunerated fulfilment. He felt set up. Perhaps he had been.

'What's up?' asked Rafferty.

'I'm thinking about the fact that we've still got nearly two grammes of coke.' Brian issued instructions concerning its administration. They lasted until mid-morning the next day, chatting about MTV and then about how typical it was that they were rubbing their gums with the dust off the coffee table, and then about how typical it was that they were talking about this, until they were tired enough to get stoned and lie down. The last thing Brian knew, Rafferty was somehow out to lunch.

Chapter 5
'New Labour New Coffee'

1–2 May 1997

Brian could never think of himself as 'Trooby', but that is how he'd quickly come to be known in Illeshall. Over drinks with some members of the Constituency Executive in The Red Queen, he'd told them about the meaning of 'Brian'; and then that his surname, Harper, meant 'Well, "harper" really. Or "harpist". They were poets, really, like those epic guys with their lyres, or those troubadour fellows with their lutes, or whatever they had.'

'So you're a high-born troubadour, are you?' asked Trev Gerrard, a paunchy, jowly man with bristling grey hair and a full, brown, but greying, moustache. 'That's what we'll call you,' he said, laughing and resting a hand on Brian's shoulder, and 'Troubadour' being rather onerous to pronounce, and '-y' being a suffix liable to be appended to any name whatsoever in a spirit of familiarity, 'Trooby' he became, in Illeshall.

It was the call of 'Trooby' he heard now, in tones of high-pitched friendliness. Brian went over to the window and looked down to the other side of the street, where three girls in their twenties in Ginger Spice-style Union Jack hot pants, bikini tops and stilettos clung together. Brian didn't know why they hadn't rung the bell of the Constituency Office, except that when girls went out in Illeshall they tended to decline any option that reduced the opportunity for giggling and singing out. Brian knew at once that something was up: clutching at the arm of their spokesperson was Jo Sangarillipai. Brian had had occasion to observe that the preferred method of seduction of Illeshall girls was to provoke something like drunken sexual assault. He thought of Nicola and Sharon, both of whom had appeared to prevaricate over the question of a date but had, in the former case, subsequently adopted a hip-dislocatingly exaggerated gait whenever she knew he was behind her or, in the latter instance, taken to wearing tight leopard skin and pouting whenever she knew he was going to be around; until abruptly, then insistently, they presented themselves close enough to grab. He imagined this was what it must have been like in olden times. He and Jo had got acquainted over the bar of The Red Queen, and asking her out had set in train a sequence of events he now realised was significantly predictable. Having been told that Brian would call from London to make specific arrangements, she had, he'd been told, created a huge to-do every time the phone had rung, consulting all and sundry as to what she should do about this embarrassing attention. Brian had then given up trying to contact her, assuming she was not interested. After a week or so, she had then accompanied her friend, Sara, on a trip to the Constituency Office, ostensibly to pay a call on Sara's sister-in-law, Anna-Marie, during which she had stood outside the door, out of sight. Then, as Sara said her goodbyes, she had leant low around it, in a manner that could not have been more effective if it had been adopted with the express intent of displaying the extent of her quite substantial breasts in the low-cut top she happened to be wearing, in order, apparently, to bid Brian 'Hi!... Bye!' Now she was standing next to a woman who was asking what he was going to be doing to celebrate victory, as if she didn't know.

'I'll be at the count until about two; then there's an all-night party in the council function rooms. If we win.'

'We will. Can we come? My dad's a member.'

'If you want to. I don't know whether it'll be your kind of thing. And you might be tired out by the time it gets going.'

'We're never tired,' affirmed Jo.

Brian had asked Jo out not only because she was very attractive and seemed to have even more time to talk to him than was the Illeshall norm, but because she was a bright girl, studying Media at Illeshall College of Higher Education, and read books. But this was not uppermost in Brian's mind that night as he tried to work out the appropriate amount of attention to pay her as she performed a dance that consisted largely of quite vigorously shaking her breasts, although it included some swaying from side to side. The key to approaching the situation correctly, Brian knew, was to concentrate on looking into her eyes when he glanced in her direction, since his own eyes would in any case divert involuntarily from time to time. 'Things Can Only Get Better', she was mouthing, or shouting. Brian thought of 'Voodoo Ray', considering by contrast the striking affirmative whiteness, the emotional clarity, not to say one-dimensionality, of New Labour's campaign anthem; and, more broadly, the development of house as a style of bland mass appeal, wondering whether it had been assimilated and neutered, or whether it was also transforming the mainstream. Before he had got to the bottom of these speculations 'Boombastic' was blaring and Jo's backside was thrust, grinding, into his crotch.

For the first time in his life Brian wondered whether to be embarrassed that he had *not* got an erection in public. He was at a loss. To merely stand there while Jo gyrated seemed a rather limp response; on the other hand, he felt sure that the majority view among Illeshall Labour Party's finest would not be that it was appropriate for him to grind and thrust back, natural reaction though this might be. The only way he could think of to escape this dilemma was to take her in his arms and kiss her, before leading her by the hand into the beckoning dark.

Brian hurried to climax as the people of Britain were once again tunefully assured that 'Things Can Only Get Better', to be greeted by the sight, on the TV, of Rafferty dancing alongside Neil Kinnock and John Prescott. He was struck by a sense of how near and far at once from history he was. As Tony Blair greeted a New Dawn for the nation, Brian thought of Wordsworth: 'Bliss was it in that dawn to be alive, but to be young was very heaven.' He thought of Manchester, caressed Jo's lovely backside, and wondered whether she would be the one to free him of his yearning.

The absence of Rafferty, and indeed his other friends, had been the first thing Brian noticed about Illeshall, although he felt the absence of such attunement as a relative lack of interest in the people he had met there thus far. His relationship with Rafferty had ceased to be sexual some time before – they would never be sure exactly when, or which gesture by which of them had announced its end to which, and it felt, indeed, rather like something they had simply grown out of – but she remained his closest friend. The next thing Brian noticed was the extent to which people talked to him – people he passed in the street, people in the pubs and cafes – and thus the degree to which he had to talk back. He had been so disconcerted initially by the amount of talking required of him that for some time he avoided going to the same newsagent's two days running for fear of what greater familiarity would bring, until he renounced his lone struggle against the tide of talk. He had formulated, in order to resist his desire to say to one of these talkers that, actually, he was doing something here, that he didn't know if they'd heard of it, but it was called *thinking*. Illeshall was no place for a *flaneur*.

Certainly Illeshall was not on a cerebral jag. Jo was a partial exception. Shagged out, she had risen to examine his books, and now held up a copy of Will Hutton's *The State We're In*.

'Sounds like he feels like us,' she smiled. Brian smiled back.

'What's it about, then?' asked Jo.

'How Britain is held back by the past. That we must modernise or die, send the aristocracy to the guillotine, reduce income disparities, that kind of thing.'

'Can I borrow it?' Brian's heart lifted.

'Of course you can; keep it as long as you like.'

'What about this?' asked Jo, brandishing a copy of *The Blair Revolution*.

'Much the same.'

'It's a funny picture of Tony. It looks like he's wearing a beret with a red star on the front.'

'I think that's the way the silkscreen makes his hair look. It looks like that famous image of Che Guevara, doesn't it?'

'Never heard of him.'

'Oh well. It just suggests that the people behind this book know the old tunes, that's all.'

It was a warm and sunny day, and the red brick of Illeshall looked bright and gay as though it had done itself up in honour of New Labour. On the way, they bumped into Celia, a general, blithe, soft-lefty loyalist whose head and body were round, indeed almost snow-person-like, with a round nose and eyes, rounded off by something that might have been called a rounded bob were it not better known as a pudding-bowl haircut. Celia had a disconcerting way of making remarks that were apropos of nothing Brian could think of, and she didn't fail today.

'Clouds on the horizon,' she remarked, breezily. There were no clouds to be seen.

'You mean the burdens of office will weigh heavier than we think?' tried Brian.

'Oh no,' replied Celia, and resumed her trundling.

'Now she's seen us, there'll be talk,' said Jo, knowingly.

'After last night, I should think there'll be talk anyway,' replied Brian.

'Sod 'em,' said Jo.

Coffee in Illeshall had begun a couple of years earlier, but Costa Coffee was still a destination venue. Brian had picked up most of the papers at Smith's round the corner, and plumped them down gratefully. 'Hi Sara,' he said to the young woman behind the counter. 'A couple of cappuccinos, please.'

'Two?'

'Yes, please.' Brian had learnt to accept that, in Illeshall, 'a couple' meant 'a few'. It seemed to him a manifestation of a culture that had not fully mathematicised the world. It had not gone down well when he had tried to explain that you described two people who were together as 'a couple', that you 'coupled' two train carriages together, and the like: Illeshall would have its way in Illeshall.

'You going to write a victory poem for the *Advertiser*?' asked Sara.

'Dunno. Maybe. Depends whether inspiration takes me.'

'It should do. Doesn't it feel fantastic? Like having a terrible burden lifted off your shoulders, getting rid of that lot.'

'Christ, yes; and giving them a right bloody stuffing, too. Imagine if we never had to put up with them again?'

'Feels like we might not have to, today.'

Brian took the coffees over to their table, and Jo took a sip.

'Do you know,' she said, 'it's almost disappointing coffee doesn't taste different today.'

'Oh but it does,' protested Brian. 'New Labour New Coffee.'

Jo smiled, although the joke had already worn thin. 'New Labour New *Everything*,' she whispered.

'Oh yes, that too,' said Brian, taking her hand across the table.

Brian had calls to make, on the mobile phone that continued to be a source of mirth in Illeshall despite his protestations that Peter Middleton had asked him to get one for work. When he clipped it to his belt, they said he looked like a plumber, but if he kept it in his pocket, it was uncomfortable to sit down, and if he put it on the table, they mocked his ostentatiousness. On this point, he had abandoned the attempt to evade ridicule, and now he flicked it so it span around. Jo left him to it with a kiss. First, his boss.

'Hello Peter.'

'New Labour New Brian!'

'Peter, the moment is past for that joke, even in private.'

'Well, it's a special day. An historic day.'

'Yes. I don't suppose I need to go through the papers for you, today, do I?'

'No, not really. But you might tell me where you got to last night.'

'I was engaged in private celebrations.'

'Is that what they're calling it now? I'm not up on these things.'

'Yes, well, anyway: what do you want me to say to Peter?' This second Peter was Peter Weston, the editor of the local weekly, the *Illeshall Advertiser*. He'd be looking for a comment from the local MP.

'Well, use the "We campaigned as New Labour and we will govern as New Labour" line. Reassure all my new swinger friends.'

'Peter, you shouldn't use the phrase "new swinger friends", even in private jests.'

'No. Well, something about education, training, creativity, a vote for the future: new employment opportunities in new industries for Illeshall. You know the kind of thing.'

'So: New Labour New Illeshall.'

'Yes. Though you shouldn't use *that* line, should you? Even in private jest. And don't give any hostages to fortune: "We have promised only what we know we can deliver," you know.'

'Yes, Peter. I've got that bit of the manifesto written on the inside of my eyelids.'

'Anyway, do you want to pop round later, have a bit of supper?'

'Probably. Though I might be otherwise engaged.'

'Oh no, here we go again. Give us a call when you know what you're up to, anyway.'

'OK, cheers then. Bye.'

'Bye.'

Brian decided on another coffee before he called Weston. He had made it his business to seduce him into a friendship in which, Brian thought, Weston's jokey irony was primarily a way of maintaining his pride in his journalistic objectivity; especially since his objective views included considerable enthusiasm for 'The Project', albeit mixed with a bit of chuntering about 'working-class values'. After a spot of scribbling on the margins of *The Guardian*, Brian pressed the 'dial' key.

'Peter Weston.'

'Peter, how are you? Thought I'd give you a call rather than get taken unawares by your bloodhound-like pursuit of me.'

'Brian! I'm good. I mean, "A new dawn has broken, has it not?"'

'Peter, he was joking. A new dawn was just breaking.'

'The man is made out of soundbites.'

'Well, you've probably got to be, if you're going to be a twenty-first-century prime minister.'

'I know. I just get a kick out of being cynical.'

'Cynicism is the enemy.'

'I know. My professional deformation, as you would say.'

'Well, at least you know it. Do you want to know what Peter has to say about all this?'

'A new dawn for Illeshall?'

'Something like that. He says "Illeshall elected me as New Labour, and I will represent Illeshall as New Labour."'

'Very poetic,' interjected Weston.

'Workmanlike,' parried Brian. '"I look forward to working to provide the people of Illeshall with the educational and training opportunities to fit them for the industries of the future."'

'Big on education and training, isn't he?'

'We all are. It's the key to getting ahead in a globalised world.'

'Ah. Globalisation.'

'Well, Peter, globalisation's happening whether we like it or not. People know that. The question is, what do we do about it? What works?'

'Yes, I know.'

In truth, Brian was a little too tired to cope with Jo for a second night in succession, and so he made his way to Peter Middleton's, a large semi-detached villa on the edge of town, with leaded windows and a garden that could almost be pluralised. His daughter, Hermione, a pretty, raven-haired girl of ten, opened the door.

'Hello, Brian. We're out on the terrace,' she said, and led him through the house. Peter Middleton was a tall, svelte man in his early forties who had suited a moustache but had shed it in a bid to appear trustworthy. His hair was fine and dark, with a slight flick to it, his features handsome enough, but he had an unfortunate tendency to look more pleased with himself than he actually was. He was sitting, the acme of relaxation, across from his wife, Cécile, whose blonde hair belied her origins in the south-west of France, and Allegra Beaufort (who went by 'Ally'), Middleton's Westminster researcher, who was in her mid-twenties, very slender, with notable cheekbones and auburn hair. She had an abstracted air that men tended to take for dreaminess but which in fact was an index of her complete lack of interest in anyone who was not useful to her.

'Brian! Just in time for a spot of Chablis. Chablis socialists, us! We're going to have cold tortilla and salad later. As much tortilla as you can shake a stick at.' Brian was pleased. They knew he loved tortilla, especially cold, and it was just the kind of evening for it, still so bright and sunny it seemed like lunchtime. He sat down by Middleton.

'Worn out from your celebrations, then?' asked the MP. Allegra deigned to smile.

'Something like that,' smiled Brian, wearily.

'Well, you're a young man still. Still got the energy to celebrate.'

'You're still young, Peter,' interjected Allegra. 'I saw you on the dancefloor last night.' This set off Cécile: 'Oh, Peter and his dancing!'

The evening was a quiet celebration of the more than doubling of Middleton's majority, for which he paid fulsome tribute to Brian. 'You're ideal for this job. You'd hate Westminster. All those egos to stroke. That's Ally's forte. You're a man of substance; a man of many parts; a real campaigner. So: you're ideal for the job. Now we have to make sure the job's ideal for you. Now, I'm sure between us me and Terry can sort you more money, but what I'm really thinking of, going forward, is using you to power me up, intellectually speaking. How about looking into this "Third Way" business people are talking about? I mean, I know I support our policies, but I'd like to know *why* I do. Philosophically speaking, I mean. Maybe you can turn up something those narrow London pointyheads are too on-message to know about. Make me look clever.'

The evening darkened and chilled, and Brian said his goodbyes and made his way home. He thought of calling Jo, but it was getting late. He called Rafferty, who was now earning a living slagging off celebrities in a mildly recondite linguistic register, but she didn't pick up. He found himself watching QVC. The TV said:
  'It's a work of art… without any artistic effort.'
  'Yes. With Bowmaker, anyone can be creative.'
  'There's never a time of year when a bow would not be… well… practical.'
  'What's great is, we're using colours traditionally associated with spring… all the year round.'
  'Yes. The thing is, it's undying… I mean, when the flowers die you can just undo it, get some fresh flowers and make it up again.'

It was strangely consoling, in a hopeless sort of way. Brian resolved, rather differently, to get himself one of the smiling dancing flowers they had always had jiggling away to house music in the *Mancunion* office.

Chapter 6
'Opium is the opium of the people'

June 1998

Brian, who was wearing a tiara himself, noticed first that the room seemed to be full of blonde women in their early thirties wearing camouflage pants and Engerland shirts. Of course they were wearing tiaras, too – universally fancier and more lustrous than Brian's rather tarnished junk-shop relic – but they most reminded Brian of the crowds that, in the last couple of years, had started to congregate to watch international matches in pubs 'for the atmosphere'. Brian, whose passion was for The Arsenal, and who supported England precisely as far as he felt objectively implicated in their humiliations, had taken to declining invitations to attend such affirmations of communal identity.

'We're not all going to sing "Vindaloo", are we?' he asked Rafferty, plaintively.

'No, darling; but don't you think it's an interesting hybridisation of English identity?'

'Well, I suppose; a loutisation too.'

'It's carnivalesque, darling; we don't have louts any more; no high and low culture. This is Cool Britannia, right here, right now! Now, doesn't everyone look lovely with their twinkly toppings? All in honour of lovely Diana,' enthused Rafferty.

'Yes, lovely,' agreed Brian, who had never dared confront Rafferty over what seemed to him a worrying level of identification with the People's Princess. In any case, he was more concerned with the rest of the crew. One thing he had come to notice about Rafferty's parties was that few of the women seemed to want to have sex with him, which was beginning to dent his confidence. Not his sexual confidence – elsewhere, there was sufficient evidence that he had retained his charms – but a vaguer sense of a diminution in his worth and standing, although, since these had never been preoccupations of his, this was as yet obscure to him. He just wasn't sure of his depth.

'Are the others here yet?'

'Oh yes; you're the last to arrive, as per.'

'Sorry darling; but it's a long way from Illeshall.'

'Oh, Illeshall's another planet! We've got some Es, darling, just like the old days; no more of that nasty old cocaine.'

As they weaved their way through the spacious living room of Rafferty's Baron's Court mansion-house flat, it became clear that the main body of the party had by no means sworn off the coke. The conversation was loud, and about work:

'I didn't want to *ninetiesify* it, I wanted a certain *basicness* there';

'Honestly, I *swear*, it was the *worst* meeting of my *life*!';

'I've been given the opportunity to grow the interactive team.'

In a corner, a group of gay men, snake of hip and envenomed of tongue, were engaged in a competitive discussion of 1970s children's TV. Madonna's 'Ray of Light' was playing, as it would seem to have been all night each time he noticed it. At last they reached the L-shaped sofa on which the crew had ensconced themselves, and Rafferty left Brian to be embraced and settled down.

'Have you heard about Rafferty's new job?' asked Colleen, now fundraising at the Tate.

'No. What's she up to now?' Colleen giggled.

'I knew she wouldn't tell you. She's left it up to us.'

'Oh yes?' said Brian, interrogatively.

'She's going on Live TV. She's going to give short talks on the elementary principles of critical theory, with reference to the cultural events of the week.'

'That sounds a bit highbrow for Live TV.'

'In her underwear. Her underwear, glasses, a mortarboard, a cane and thigh-high boots. They wanted her to do it naked but she pointed out that she's turned thirty. They think the sky's the limit for a busty blonde with an extensive vocabulary and a firm manner.' Brian laughed so hard he thought his face would burst. As he was still easing up, the thought came to him that Rafferty would be not a sylph, but a SILF – a Schoolmistress I'd Like to Fuck. It did him in again, glad he no longer wanted her, although what he sought was still shaped in her image. It occurred to him that it might prove rather too valuable a commodity for such as he.

When he'd recovered, Martin announced, 'I'm in the mood to impart some genetic information. Quite vigorously. You coming scouting, Brian?'

'Oh no, not tonight.'

'Come on! Shirley's history now.'

'I know. I'm just a bit dispirited about the whole business, just now.' Just then Charlotte Raven sailed over, Julie Burchill in tow, who exclaimed: 'Martin! Deconstruct champagne for me!' They'd met one coke-and-Absolut-fuelled night at the Groucho, when Martin had convinced her that his failure to define postmodernism *was* postmodernism; and Burchill liked to say that he was a 'proper intellectual, while I'm just like a polytechnic lecturer.' Brian found her rather Burchillesque, and slipped off to find Rafferty.

Rafferty was coming back the other way, ushering Allegra into the midst of things.

'Brian! Look after Ally while I find someone for her to talk to.'

'Hello Brian,' said Allegra, and they gently bumped cheeks. 'Thanks for getting me invited.' She was wearing an England shirt and camouflage trousers.

'A pleasure,' said Brian. 'It must be nice to get out of the Westminster whirl.'

'Oh, yes. I envy you the peace and quiet of Illeshall. Time to think. A finger on the pulse of the real Party. But you're so much better suited to it than I would be.'

'Are you implying I'm a sedate kind of guy?' smiled Brian.

'Oh no; that's not what I meant!' Allegra fleetingly placed two fingers on his arm. 'I meant you're more of a thinker than me. Thinking things through. I'm more on the surface of things, surfing around on waves and currents of information, gossip, rumour. I sniff a policy paper here, skim the emails from Central Office there, sit in on meetings with policy wonks. Pick things up.'

'Or grasp the essentials,' ventured Brian.

'Oh no, that's not what I'm saying, not intellectually. But I do think perhaps I'm a little more intuitive. More like a broker to your analyst.'

'They say in the banks that analysts are ten-a-penny. It's the people with instincts, the brokers, that bring the money in. And make the money.'

'Yes, I suppose it is,' smiled Allegra, dreamily. 'But that's *banking*. It's not about *ideas*. Not about the important things in life.' Brian had his doubts about just how unimportant Allegra, who had been engaged to a banker, thought money was, although he had to give her some credit for having chosen the Labour Party as the start of her career path. He decided he wouldn't remark that it was bankers, and brokers specifically, who had just brought the world economy to the brink of collapse, in the form of the Asian financial crisis. Just then Rafferty returned with Toby, a TV producer to whom Brian had, in the past, confessed, in a manner construable as proud, his lack of a visual sensibility. Having said hello, he returned to the sofa.

A woman of a certain age, a writer of lifestyle features for the Sundays, dressed all in pink satin, was engaging the crew.

'The thing is,' she asseverated, 'you're all intellectuals. You think happiness can only be found through world revolution, rather than a new sofa.'

'Only Kieran's a revolutionary,' objected Colleen, referring to the sole former member of Moss Side Labour Party to remain thus committed.

'The rest of us are reformists.'

'I think my point still stands,' maintained the woman. 'I'm Marina,' she added, smiling at Brian. Her lips were strangely full and resumed their form in their own good time, like cushions filled with dense foam. 'What do you do?'

'Oh, I work for an MP,' said Brian, quietly.

'Another revolutionary!' cried Marina.

'Not really. I'm more an exponent of the "Third Way".' This was greeted with cries of derision and a general opinion that this was a meaningless expression.

'Well, it's true that it involves acknowledging the force of some of the claims that have traditionally been the preserve of the Right:

that we need individual initiative, enterprise, economic efficiency. But it also means it's all to play for in the social and cultural spheres. Good public services, early intervention to ensure equality of opportunity...'

'The thing about the Third Way is it doesn't answer the question of where it's a way to,' interjected Martin. 'It has no vision of The Good Society.'

'What it does,' added Kieran, 'is capitulate to capitalism, to the bankers who are currently wrecking the world economy. The Prime Minister is no longer even Chief Executive Officer of UK plc, just its Head of Human Resources. And when it all comes tumbling down, then where will you be?'

'*If* it all comes tumbling down,' objected Brian. 'The world economy only has to catch a cold and the left-wing press is full of prophets of doom predicting the end of the world.'

'If the collapse isn't fatal,' averred Kieran, 'it will be next time, or the time after that. All the economic experts were saying, around the 150th anniversary of *this*' – tapping firmly on Verso's recent new 'designer' edition of *The Communist Manifesto*, strategically set upon the coffee table – 'just how stunningly prescient it was.'

'Well,' said Brian, who had discovered, since their Socialist Campaigner days, and to his considerable surprise, given how much political argument he generally engaged in, that it made him uncomfortable, even upset, to argue with his friends, 'we'll see.'

'We will,' agreed Kieran.

'Intellectuals!' said Marina. 'The best-informed lefty I know says the really scary thing about Blair is that he really means what he says.' She departed with a cushiony smile.

'I'm looking for a woman who will bend over forwards for me,' said Martin, changing the subject.

'Oh, give it a rest,' sighed Brian. 'Anyway, you'll be quids in with your new job. Grad students queuing up for it.'

'You've got a new job?' asked Michelle.

'Yes. In the States. White's,' replied Martin.

'How did you swing that, then?'

'By managing my thinking astutely. Seeking out gaps in the intellectual market. Forsaking the moralism by which, as the dominated fraction of the dominating class, academics seek to empower themselves, I embrace at once a Blairite realism of the mind and an emotional lament we have come to such a pass. I laud the Labour Party's abandonment of Clause 4 as its recognition of the End of History, the triumph of market economies; while lamenting the loss of philosophical foundations which necessitates that the Third Way is no more than a progressive aggregation of actually existing social sentiment. I am an entrepreneur of despair and dehiscence. I reject all talk of transcendent values; but I also condemn the rhetoric of "adding value"; of subtracting value too. I talk of relishing the aroma of value in decay. Benjamin's Natural History. Value as that which has a half-life, that which *endures*, in all senses; what *subsists* as a vagrant, transitive humanism.'

'So why the States?'

'Well, I think what's probably brought me the call is my recent work on detumescence. I argue that Derrida's notion of castrated thought implies a projected view of female aggression, the *vagina dentata* and all that – incidentally, how can men be scared of the toothed vagina when they like blow jobs so much? Detumescence is more redolent of an inner inadequacy, I contend. The feminists love it, although some argue that it evinces a misogynist lack of interest in the feminine. It's all column inches.'

'Sorry to be obvious,' said Michelle, the doctor, 'but you sound quite cynical.'

'Well, it's British academia that's done it to me. The RAE, the Research Assessment Exercise, means that the quality of British research in the Humanities has plummeted, because the model of production is that of the sciences, where half the time you're just writing up results. What's more, our research council is run by historians, the plodders of the academic world, who don't waste time thinking. It's all quantity not quality, more or less the rote production of what once would have been undergraduate dissertations. An interest in ideas is a positive disadvantage. My British colleagues are interested in ideas the way accountants are interested in numbers. By going to the centre of late capitalism, I actually gain myself time to think, because they expect their academics to produce at a rate attuned to the nature of their thought. I can work on my book on style in Cioran, for which I plan to learn Romanian. That would be professional suicide over here.'

They surveyed the scene in silence for a while. After a while, Martin said, impressed: 'These are *sharpened* people.'

'Polos,' said Kieran.

'Polos?' Brian asked.

'Power-oriented little zeros,' explained Kieran. His features folded in on themselves in a contempt that somehow seemed to have as little to do with him as it implied he wanted to do with the world. It was the disappointed look of a lonely man. To have remained a Trotskyist had been to condemn himself to a circumscribed life among freaks and weirdos, and it had taken its toll. Brian clapped him on the knee. 'It's way past time we necked some pills.' Before he had time to get up, Rafferty was upon them, brandishing a plastic container. 'This is full of pills and we're gonna neck 'em!'

'Well, perhaps not all of them,' moderated Brian. 'And can we have some coke to pick us up, first?'

Inevitably, they ended up snorting it off Rafferty's slick copy of Marx's jeremiad. 'These days, opium is the opium of the people,' remarked Brian, not altogether accurately. He began to ponder whether what they were doing was in accord with or contrary to the spirit of the age, before deciding it was best to dismiss it as a random event. These days, you never knew with Rafferty which level of irony would be regarded as fundamentally imperceptive.

The next day, Rafferty decided she wanted some fresh air: they would have a picnic in Kensington Gardens, by the round pond. Acolytes were despatched to secure supplies. Rafferty was all for taking her new car, a black Saab convertible, a choice which Brian felt must say something about their affinity, or demographic, since it had been the only car he had ever knowingly coveted, and was now the only thing he consciously envied Rafferty for; but Brian could see no way, given the list of provisions she had ordered, that they could safely return in it, and so they took taxis.

As befitted their pastoral setting, they discoursed of love. Brian had noticed that now they were in London his friends talked faster than they had before. It was as though they were deliberately trying to shout each other down; but Brian realised, from his own experience, that if they didn't they would never get to say anything. A couple of joints slowed them down, however, and Brian told them how sex with Shirley had come to seem an increasingly silly and mechanical business. His theory was that he had matured emotionally, and that once he could no longer see a serious future for their relationship, having ceased to find her interesting, his sexual desire had waned. 'Perhaps love,' he opined, 'is the mysterious capacity to forgive one another for the indelible silliness of sex.'

'Nonsense,' said Rafferty, 'you've had sex with shedloads of people you weren't in love with. Lust is what overcomes our sense of the indelible silliness of sex. *Love* is the mysterious capacity to forgive one another for it.'

'Well, I don't know. I don't seem to be feeling much lust these days, anyway. Not compared with before.'

'You're growing old, Brian,' said Colleen, smiling. 'In that case I'm *not*,' said Martin. 'Any attractive woman I talk to at the moment, I want to say "*Shut your mouth and open your legs. Tempus fugit. Carpe diem. Get your coat on and your knickers off.*"'

'Have you considered procuring the services of a prostitute, Martin?' asked Rafferty.

'I have, actually, but I don't think I'm made like that. To get aroused, I need reciprocal desire. Although, come to think of it, maybe just the signifiers of reciprocal desire. Actually, going to a prostitute would be an interesting exploration of the capacity of artifice to supplant nature. I mean, it clearly works for some men.'

'I hope you'd go for a high-class prostitute, a proper professional,' probed Michelle.

'Oh God, yes, I'd want to feel it was an ideal capitalist exchange between free agents, not a grubby transaction with a bedraggled drug addict. I'd want to feel she was getting a proper return for her *outlay*, as it were.'

'Someone else is going to be selling sex for money, I hear,' goaded Brian, fixing Rafferty with a smile.

'Brian, darling: when have you ever known me refuse an invitation to strip to my underwear? Besides, it affords me the opportunity to make interventions into the culture.'

'Interventions into the fantasies of grubby little pervs,' objected Brian, to which Rafferty replied: 'Brian: is it your contention that you are *not* a pervert? I have information to the contrary.'

'I'm sure you'll be a massive hit,' conceded Brian.

Beethoven's 'Ode to Joy' was drifting over from the bandstand, prompting him to add: 'You may even herald the revolution.'

'Ooh,' ejaculated Rafferty, 'I hate this! It's so noisy! And masculinist. The throttling, murderous rage of a rapist incapable of attaining release.'

'*What?*' asked Brian, incredulous.

'I read it somewhere,' explained Rafferty, 'but it's an overstated version of my feelings.'

'It *is* a hymn to universal *brother*hood,' chipped in Martin, 'and we know what Carol Pateman had to say about that excluding women.'

'But it's also an aspiration to the reconciliation of individual and collective voices,' protested Brian.

'Yes, and we all know who gets the blame when that vision isn't realised,' objected Rafferty.

'But it's a work of art,' persisted Brian. 'The reconciliation can't be anything but fleeting and gestural, that's the point of it.'

'It was the Nazis' favourite piece of music, played on Hitler's birthday,' was Rafferty's rejoinder.

'It's also the sole work of art Bakunin wanted to save from Western culture, so it's anarchist, too; and the First International almost chose it as their anthem, rather than the Internationale,' Kieran pointed out.

'Yes,' said Brian. 'It represents not any particular political position, but politics per se, or The Political: the striving to forge alliances out of disparate viewpoints for the furtherance of social good. Maybe sometimes, depending on the particular politics it's embodying, you'd want to stress dissonance, the irreducibility of the particular; but to resist it *tout court* is to be ahistorical, apolitical. It's compromised; but that's the world for you. It doesn't put an end to hope and striving.'

'It's also the anthem of the European Union,' said Colleen, mischievously.

'Well that seals it,' pronounced Rafferty. 'Right here, right now, I declare myself dissonant. I have an ear for the instrumental.'

'And an eye for the main chance,' rejoindered Brian. 'But the European Union is a complex and contradictory phenomenon.' And so, being who they were, the talk turned from the otiose to the business of negotiating the world – the bomb plot against the World Trade Centre, the Oklahoma bombing, Pakistan and India testing nuclear bombs, the US bombing of Sudan and Afghanistan, US threats to bomb Iraq, President Clinton's sex life and the Good Friday Agreement. That night, to Brian's obscure disquiet, Rafferty relieved Martin of his sexual frustration, as a way of saying goodbye. Brian felt as though hulking shapes were gliding, silent and unseen, beneath the surface of his mind.

Chapter 7
'She wants me to put up shelves!'

October 2000

'Isn't that a bit egotistical?'

Brian's heart sank. Probably he should have known, but still, he hadn't expected his expression of a desire to be buried in the style of Sutton Hoo to be taken seriously. His interlocutor and girlfriend, Judith Hargreaves, had many qualities, ranging from compassion to cardiovascular fitness; but a lively appreciation of hyperbole and heterosexual camp was not among them. (Brian couldn't help but follow his dad in approving of her spelling of the diminutive of her name as 'Judy', rather than 'Judi', though with rather less fervour – 'She's not a "Jud*i*" is she?' – the last syllable abruptly and excessively shortened and heightened and emphasised – 'Not one of these "Look on the spelling of my name, O ye pre-contemporary prisoners of the spelling 'J-u-d-y', and despair, you poor benighted fellow-bearers of the name of 'Judith'!! I am the 'Jud*i*' of a New Age!! A New Model 'Jud*i*'!! Jud*i* in the Sky With Bleedin' Diamonds!! ATTEND MY EDICTS!!" No? Well that's alright then.')

Brian had once quoted, in response to Judy's deprecation of his predilection for 'fancy words', Wilde's dictum to the effect that 'The man who calls a spade a spade should be condemned to use one,' and been firmly told that he shouldn't look down on manual labour. Wilde had no business flaunting a flightiness subsidised by the toil of others. Brian had proffered Seamus Heaney's 'Digging' as an example of a bid to undermine the 'bourgeois' opposition of mental and manual labour; but Judy had refused to concede that digging needed any more justification than it already possessed by virtue of its utility.

A similar apparent indifference to questions of aesthetics had manifested itself in relation to Brian's kitten, Peg. A rarity, a ginger female, her antics had moved Brian to reflect on the disparity between our sentiments in respect of young animals, or indeed animals in general, and their essential nature: Peg, he had realised, spent almost all the time she was not sleeping next to him, or eating, in practising hunting, chasing and killing things. 'Perfect Peg in every part,' he had said to Judy, and given her several of Ted Hughes's poems to read, but, although she had consented to look at them, they had been returned with the words 'She's a *kitten*,' as though Brian's thoughts were both self-evident and irrelevant. He had briefly fancied himself the suitor of an Ice Queen, blasted by the wintry chill of her disdain.

She was a fitness instructor at Brian's gym, his age, but lithe, lean, supple. They had exchanged smiles for a while, got chatting and Brian, fortified by his estimation that he might seem to her a good match, had asked her out and, unusually, the whole thing had proceeded perfectly straightforwardly. Indeed, Brian mused when she asked him back for coffee after their third date, it was almost according to the book, or even *a* book. Brian didn't mind the orderly and methodical: they were very much part of what he felt was missing from his life in Illeshall. Indeed, Brian had become quite clear about what he needed to sustain himself in what he, as he never had before, now firmly thought of as The Provinces: a wife. That is to say, in his mind, someone he could talk to without fear of reprisals or scornful indifference.

If he had mentioned such a hope to most men in Illeshall they would have laughed at the notion that marriage could be free of reprisals, which was usually merited. As it was, his expression, once, of a general desire for the married condition had been enough to provoke such an avalanche of amused references to wedlock that, even now, he could not help but hear or imagine a mocking resonance in most references to someone's 'wife'. Perhaps, he thought, Judy could remedy his sense of isolation and lay to rest such fearful interpretive ambiguities. When he had once confessed to loneliness to local Party member Rob Jackson he had been brusquely advised to take a walk down Connolly Street where, he was assured, he could not fail to get his cock sucked. At the time he had found this a shocking rebuff, testament to its expressor's emotional inadequacy. But subsequently he had come to find his solitude substantially corporealised in the urgent tenderness he periodically felt in his penis and realised, when Judy's lips first closed around him, that he did indeed feel considerably less alone.

That counted for little now, sitting next to a peeved Judy on the L-shaped sofa that was his major contribution to the furnishing of his flat. Buying the flat had been a bid at a fresh start, with the additional benefit of serving as a sop to those who resented his failure unreservedly to pledge his future to Illeshall. He thought of it as a New Labour flat, in a red-brick development in the centre of town, with balconies and coloured ceramic motifs of a kind that had for some time been springing up in Britain. After the exertions of the move, he had found himself unable to take much further interest in the place, and most of the furniture had been inherited from his neighbours, who were constantly upgrading, and who made room for new arrivals, as well as doing Brian a friendly turn, by shuffling off to him their newly spare bits and pieces. Brian was happy enough to be saved the bother, but lately his acquisitions had taken on an alien aspect rooted in his consciousness of what felt like their mute indifference during his and Judy's bouts of sex. By contrast, there sat as sentinel over their union a peace lily Judy had bought him and expected him to nurture (peace lilies being very forgiving of neglect), next to a dancing flower whose dancing days seemed to be long gone. Brian had come to know again an experience he had first undergone with Shirley: a sense of the absurdity of sex at a polar remove from its rightness in a blissful bower.

Judy was fed up because Peter Middleton, back late from – rarest of rarities – a tête-a-tête with Tony, wanted to see Brian to talk it over. Brian sighed.

'I'm going to call him back. Say can't it wait until tomorrow?'

'No Brian; it's your job, you've got to go.'

'No, I'll just call him.' When he did, Peter guessed at once that it was a question of Judy.

'Bring her over. She can talk to Cécile about her new fitness regime. She won't blab; she won't even be interested.' So they dropped little Sean, Judy's boy, off at her parents', and made their way over.

'So?' asked Brian once they'd sat down.

'Oh, I don't know. I never do.'

'Oh dear; playing through all the roads not taken?'

'Yes, I suppose. Said he wanted to sound me out about our message in the Election. I said, what about our first-term record on the economy and fulfilling our pledges? He said he wanted something to enthuse our voters, who've become a bit apathetic, a bit disappointed. Oh! Put it this way, I wasn't gung-ho about competition in public services, the way you would have been.'

'Ending government monopoly is the only way to improve services while increasing efficiency. Look at telephones. It used to take you three months to get a bog-standard Bakelite number. Now it takes you three minutes to get whatever tickles your fancy, at a market rate.'

'Yes, but healthcare isn't telephones.'

'Hmm. In any case, it's a minority view. Nationalisation is still religion when it comes to the NHS. A stopgap technical solution elevated to the status of a religious principle because, in the absence of any other ideas, it looked for a while like a waystation to socialism.'

'Yes, well, as you say, a minority view.'

'It's Tony's.'

'Yes, but where's that going to get me? He's not going to make me Secretary of State for Health, is he?'

'Playing the long game.'

'Yes, well, I mean, we all know who's going to succeed Tony, don't we?'

'Exactly. I think you're right.'

'You do? Livy thought so, too.' Livy, or Olivia, was Peter's replacement for Allegra, who was now an Assistant Producer on *TFI Friday*.

'So I just said something noncommittal like, "Of course, we must ensure the massive investment we are starting to make in public services is used wisely." Then – Oh God! – I mentioned the Leylandii.' Brian burst out laughing.

'What did he say?'

'Well, he was noncommittal. Said he thought it was one to follow the *Mail* on. Suburbanites loving their privacy and all that.'

'I'm sure we can finesse it.'

'Yes, Brian; I'm sure you can.' Peter was silent for a while, then said, 'You know, he's a funny sort. Kind of oscillates between despair and belief. At first, you'd have thought no government had ever gone behind in the polls before.'

'Well, *he's* never been behind in the polls before.'

'No, but, well it was the fuel protests and "Ah! They're all against us". The police, the press, the oil companies, private enterprise. Really embattled and gloomy. Then you suddenly realise he's hardened and brightened, like steel, and he's full of wanting a resounding mandate for a fully "post-Thatcher Britain".'

'So you think oscillating between hope and despair is strange, do you?'

'Well, I dunno. Maybe it's what you need, to be a leader.'

'So: how were you feeling when we came in?'

'Not great.'

'And how do you feel now?'

'Better.'

'So: not *entirely* strange, then.'

'But I don't have the depths and the heights.'

'Peter, you know better than most: a middle course is best.'

Peter had left his chat with Tony with another idea. 'Tony has someone watch the soaps for him and keep him abreast of the characters and the main plot developments.'

'Oh yes,' said Brian, suspiciously.

'Well, it's the kind of thing you could do quite easily.'

'Hmm. Why don't you ask Livy to watch the soaps, they're her kind of thing, I'm sure.'

'Are you scorning the pleasures of the electorate?' Middleton smiled. 'I bet your smart media mates watch the soaps.'

'They're not smart media mates, and I've no idea whether they watch the soaps.' Brian had some idea, really.

'Thinkers.' Middleton smiled again.

'Yes, they do tend to think.'

'Too much.'

'Such men are dangerous. Though they're not all men. Or particularly dangerous.'

'And you're not lean, Cassius. Though are you hungry?'

'*Julius Caesar!*' said Brian, with mildly surprised emphasis.

'Yes, I saw it in Newcastle with Jack Cunningham and his dangerous daughters.'

'Oh yes?'

'Too dangerous for you. Shall I go and get a curry?'

'I'll go,' offered Brian.

'No, it's alright. Good to be seen out and about. Pleasures of the common man and all that.'

As they ate, Brian resumed his defence of himself. 'I don't not watch soaps because I scorn the pleasures of the electorate. In fact I have many times tried to watch soaps. I admire people who manage to pay them enough attention to find halfway intelligent things to say about them. But I'm just not interested in them. And then I wonder whether I'm insufficiently interested in people. And then I remember that the people in them aren't much like people. Certainly not as much like people as the people I read about in "my books", as you call them.'

'I watch the soaps,' ventured Judy. Brian stopped himself from joking that she didn't find anything intelligent to say about them; it might have been too close to the mark.

'Of course you do,' gasped Middleton. 'And I bet you could write me weekly summaries of them, couldn't you? For a suitable fee. Just a line or two for each. Just the main ones. I'm sure you know which ones I should know about.'

'Oh yes,' said Judy. 'I'd love to.'

So Judy hadn't been bored at all, indeed had seemed engrossed even during the more political moments; and her eyes sparkled as she proposed, on their return, that they open another bottle of wine. Brian readily agreed. She was full of praise for his cleverness and acuity, and excitement at her new involvement, and after a while turned wanton. Perhaps, mused Brian the next morning, this was what real relationships were like. Periods of indifference, even almost antipathy, punctuated by revivifying sex. Perhaps he was growing up, he wondered. He called Michelle with this theory. 'How ya doin' sweet thang?'

'Oh honey, don't: I've just been made a consultant!'

'Wow! Excellent! Ha ha! We rule!'

'Ha ha, no! "Too cool to rule".'
'"Too cool to rule", that's us, baby! Which mustn't, of course, distract us from the serious business of constructing a hegemonic democratic alliance.'
'Oh no, no; of course not.'
'Michelle, I've been wondering: do you think I'm growing up?'
'Oh darling, you've always been all growed up.'
'No, but I mean, coming to terms with reality emotionally, as well as rationally.'
'I don't know if any of us ever does that, sweetest.'
'Well, not altogether, or else there'd be no impetus for social change. But I mean, developing a working accommodation.'
'Well, you seem to me to have accommodated quite well.'
'Yes, but you know how *bored* I am in Illeshall, away from you lot.'
'Yes, but *I'm* bored, a lot of the time. Boredom is an ineluctable fact of human life. Part of the human condition.'
'Hmm. Maybe I should get back into existentialism.'
'Yeah, maybe.'
'Not that I was ever into it, in the first place; but I did the reading.'
'Maybe you should do it again.'
'Maybe. Not much else to do but read.'
'How's Judy?'
'Oh, Judy's fine. We're on an up at the moment. That's what I was thinking. Just because it mostly rumbles along at a low level, doesn't mean we don't have peaks.'
'Maybe you're just a low-level kind of guy.'
'Maybe.'
'Well, I don't know. She seems nice, and you've been with her longer than you have with most people.'
'Yes, but she still finds it odd that I'm not from Illeshall. And she's still trying to lick me into shape as an Illeshall man. She wants me to put up shelves! She doesn't understand why I don't always want to be going round to see her family.'
'What's wrong with her family?'
'Nothing. Just a bit Illeshallian, that's all.'
'That's a bit racist, isn't it?'

'Generalisation is the condition of possibility of all thought. Indeed, arguably it's what thinking *is*.'

'Hmm. Anyway, Illeshall's lovely.'

'Hmm.' It was something of a sore point with Brian that all his friends, apart from Rafferty, had visited Illeshall, once, and found it charming, having stayed for precisely the two days its charm could last. But then, what was life without limits? Infinitude was death.

'How's Steve?' asked Brian. This was the man for whom Michelle had recently abandoned a wealthy lover. To her considerable chagrin, she just liked Steve better.

'Oh, OK. Not so happy at Verso now Perry Anderson's in town throwing his weight around.'

'Hmm. The monk. Savonarola.'

'Well, hardly; but still. Anyway, now I'm on a consultant's salary he can pack it in and be a house husband.'

'Aha! Serious stuff.'

'You never know, it might be.'

'Oh, to be young and in love.'

'So you're not in love with Judy, then?'

'I hope not. I hope I'm capable of more than this.'

'Well, maybe you should finish with her.'

'Ah, but then, you see, I'd be on my own.'

'We've all got to learn to be alone.'

'Oh, I've learnt, I've *learnt*. "We perish each alone." A mediocre philosopher used to repeat that. Mr Ramsay in *To the Lighthouse*. He was fictional as well as mediocre, which was even more of a professional drawback.'

'It does tend to be.'

'Well, you're not fictional, anyway, consultant. Maybe I am; maybe that's my problem.'

'Yes, maybe.'

In truth, one of the things Brian noted of himself when he read existentialist literature was his lack of a besetting sense of unreality. He presumed this fitted him for practical affairs, like politics, rather than literary pursuits.

Peter Middleton had been invited to preside over two openings in the next month, both of which would please him. One was the new retail park on the site of the old colliery, fronted, as a gesture to its historical legacy, by the old pit gates. This associated Peter with urban regeneration. The other was a new engineering start-up, manufacturing computer-operated security gates, which linked with his pledge to help bring hi-tech industry to Illeshall. As a result, Brian would be in credit for a while without needing to make too much effort. So he called Rafferty, who did not regard Judy as a serious match for him, for a moan about Illeshall.

'So how are the salt of the earth?' she asked.

'Oh, I'm too sweet for them, honey.'

'Ooh, me too.'

'You know, when I got a job in the north-west, I thought I was so lucky, that it would be just like Manchester. But the thing is, in Illeshall there's no outside influences, just people from Illeshall and its surrounds. Practically, it's a place *no one* is drawn to economically. Apart from me. So everyone's an Illeshallian, even the people who *are* from outside. Nature's Illeshallians stay. Because outsiders are perfectly welcome *if* they behave like an Illeshallian. A life of 'banter'. And shouting. And sentimentality. A life of banter and anger and sentimentality. It's not exactly thronged by people fizzing with dynamism – people here stand on both sides of escalators, as though no one would ever think of walking up or down them. There's no ambition. You know, I wanted to try and make this the biggest Constituency Labour Party in the north-west, make this a safe seat. But they're not interested. "We did alright last time, so where's the need?" I used to think that all the people saying "I don't live to work, I work to live" were expressing an admirable commitment to a work–life balance. Now I just think they're lazy bastards. The only thing they seem to get competitive about is new kitchens. We've had a rash of them here, and I keep getting invited round to see them. What can I say? I mean, I try to understand them as exercising the same faculties as I do, so I say to myself, getting a new kitchen, or doing up your house, is an exercise in imagination. But then I say to myself, can't they be imaginative about less banal things? It bespeaks a lack of lively minds. Unless the liveliness goes into all the jokes. But then the jokes aren't very good. Comediocrity is the bane of my life at the moment, in fact.'

'It's probably the same for them, darling.'

'Yeah, probably. It's probably just summer being over... Do you remember that summer when "Only Love Can Break Your Heart" was playing *all* the time, when it was *so* sunny?'

'Yes. I think it's the only thing I *can* remember about that summer. Or rather, I can't connect it to anything else but sunshine and open windows–'

'–from which it wafted on gentle zephyr,' interjected Brian.

'Are you being Miltonic?' asked Rafferty.

'Only a bit.'

'That's alright then!' she said, in a tone of comic abruptness.

'I like St Etienne,' said Brian.

'Yeah, so do I. But a bit clever. That's why you don't love them.'

'Yeah, media-y.'

'Postmodern!! Oh them media people,' sighed Rafferty, who was now writing a TV column.

'I know, honey,' said Brian. 'Anyway, they *do* know how to write proper tunes.'

'Yeah. And "Only Love Can Break Your Heart" *may* be the best cover version ever.'

'Maybe.'

'Anyway, I have unburdened my freight of emotion like a true docker's son.'

'A stevedore.'

'And you've put in your shift. Without giving me short shrift.'

'Yes, darling. Anyway, it's time for my bed.'

'Yeah, me too. Goonight honey, she yawned; goonight, goonight, sweet prince.'

'Goonight honey.'

Brian thought about giving his dad a ring, but while his dad was a solid pragmatist who in general regarded criticism of the Party as the stuff of dilettante wankerism – 'Remember,' he had always said, 'the wankers only like us when we're out of power, not responsible for any difficult decisions' – he was of a generation which had inherited a view of the market that combined the residue of a religious abhorrence of sin with an aristocratic disdain for trade. Of course, that had depended for plausibility on a belief in rational state planning as an all-purpose workable alternative, and no sane person still clung to that view, not now even the Chinese had turned to the market. Nonetheless, he would find any talk of public service reform, imperative though it might be, unappealing.

Chapter 8
'That's differently interesting'

31 December 2001–1 January 2002

In search of drugs, they were listening to music that dignified their paranoia by giving it form. 'Intelligent Drum 'n' Bass', Martin called it. It stripped them of the inessential, the atypical, and left them like gold leaf, cool, airy and thin as two dimensions in a city turned to celluloid. It gave them a place in the world. The cityscape dipped, turned and swooped to its latest soundtrack. The music seemed distant but so were they.

gof'I can't believe we're running out of coke on New Year's Eve,' lamented Brian.

'Calm down, dear,' chided Rafferty gently; 'It's early yet, and Jazzer says he's got a mountain. I've had things on my mind.'

'You've always got things on your mind since you hooked up with that Seb.' Seb was in advertising, and had 'a way with creatives'.

'Speaking of which, why isn't *he* getting the drugs?'

'Because I said *I* would. A relationship is a partnership between equals, rooted in mutual respect.'

'Hmm. I don't exactly call it respectful to start a stopwatch every time you begin talking.'

'But he's right. I *do* go on; and he stops it every time I say something funny, a category he applies with benign interpretative latitude. Firm but fair. That's why I love him.'

'You *love* him.'

'I think so, yes. No doubt it's partly because I've got the urge. Hormones and all that.'

'Hormones?'

'The biological urge. The urge to reproduce. Especially since Michelle had Sean. Matt's got three already, and they're almost grown up!'

'So you're planning to have kids with this guy?'

'I think so, yes; I've stopped taking the Pill.'
'Does *he* know about this?'
'Of course he knows. No more acting unilaterally for me!'
'Hmm.'
The city flowed past, dark and brightly lit. A feathered moon in the middle distance became, close at hand, something more geometrical, a clock. Just gone eight. 'What happened to the lawyer?'
'Well, he was a passable conversationalist, so I passed him. To Ally. She's pregnant.'
'Not another one. Jesus... Well I have to say, I'm ambivalent about Seb.'
'I've always *loved* ambivalence!'
'Hmm.'
'Look, let's get the drugs. Then we can talk.'
When they had, Rafferty pulled into a side street and chopped out a couple of big lines on a street atlas. Then she broached her subject.
'He's *wise*. He really is. He gets things right. Not always, immediately; he's open to discussion. But when he decides, it's the right thing. He's someone I'm happy to yield to. Sometimes I yield to him to save an argument.'
'You're *avoiding* arguments?!'
'Yes; it's a blessed release.'
'You used to complain that I wouldn't give you an argument.'
'Yes, but you were wrong.'
'Hmm.'
'I need to be kept in check or else there'd be nothing but my endlessly finding things wanting. Just me and the infinity of lack. I can't face it.'
'So you avoid argument.'
'Yes, but not so I'm hemmed in. Seb checks me at just the right points. Or just the right amount. Or just the right way. I'm not sure what the operative principle is, but the point is *what works*.'
'Hmm. I suppose there's no arguing with that.'
'Brian, you and me, we were two drunken neurotics; a meeting of messes, not of minds.'
'Hmm.'

'Brian, darling. My best thoughts are in your keeping.'

'Hmm.' Brian didn't notice it at the time, perhaps buoyed up or insulated by the cocaine, and when he later tried to think back he would not, for whatever reason, focus on this moment; but there came a time when he knew he had been hit in the pit of his stomach by something that spread and stained and stayed like liquid spoiling something porous. Something that reeked sour and bitter.

Back at Rafferty's, they bumped into Kieran first. 'Whassup Kieran baby?' asked Brian.

'Not much. I'm doing an MBA in the States.'

'What, another one?' Brian held his fist in the air.

'Organisers of the world, unite.' Nearby, some gay men were bolstering their self-esteem by discussing which philosophers they would be prepared to have sex with. Derrida was a clear favourite. Suddenly Rafferty erupted, for no ostensible reason, at a youngish man with a bald head: 'You! You are a little worm, and I see you've brought your mates along. I am beset with vermicelli! Get out and stay out!' Several youngish men exited shufflingly. Rafferty, by way, apparently, of explanation, remarked, 'I hate mediocrity, so naturally enough, mediocrity hates me.' Brian resolved never to hate her, which he needn't have done.

In the living room, people were moaning about the Labour Party. Brian thought of his dad. 'Remember,' he had said, 'they always like the Labour Party when they're out of power. That's when it's easy, that's when it's just about protest; not about responsibility, not about choices.' The principal pretext for complaint was 'Spin', specifically Peter Mandelson's remark that the purpose of spin was to 'create the truth,' which was generally held to be a piece of shocking cynicism.

'But that's just philosophical common sense,' protested Brian. 'What on earth are truth and reality independent of our conceptions of them? We have literally *no idea*.'

'Doesn't science seek to investigate reality?' remarked a journalist.

'But scientists are continually finding that things they thought were true aren't true. Arguably that's a definition of scientific progress. But if truths are continually being discarded, then perhaps you'd better find another name for them. The only thing wrong with what Peter Mandelson said is that it didn't have the word "truth" in quotation marks.'

'But if you can just make stuff up, isn't that a licence for the powerful to impose on the rest of us?'

'What do you think they've been doing for the whole of human history?' asked Brian, urgently. 'In fact, the very fact that such a question can hove into view is a sign of the democratisation of truth and reality. No longer can anyone pull the "god trick", pretending they are looking at the world from no particular time, place or set of assumptions. Instead, they have to seek consensus as to what is the case. Which is all Peter Mandelson is talking about. Politicians and spin doctors are professionals seeking consensus as to what is good in the way of belief. Which is the opposite of decreeing what truth is by divine fiat, which would seem to be the fear that motivates your complaint.'

'What about when Blunkett announced £19 billion of spending on education, rolling up all the increase since Labour came to power, when the total *new* money announced was only £6.7 billion?'

'Well, one, the fact that you can make that objection shows that they aren't getting it all their own way when it comes to creating truth. And, two, it was less a lie than a piece of boastfulness testifying to an underlying insecurity about our treatment in the press. Which brings me on to another thing about spin, which is that the press object to it so strenuously because, deep down, they see it as an arrogation of their own right to create the truth. The spin doctor is a response to the power of the media.'

'So you think we live in a mediatised hyper-reality, a Baudrillardian nightmare?' asked Martin.

'I do not. I think Baudrillard is a Platonist, nostalgic for absolute truth, which I don't think ever existed. A tyrant's *Paradise Lost*. It's gone the way of 'scientific' Marxism. I don't see anything going on in the media which doesn't go on in common gossip. It's no worse, even a little better. The "higher gossip", perhaps.'

'Baudrillard is detumescent, I feel.'

'Very much so. But it was only ever an *appearance* of solidity in the first place; whereas your penis, from what you keep telling us—'

'—is very much *my* concern, when we are in company.'

'Speaking of which,' prodded Matt, 'how is life in the groves of US academe?'

'Well, talk about gossip. I think life in an American college town is my idea of hell. Still, I make sure I don't spend much time there. I keep myself trotting about. The most surprising thing is finding oneself identified as English. I mean, I suppose I *am* English, but not in *that* way... And after 9/11, it was bizarre. I'd only just got there because, as you know, I was paid extra money with no teaching to stay on in London long enough to count in the Research Assessment Exercise; and it was a bit like that scene in *White Noise*, after the Airborne Toxic Event, when people are looking at each other to see how frightened they're supposed to be. Except that I was looking at all these people who were terribly shocked, and I wasn't shocked at all, and their shock couldn't make me shocked because we came from such different places, and I didn't really know them from Adam, so I had no idea what I thought about their reaction. It was a very dislocating time.'

'How are your students?' asked Michelle.

'Well, that whole Emo–David Foster Wallace thing has kicked right along in terms of graduate applications. So I get serried ranks of intense post-adolescents wearing Kurt Cobain badges. In research terms, I increasingly make a virtue of my lack of capacity for abstraction. My new book, *Lethal Competence*, attacks literary academics as civil servants of the heart. It's from Cioran, you know: "To see everything from the outside, to systematise the ineffable, to consider nothing straight on, to inventory the views of others!... There was a time when the professors chose to pursue theology. At least they had the excuse then of professing the absolute, of limiting themselves to God, whereas in our century nothing escapes their lethal competence." I have been called a Benjamin for our times. Accordingly, I drop hints that I have dabbled in kabbalah. Thus the rumours that I am on friendly terms with Madonna. "God save me from being a useful man," I say, after one of the French decadents, but in truth I'm jealous as all hell of Brian. I give everything I don't need to live a suitably though modestly capricious life to the Labour Party, though that's a secret.'

'A secret you can't keep,' prodded one of the journalists.

'My professional deformation is pedantry. Yours is smart-arsery. And no one likes a smart-arse. Don't pretend you're pleased about it or you'll become Piers Morgan. Who knows? Maybe that's what you want. My problem, and it is a problem that feeds the sensibility that informs my career, is that I am in exile, marooned, cut off from my cohort and thus condemned to a life of conscious artifice, like a sex worker.'

'Sounds like being a spin doctor,' remarked a journalist. 'What do you say, Brian? You are one.'

'Me? No, no; I'm nothing as grand as that. Just a researcher and organiser.'

'Though you're writing a book, aren't you darling?' interjected Rafferty. 'What's it called again? *What Is To Be Done?* or something, isn't it?'

'No, no. My editor keeps insisting it's called *Twenty-First Century Labour*, but that seems a bit presumptuous to me. It's not like I have anything momentous, or even terribly original, to say.'

'You mustn't let that hold you back!' averred Martin. 'If I worried about things like that I'd be doing sessional work in an FE college! You've just got to trust that you will imbue things with a certain style, a certain spin. That's what finding your voice is.'

'Well, maybe. I've just made notes so far, anyhow.'

'Stop with the notes and just write!' cried Martin, urgent and imploring.

'Ah, well, maybe,' was all Brian could say.

Mention of a book was enough, it seemed, to get him into conversation with a model, or ex-model, she wasn't sure which. Her skin was so pale it showed the darkness beneath, like ice cubes melting on a table. Brian was moved to ponder Wallace Stevens – 'Death is the mother of beauty' – and in consequence remarked that it was not at all true that we in the West cannot face up to death, that in fact we are inured to it by constant change, above all in the form of fashion. What is more, he went on, our preoccupation with fashion is an enactment of our fear that our subjectivity may not be attuned to the historical process, an anxiety consequent upon the relatively fluid nature of our identity in a situation where social determinants, and thus identities, have been pluralised. Our obsession with fashion is the burden of our freedom.

'That's differently interesting,' responded the model.

'This coke is top-notch. Personally, I love Dior's new range.'

She went on to explain that she, personally, was opting for the simple life. All she wanted in a man was kindness and £70,000 a year, which she, personally, thought quite a modest sum. 'I'm such a sentimentalist,' she laughed. 'Anyway, I haven't got one yet. I must be very bad at expressing myself.' Suddenly she broke off. 'Oh *Christ*, how did *this* happen to my life! Am I going to be a *good* person?'

'Virtue is its own reward,' said Brian, at a loss. He wondered whether she was sizing him up but decided, on balance, she probably thought he was gay: whatever, she was used to granting audiences.

'So: what college were you at?' she suddenly asked.

'College? Oh, I was at Manchester.'

'*Manchester*? But I don't understand. You seem really intelligent!' Brian recalled Rafferty telling him about conversations like this: the hopeless affrontedness of confronting a world that doesn't understand the choices you have made. 'Because Manchester's motto is "Kick the fuckers in the knackers",' he said.

'Cool,' she remarked. Just then someone not afraid to be thought prematurely middle-aged put on Howlin' Wolf singing 'Backdoor Man', and the model, whose name Brian would learn was Clarrie, began what looked like an impression of Salome, to which Brian responded as best he could. When it had finished, she sighed.

'That's the thing about the blues: you're always pleased to hear it, but you don't want it to overstay its welcome. Anyway, I'm sorry to be abrupt, but do you fancy being my backdoor man?' She was a little diffident and very confident. Brian couldn't see a way of saying no, and didn't want to in any case.

'Come on, Brian; if you're going to go for the win, you have to be honest.'

What Brian chiefly remembered about that night was how vocally responsive Clarrie was to the merest brush of his hand. She would tell Rafferty that he was afraid of her passion; but the truth was he didn't believe in it. When he awoke, two Chinese people on the TV were telling him about the dollar, and he slipped back to Rafferty's. Most of the crew were still up, though Michelle had left to tend to her child. Rafferty was talking about her days in the SWP.

'I got into it, got out of it, shook it all about a bit.'

'Sounds like the Haçienda,' remarked Brian.

'Oh no. The Haçienda was a *much* more cerebral jag. Speaking of cerebral hags, how did you get on with Clarrie?'

'Well, I didn't hate it like poison. More like a mild emetic.'

'Oh dear, so it's back to good old Judith, is it?'

'That's my estimation.'

Rafferty gave him a 'despairing' look, then suddenly brightened. 'Hey, Brian. Do you want some poppers?'

'Ooh yes,' said Brian, keen to consign his toils with Clarrie to history. Sebastian piped up. 'Amyl nitrate epitomises the incompatibility of intelligence and happiness. It makes you stupid for a short while. The amount of brain it destroys, it must make you stupid in the long run. This frisson must be its appeal in the medium term.'

'No,' said Brian. 'Its appeal is that it makes you laugh your fuckin' arse off.'

'I am the vampire of my own heart,' quoted Martin. 'Condemned always to laugh, and never to smile.'

Somehow they meandered back onto the Labour Party. Rafferty confessed she was no longer going to her branch meetings.

'Why ever not?' demanded Brian.

'It's my nerves.'

'I'm surprised you find branch meetings so nail-biting.'

'No. There's a woman I see on Wednesday evenings. She can't make it any other time. She's very exclusive, booked right up.'

'She must be very good. What is she, a therapist?'

'Of a kind,' confessed Rafferty, half abashed.

'Acupuncturist?'

'No.'

'Yogi?'
'No.'
'Well, what is she then?'
'Not a fitness instructor,' said Rafferty pointedly.
'*So?*' asked Brian, fixing her with a rare look in response to her jibe. Rafferty felt that, having given offence, she owed him the truth.
'Aromatherapist,' she said defiantly.
'Aromatherapist?!' Brian laughed.
'Aromatherapist to the stars,' modified Kieran.
'I would just like to say,' said Rafferty assertively, 'that at this point I think we should get drunk again,' and started sploshing out Absolut.
'Hurrah!' shouted Martin. 'Anyone fancy some modafinil? Keeps me awake when I'm writing, though I can't overdo it if I'm going to get melancholy enough to have something to write about.'
'Are you mad?' asked Brian, fetching a large wrap from his pocket. 'If you can write while you're on it, I want no part of it!'
'Maria, dear, don't we want to be getting to bed?' protested Sebastian mildly.
'*I* certainly don't,' came in response. She looked to the others for support. 'I may be being egotistical, but how else is one to judge what's in one's interest?'
'*Your interests*, darling, and *what interests you*, are often quite distinct things,' Sebastian remarked, though in an observational rather than argumentative manner.
After a while, thoroughly wrecked but still civilised and lucid, they were onto public service reform.
'I'll tell you something,' affirmed Brian, 'what we're going to do is a heck of a lot different to what the Tories would do if they were running the show. We want a spot of market forces for the sake of diversity and innovation. They just want to flog it all off to their mates!'
'What I don't understand,' said Sebastian, 'is why, as intelligent people, you think your opinions are worth so much? The swarm knows best, as mediated by professionals who depend for their livelihood on getting it right. Your views can't claim to be scientific, you're not divinely inspired: there's only the averaged norm now, or eccentricity; and your backgrounds as the sons and daughters of rad-

ical intellectuals, trades union and Party officials and the like have formed you such that you are blind to the way history has moved on. You're oddballs, clinging like teenagers to a badge of identity. "'Ave they got any politics?" you ask, meaning "Are they left wing?", then you despise the most consummate political professional your party has had for decades, precisely because he's got enough politics to know it's suicide to listen to you lot and not the public. The man who was clear-sighted and brave enough to go to Red Wedge and tell them they needed to be reaching out to the people who were listening to Duran Duran.'

'I must say I've modified my views on Duran Duran,' said Brian.

'Yes, and you're the one who's modified their politics the most, because you're a professional, which means you've got to be *serious*.'

'Isn't it sad how, these days, cynicism seems to be cynicism-lite?' sighed Colleen. 'It's no longer agonised and romantic, the preservation of ideals in the form of disappointment, but their maintenance as nice ideas on which no grown-up would ever act. It's like Peter Sloterdijk says: "They know what they are doing *and still they are doing it*." I think you're being cynical in a way that is above your pay grade, Brian.' Brian, who was quite proud of what he earnt, which, unusually for someone in his line of work, was more than most teachers his age, frowned involuntarily.

'I'm serious,' growled Martin. 'I'm a dangerous man. I'm an intellectual with convictions. Like the Narodniks. I would have shot Thatcher, suppressed the anarchists at Kronstadt, quelled the Spartacists in 1918. Put me in the right place at the right time and I'm a militant for achievable progress.'

'But you never shot Thatcher,' said Colleen.

'I had no idea how, and I didn't suppose I was clever enough to work it out. But if you'd shown me a plan, given me a weapons manual, some training, something like that, if you'd given me the wherewithal, no question.'

'So you're a potential suicide bomber?'

'No! That's not about achievable progress, that's about anger and revenge and a desperate need to assert a clear identity. Don't get me wrong. You need those things. And I've sure as hell got them. But achievable progress is what it's about.'

'But how do you judge what's achievable?' asked Kieran.

'You leave it to the professionals,' said Sebastian, who had given up trying to sleep.

'I used to love *The Professionals*,' said Rafferty. 'They were real men. Like Liam Gallagher.'

Chapter 9
'First Iraq and now this!'

March 2003

Brian would ask himself why he was still with Judy, but what he knew consciously was reason enough. She was an attractive woman in many ways. The tautness of her physique was topped by a well-made face given charm by the large, Lady Di-ish conk in the middle of it. The resemblance would have been more marked had she worn her hair blonde or in the sculpted loaf-helmet of the girlfriends of his youth, emulous of the princess-to-be; but it was a mixed brown and longish, generally bunched up behind but, when loosed, tumbling round her shoulders as silkily as her shampoo said it should.

Convention would have it also that Judith defied the scorn of Rafferty, and was not only kind and capable and possessed of that admirable straightforwardness which is an absence of tricks and ways, rather than that bluntness which is so often a narrow imposition of self – which she was; but engaging, lively and possessed of an intuitive understanding of the heart and soul of man which compensated for her lack of the sophistications of book-learnin' – which she was not. She did not know nuffink; indeed she was possessed of a good average of the range and depth of knowledge her school had deemed relevant; but she had a less vivid conception of life outside Illeshall than she did of the comforts and privileges afforded those who broke into the magic circle of celebrity. She had no fantasies of joining this circle herself. For her it was merely something to gab about with the girls, a leisure activity, just as they might tour the sheening counters of John Lewis in Liverpool or The Trafford Centre. She was content with her lot of bounded aspiration and believed, like most of us, in 'bettering herself'. Rafferty held that Brian's continued association with her was a sign that he had become complicit in his own torpor. In his more sullen moods he would agree with her to the extent of reflecting that he had never known there were jobs that could land you in places where no suitable women existed – indeed, that the idea of such a place had never occurred to him. Self-pity is a considerable defence against guilt over such things as infidelity.

Even at his most piqued he hadn't come close to spurning her, for the moment he glimpsed such an urge beneath the surface of his mind there rose before him the prospect of being a single man in Illeshall. To think of being one of those blokes in their fifties, greying, paunchy, shuffling around pubs around town till they met up with others of their kind, no friends, no prospect of a woman, only drink, and drinking buddies. What is more, for all her lack of heft or precision as a commentator on the human condition, Judith nonetheless served as a confidante, someone to whom he could commit thoughts that would not have been innermost save that Illeshall was the most talkative place he had ever experienced. No confidence was ever kept, it seemed. 'Everybody knows everybody's business here,' Nicola, his co-worker in the constituency office, had assured him brightly shortly after he arrived, and had meant it as a boast.

What is more, she was a haven in a world where the passions and the humours, whether good or bad, were more unconcealed and less alloyed than he had known outside his parents' marriage. It seemed to him that, while he did his best to remain upbeat and bright, others saw this as precisely the magnet for the iron filings of their angers, moodinesses and depressions, like toddlers with a parent. Or at least, that is how he saw it sometimes, when he had not let himself become convinced that there was a low falsity to such 'Hail fellow well met antics,' as Rob Jenkins described his efforts. Brian tried theorising all this as a matter of cultural difference, as a clash of sensibilities or structures of feeling; but to live it was wearing, and never ceased to be so.

Nor did the need continually to demonstrate he was not 'up himself', evidence of which, given that he was from London, could be anything at all. What really made this distressing was that it was a demand that was not entirely external to him, that it created in him a constant desire to justify himself. For Brian was not 'middle class', as he was constantly told he was in Illeshall, in any simple sense. Culturally highly aware of the modes of bourgeois culture, he was nonetheless only one generation away from the Manchester slums. He was a hybrid creature in a rigidly dualistic world of 'snobs' and the 'alright'. He was on the side of both, while it sometimes seemed everyone was against him, or always liable to be. However he behaved, he would always be reflected back to himself as by a mirror in a House of Fun. Observing how hard everyone worked to ensure everyone stayed in their place, to enforce social norms, and how so many of the people who surrounded him were determined to make him as unhappy as they were, or to allow him to be happy only on their terms, the fundamental tenet of Brian's political credo – that virtue resided with the poor and oppressed – was sorely tried. Once, it seemed to him, he had believed in the illimitability of human potential; and now, he occasionally felt, he found himself mired in human nature at its most petty and least noble. He pondered ever more frequently Bacon's description of statecraft as the art of building a ship from 'the crooked timbers of humanity'. He called to mind Michelle, a bright working-class girl, and how glad she had been to leave her hometown behind, how wretched she now felt her life there had been.

Thus, where once, as a teenager, his model of social power being the restrictive practices of teachers, he had believed simply that the world was run by stupid, bad people who should be replaced by philosopher-kings in the form of revolutionary leaders such as he himself would surely be (strictly speaking, his own private fantasy was of being a revolutionary cadre, commander of a platoon, semi-automatic in hand but not firing, crouched behind a crumbling wall with some fleeing civilians, including a hauntingly beautiful artistic woman who would fall in love with him because of his conviction and competence) now he felt the temptation to believe that, if there were no philosopher-kings in Illeshall, it was probably because they were avoiding the place like the plague and, given the psychological and intellectual deformations of such radicals as Illeshall boasted, that he would rather take his chances with the elite. And he began wondering where he had gone wrong, that he should be so completely unhappy, since once, in his intellectual confidence, it had never crossed his mind that his life would be anything other than fine and fulfilling so long as he did the right thing. That he had gone wrong was clear, and this in itself sapped his self-confidence, causing him to wonder whether he had the right stuff at all. All kinds of talents and dispositions came to seem, if fleetingly, more valuable than those that had brought him to such a pass; which at least did him the favour of relativising the worth of those abilities he did possess.

Thus Rafferty found herself saying: 'But there are thousands of idiots here in London.'

'Maybe,' Brian replied, 'maybe. But there aren't *only* idiots in London. And in any case, maybe you just think they're idiots because they don't think the same things you do. You know you tend to do that.'

'Well, I'm right.' They both laughed.

'But I just don't think I'm that intelligent. I don't think with great scope, I don't seize on precisely the telling detail. What I can do is digest fairly difficult stuff, present it coherently and sometimes even punchily, and hundreds of thousands of people can do that. At Manchester, I read more than most people, especially about the things I thought were important, and I had a radical perspective, and I thought anything I didn't know already I would attend to in due course, and so I stood out. But at Oxford there'd have been hundreds and hundreds of people like that, and maybe I'd have been properly put in my place. When I listen to Radio 4, *everyone* seems more intelligent than me.'

To which Rafferty replied: 'They're just confident and think the position they occupy is part of the natural order. Anyway, I think you're being silly and you should just come to London. It's no good trying to combine the sensibility of a spiritual aristocrat with the sociology of an MP's skivvy. If you don't value yourself aright, you'll get valued at the world's estimation. Or I could say, conversely, that while you say you're desperate to get to London, you don't seem dynamic enough to get here: you won't grasp opportunities, let alone make them.'

'You're not rousing me to action, you know. You're making me feel thoroughly misunderstood.'

'Well, that's not necessarily everybody else's fault. It sounds like self-pity.'

'Maybe. You know, it is possible for someone not to have an obvious way out.'

'Well the way out may not *be* obvious. Especially when you just see the downside of everything. What would be so bad about being a teacher? Millions of people are.'

'I really can't bear the thought of all that talking, and having constantly to win the kids over and keep them onside. And keep discipline. My god, it sounds like a nightmare.'

'It sounds quite a lot like the job you already do.'

'Oh, but not in the same proportions. The trouble is, I want exactly *this* job, but exactly not here.'

'What about another MP?'

'Well, for a start, I'm not going to another small place. In other words, nowhere but London. And in London it's a young person's game on a young person's money... I know I sound like someone finding reasons not to do things, but I really do think it's actually because there are reasons not to do them; I am not boxing myself into a corner, I am objectively boxed into a corner.'

'"Everything Must Change."'

'I suppose so. Eventually.'

'Patience, *mon cheri*.'

Adding to his 'patience' was an attachment to Illeshall that was a stubborn adherence to his life choices, choices based in his conception of virtue, derived from his father, and involving thus both a desire to prove his father right, and proving himself to be right with his image of his father. It almost amounted, he came to realise, to a desire to live his father's life in, he was coming to fear, circumstances that were no longer propitious: perhaps his parents' life was contingent on the post-war settlement, and its rewards were for the educationally adept working class to remain in the service of the state rather than aspiring on their own account. Thus Illeshall appeared to him as both a test of his spiritual mettle and a possible fool's errand, and Judy was both enabler and emblem of this.

When Brian considered Illeshall under the latter aspect, he was by no means immune to the irony of the fact that, instead of a gifted working-class child getting out of a small Northern town, he was an ambiguously middle-class man, approaching middle age with, though he allowed it himself, gifts of his own. It seemed unfair to him that cultural poetics should require that he feel guilty for his desire to do as the child. Yet this was blindness. His parents' guilt at their own versions of this self-betterment had been the irregular bias in the course of their lives, the momentum of which, conjoined with the gravitational pull of Judy, held him still. A more complicated equation than that of the high enslaved by sexual desire for the low, the favoured son by the comely wench.

What Rafferty called torpor was, all the same, vivified periodically by sex, which principle, conceived by Brian as Lawrentian, could be activated by, for instance, the nondescript sheepskin boots Judy sometimes wore, which for Brian were imbued with the aura of all the cute inappropriate girlies he tried not to look at for an instant too long as they tootled in and out of his gaze. The rest of the time they were like two cats, he rereading *The Portrait of a Lady* yet again, she scribbling notes on a soap; or of a Saturday night enjoying the pleasures of a lamb satkora and a chicken tikka masala at the local balti; or rooting round a car boot sale on a Sunday and returning empty-handed, in almost mute animal singularity and solidarity; like many another couple, he supposed.

He knew it would not be enough in the end. And yet he plotted not an escape, but a further narrative development. Knowing full well that they were not fully open to one another, he theorised that one is open to people who are liable to affect one's life. And so he decided to turn Judy into such a creature. Having lamented for some months, bleeding into years, that his residence in Illeshall was depriving him of whole phases of life, that if at times he was troubled by the mood swings and diffuseness and changeability of the adolescent it was because his lot was similarly liminal, unintegrated, he resolved to integrate himself good and proper. Feeling cast adrift, he willed instinctual unity: he would have a baby with Judith.

And so one night, having broken open an extra bottle of Chardonnay and observed their mutual consumption of half its contents, Brian asked Judy why she hadn't ever broached the subject of children.

'Well, I've already got one; and if I just wanted to get knocked up there's plenty of men down the gym willing to do the job.'

'Would you like one with me?' Brian asked.
'I don't know. Maybe I need persuading.'

The news – not that Judith was pregnant, but that they might try – got a predictably mixed reception.
'That's wonderful!' cried Michelle.
'Well, it's about time you settled down,' said Colleen.
'Congratulations,' said Martin, Kieran and Matt.
'Oh Brian, what on *earth* are you playing at? What is she? Calypso? Or *Circe*?' asked Rafferty, aghast.
'Well; she's certainly enchanting.'
'First Iraq and now this!'
'Well, they're both happening and that's that.'
'Like it's up to you.'
'Well, one of them is. I shall exercise my rights as far as my authority extends.'
'I'm glad you're thinking about it in legal terms. I've been doing much the same. I was flicking through a copy of C. B. Macpherson's *Political Philosophy of Possessive Individualism*, and it got me thinking about penetrative sex.'
'There's not a lot that doesn't, is there?'
'Yes, well, no. I was thinking: if no man has a right to "invade" the property of another, and the possessive individualist sees himself as having property in his body, then by virtue of my position on rape, I'm a possessive individualist, i.e. I'm a liberal feminist.'
'Yes, well, socialist feminism doesn't *deny* liberal–'
'I mean, having someone inside you *is* quite an invasive thing, if you think about it the wrong way. It's very much something someone has to earn the right to, whether by beauty or character. My husband has a standing right to invade me, of course, unless specifically rescinded. When it comes to interpretation of my attitude in respect of said invasion, there is a presumption in favour of his rights as my husband, though these are always subject to review. And I'd be angry with him for retrospective invasion if we split up, naturally. I expect that's where the spite of divorcing women comes from.'
'Well, there's generally a sense of emotional betrayal, isn't there?'

'Oh, I suppose so. Anyway, where *do* you get the right to invade Iraq from?'

'I'm not doing it personally! And it's not a sexual thing.'

'Are you sure?'

'Anyway, from the fact Saddam is a truly awful tyrant and is in contravention of yet another UN Resolution, 1441, which allows for "serious consequences" for non-compliance–'

'But they didn't get a second resolution!'

'But a second resolution was politically desirable rather than legally necessary. It's only because we tried so hard to get one that people think we *needed* one. I thought the Left believed international law was a bourgeois illusion, anyway. Who wants their foreign policy determined by Russia and France, who are up to their necks in oil and financial business in Iraq? And who specifically failed to get a resolution debarring military action on the basis of 1441. In any case, those against the war argue the necessity of a second resolution, and those for it point to 1441, and there's no legal body to adjudicate the case.'

'But it's an act of imperialism against the Muslim world!'

'No, it's not. It's an attack on perhaps the most brutal dictator in the world, with the support of the Iraqi Left. Why should the experience of actual Iraqis be trumped by the stance of a peasant in Pakistan, be subsumed in some self-aggrandising global drama of Muslim injury, some further step in the ongoing endarkenment of the Islamic world? In any case, we didn't have a resolution for Kosovo, and Robin Cook and Clare Short went for that; *and* that was *defending* Muslims. You seem to think these people are the oppressed fighting for freedom. But they *hate* our freedoms, they hate the very things about our system that we leftists approve of. The freedom they want is the freedom to throw acid in the faces of westernised women in Kabul.'

'But it will destabilise the Middle East and expose us to further terrorist attacks. It's reckless militarism. Saddam will probably use his WMD.'

'The Middle East could do with destabilising. It's badly in need of modernisation. And as for WMD, it's better to pick a fight with Saddam at a time of our choosing rather than his. The only persuasive force that got him to let inspectors back in was 250,000 Allied troops, and we'd better use them while we've got them. And that means before the Iraqi summer. You have to understand: everything's new since 9/11. We simply can't take the risk of links between Saddam and Al-Qaeda.'

'Saddam is too secular for Al-Qaeda.'

'I wouldn't be too sure. Everything's new; we can't depend on received wisdom. Think of Bali. They're against people *dancing*.'

'They're against people nicking their oil.'

'It's not about oil. If it were about oil we could have cut a deal with Saddam in the blink of an eye. It's about liberation from *evil*; a New World Order.'

'About the Project for a New American Century, more like; and you're all lapdogs of imperialism.'

'And you're an appeaser. Tony's been talking about Saddam since his Chicago speech in '99. We *believe* in this cause. Liberal interventionism and neocon ambitions just happen to meet at this point.'

'But the US is the evil empire.'

'Maria, I'm not even going to address that; it's laughable. The evil is the evil that's broadcasting the protests against the war on state television.'

'Don't call me laughable! Don't you think there's something fundamentally cockeyed in trying to *persuade* a nation into a war on an abstract concept like Terror, or Evil?'

'Fascism was an abstract concept, but it has very concrete particularisations, like Saddam.'

'Or Libya. Or North Korea. Why aren't you attacking them?'

'We can't do everything; and especially not everything all at once. But we have to do something to protect against the appalling randomness of terror.'

'That's such a Western, middle-class view. Like "The Project". Where everything can be planned and executed. Do you think people in the developing world don't know randomness every day of their lives?'

'Well, poor them, and lucky us. And let's do something for them while trying to stay lucky. Let's defend our way of life.'

'"*Defend our way of life?!*" What has become of you?! You've become an American.'

'No, I haven't. I just don't see America as an enemy. In fact, I see an attack on them as an attack on us.'

'They were asking for it.'

'Asking for it how?'

'By being imperialist. By being arrogant, and fucking around with the rest of the world.'

'America is a great power, and great powers have always had far-reaching interests. There's nothing unique or extraordinary about America in that respect.'

'Listen to you! It's just realpolitik! What happened to your ideals, your values?'

'Traditional values in a modern context. And a real one.'

'Jesus, Brian; I can't have this conversation any longer. I'll speak to you when I've calmed down. *If* I've calmed down. And not before.' Although his mind had been clear, and even energised, while they argued, his body had begun to tremble, and once he had put the phone down Brian took stock of the fact that he was shaken. He didn't like to argue with friends at the best of times; and it seemed to him there had been real scorn and dismay in Rafferty's tone. What is more, he could not now call her except to recant, it seemed. His will as a cadre had crunched into his nature as a devotee.

Perhaps it was an obscure desire to compensate for this that led Brian to lend more weight to the first target of her ire. Perhaps it was the thought that he could ring her with news of revisionism in respect of Judy; but the idea of having a baby in Illeshall came to weigh more heavily upon him. It took on the aspect of a concretisation of his separation from his friends; a kind of divorce; a step he could not take however much he willed it. It showed almost at once, in his disinclination to engage in sexual relations with Judy. Whatever Brian had meant to do, it seemed to Judy that he had brought their relations with each other to a crisis, and ensured a de facto resolution.

'So she finished with you then?' asked Sara in Costa Coffee, as if satisfied to have had a suspicion confirmed.

'Single man again!' affirmed Rob Jenkins, apparently equally pleased. Brian was on his own.

Chapter 10
'Informed choices without explicit thought'

July 2003

At first the pornography pulled the gaze here and there among the numerous TV screens around the room where flesh pressed flesh and his interlocutor, Allegra, regarded him with an appraising eye.

'You get used to it after a while,' she said, a nod of the head encompassing the scenes of abandon with which they were surrounded. 'Then it becomes what it really is, something to be ignored, wallpaper, the ubiquitous ongoing film of our lives.' Brian felt like a country cousin. In the corner, one of the Spice Girls was talking to Peter York and Lauren Booth, and soon it was they to whom his attention repeatedly switched. Allegra nodded toward a television intellectual whose name escaped Brian. 'He's a great talker, but he clams up in bed. I used to fuck him for the sake of some peace and quiet.' Brian reddened. Allegra resumed her line of thought. 'If even Fredric Jameson can evoke, in his postmodernism book, the threat to our sense of ourselves that being out-competed represents, then what hope have *you* got? What's the point of being a Blairite if you have no access to power? You take the flak but you don't get in the sack.'

'Because it's what I believe in,' said Brian, with more assurance than he felt about anything else. The news that his father was dying had been like a trapdoor opening underneath his feet while, unexplainedly, he remained suspended above the white-noise visuals of the void, knowing, somewhere, that at some point he would fall. On the train on the way to visit, Brian had spent the entire time walking through carriages he now recalled as empty but which cannot have been. What he did not know consciously was that, with the prospect of the death of his father, he was facing the absence of the gaze in the light of which his life made sense to him.

'Even now?' demanded Allegra.

'Now?'

'Well, doesn't the whole forty-five-minute business seem like a moment of truth to you? It does to me. It epitomises you lot. You thought you could spin anything, that you could spin a country into war. Don't you think there's something fundamentally perverse about that? I mean, do the British strike you as a particularly pacific lot, that when their real interests are threatened they are liable to avoid war? What about The Falklands?'

'It was a piece of intelligence, passed by the Joint Intelligence Committee.'

'It was a dodgy bit of intelligence that Blair repeated about a dozen times in a one-page foreword; and the man who told the press it was dodgy is dead.'

'You're not getting into conspiracy theories, are you? This is a man who approved of deposing Saddam but talked illegitimately and loosely to journalists, then lied about it to Parliament. He was worried about being shamed and sacked. It's a tragedy, yes; but he was a Walter Mitty character.'

'That's shameful! He was a senior and respected government scientist!'

'Are you upsetting Ally?' Rafferty intervened. 'Talking about Iraq? They keep blowing up mosques!'

'You think *we're* blowing up mosques?'

'Could well be. Stir up trouble between the Shia and the Sunni, keep the national resistance from uniting. Either that or they haven't taken enough soldiers to keep order, which is criminal.'

'Can you really condemn an invasion, believe in a national resistance to it *and* object to there not being enough troops?' Brian asked.

'Well, it all just goes to show that the whole thing was ill-conceived. "*Not in my name!*"'

'Which somewhat goes against the whole notion of some Machiavellian master plan.' Rafferty and Allegra rolled their eyes.

'Even Machiavellian master plans can go pear-shaped if you've got the likes of Bush and Cheney involved,' sneered Rafferty.

'The point is,' persisted Brian, 'the prospect of a democratic Iraq means the Sunni, who are only twenty per cent of the population, face the prospect of losing their privileged position. In response, elements among them, with the help of the Sunni Al-Qaeda, are trying to make Iraq ungovernable. There's no trouble in Shia areas, which account for sixty per cent of the population, or Kurdistan, which makes up twenty per cent, though you wouldn't know that from the meeja.'

'Who says the Shia are the majority? The Sunni dispute it.'

'Well, anyway, in Basra in June, 17,000 students sat their university exams as normal. That's what it's like away from the Sunni triangle.'

'Anyway, what's all this about the meeja? Don't you like my friends? If not, what are you doing here? Still hoping to rescue me from a fate that's unworthy of me?!'

'No! I just think there's some groupthink going on, that's all.'

'Well, me and Allegra are going back to our group,' said Rafferty, putting an arm round her friend and ushering her away.

Michelle rescued him. *'Mein Irisch Kind, wo weilest du?* Come and talk to us. We're moaning about the fucking scumbag fucking middle class.'

'Kick the fuckers in the knackers,' said Brian reflexively. Then, 'Why the superabundance of modifiers?'

'Well, it's a matter of decorum. They're of no more value than fucking scumbags, but such a formulation, in imputing worthlessness, might be taken to imply mere scornful indifference, when the only appropriate emotion is white-hot, ice-cold anger: thus the second "fucking". It's only fitting.'

'Yes, I can see that,' said Brian, impressed with her precision.

When they got over to the others, disposed around an L-shaped sofa, Martin was in full flow. 'I started out a millenarian. My enemies say I have traced an all-too-typical trajectory from ultra-leftism to hopelessness, from idealism to cynicism and, they intimate, something darker; I laugh in their faces and say that my ultra-leftism was only ever a mask for my rage at the ineffable dullness of existence, and that that anger has died and been reborn as undying yet ever-changing melancholy at "mutabilitie". It keeps me in Hugo Boss. If the fashion for me ever fades, it will be because Trotskyism is on the rise once more, in which case I may well become a Trotskyist again.'

'Wouldn't you have to believe in it?' prodded Kieran.

'I probably will, if you lot can work out how to plan an economy.'

'Well, it's a question of democratisation.'

'How can that compete with the market as a coordinator of almost infinite individual preferences?'

'Well, we might not all get the precise combination of perfume and moisturiser in our shampoo that we didn't realise we'd dreamed about until we found it—'

'—so what you're saying is, come the revolution, we'll have nothing but bad-hair days. Do you think the women of the world will stand for that?'

'I think most women in the world want reliable food, water, shelter, education.'

'Ah, but come the dawning of global social democracy they'll have all that, and they'll want nice hair as well. As will I. Until Trotskyists pass the L'Oréal test, the revolution will not be televised owing to indefinite postponement. I congratulate you on the quasi-religious strength of your commitment to deferred gratification; but it's one the rest of humanity, including me, lacks.'

'Boys, boys; let's not get heated,' interceded Michelle, seating herself between them and placing a hand on the knee of each. 'I think we need some chemical enhancement. Because we're worth it.'

'Quite right, darling!' affirmed Martin. 'Too much talk of no consequence. Too much like the groves of academe. Have I told you about the new article I'm planning? It's going to be called 'Against Dialogue: Toward the Elimination of Academic Debate'. The text will consist entirely of an invitation to anyone who wants to make something of it to meet me round the back of the Hilton at midnight on the first day of the next MLA Conference; though I may specify Alan Sokal as my interlocutor–combatant.'

'But then you'd be seen as siding with *Social Text*,' objected Kieran.

'Yes, you're right; oh well, I'll just have to take them *all* on!' Brian had not yet sat down, but was looking across to where Rafferty and Allegra were entertaining some young, thin, bald men in black-framed glasses who wrote for the *New Statesman*. 'I stand like Satan in the garden, grieving at smiles,' he thought to himself, and recalled, involuntarily, St Augustine's *invidia* at the sight of his baby brother's bliss at his mother's breast.

'Do you want a summary of the posterior analytics?' he asked Martin. 'Disappearing up your own arse.'

'Ah yes; our contemporary academic plight. Although it might be truer to say that today we aim at a point at infinity, where our arse and the universal are coincident. There's no *judgement* in academia any more. Criticism requires judgement, but now it's all theory, which is to say, extrapolations and logical conclusions, which tend to the absurd. Slavoj Žižek publishes in a Verso series called *Phronesis*, which is to say, practical reasoning; but all he does is amplify Marx's diptych into a triptych: if history occurs first as tragedy and the second time as farce, in Žižek it is incarnated as stand-up comedy. Thus there's been a general apprehension that Western man has been responsible for all kinds of bad things; and that Western man is possessed of self-esteem; ergo, for many, self-esteem is bad and deflation of it is politically progressive. Well, it depends, doesn't it, on the circs, about which one must reason practically and specifically: one must judge. Certainly Marx thought self-esteem a requisite for the workers of the Rhineland.'

'So *how is* White's?' asked Colleen, smiling.

'The department is a tip. The students love it because it reassures them about where their money's going, and that our minds are on higher things – the highest things money can buy. Plus, we have a smoking policy, which is to encourage it. It is an obvious point that the smoke from a cigarette is a perfect image for thoughts drifting into the infinite, but arresting us, fleetingly, as they go. I dress like a junglist out of time – you see, black jeans, black T-shirt, white trainers – and play my students *Bitches Brew* and Glenn Gould's Bach. And they actually, genuinely, copy my mannerisms, like the way I flick the end off a cigarette when I've finished with it. I guess I'm in clover, a regular *locus amoenus*.'

'And your love life?'

'I'm having problems with Asha, chiefly because she's junior to me which, despite the fact she's ten years younger, seems to her to fly in the face of the proper order of things. At the same time, much of her interest in me is down to the fact I'm senior to her, which invests those thoughts that come to me unbidden with the status of aperçus. She wants me because she wants to beat me, but as soon as she does we'll be through. Unless I get her pregnant, in which case I can't see her ever catching up. Lack of sleep is a terrible hindrance to connected thought, and she's in postcolonial computational linguistics. For me, of course, the disconnection of my thoughts is a positive boon.'

'You're a natural,' smiled Kieran.

'Don't come at me with your outmoded metaphysics, you… you… unreconstructed Marxist!'

'At least I'm not a deconstructed one.'

'It would suit you, sir,' was Martin's rejoinder. 'Anyway, what are you retrofitting at the moment? Re-engineering? Rebranding?'

'Ah. It's the opposite of a rebranding, it's a revamp. I'm seeking to ramp up a company's understanding of the way its brand is not only a matter of its own identity, but a form of service to the consumer, enabling them to make informed choices without explicit thought.'

'Dear Lord! Get me to a nunnery! I suppose you build it into the package, make it part of your offer. What do you call what you're doing now?'

'Analyst relations,' smiled Kieran. 'PR for computer engineering. Demands intellectual flexibility.'

'Then I'm all for it!' affirmed Martin, and lifted and drained his glass.

'So you should be. After all, Tim Allan, once Deputy Director of Communications at Number 10, has moved up in the world and is working for BSkyB now.'

'Aren't we all?' sighed Martin.

'A necessary prelude to the socialisation of the means of production,' smiled Kieran.

'Itself a necessary prelude to the socialisation of women!' exclaimed Martin. 'Speaking personally, I consider myself already pretty fully socialised. I am an avatar of the future!'

'A rather dystopian vision, I hope you don't mind me saying,' interjected Colleen, who turned to Brian. 'How's tricks in Illeshall?' she asked, brightening.

'Apparently I'm a dallier.' Brian half raised his eyes. 'I enter into dalliances. I dally with women.'

'Ah.'

'Privatised women, I might add.'

'Ah. You want to watch *them*.'

'Oh, I do; I do,' said Brian with faux-wistfulness.

'Do you think you'll stay there?'

'I have no fucking idea.'

'Nice suit, by the way.'

'It's my best.' It was the first time Brian had worn a suit to a party, having come to feel increasingly juvenile amid the tailored throng at Rafferty's little get-togethers. 'It's my "man of substance" suit... You know, I was thinking the other day about what constitutes the essence of my politics, and there came into my mind an image of one time I was near the bar of a pub in town, having a drink with my girlfriend. We were having a pleasant enough time, chatting about this and that, when we began getting jostled by a mass of besuited, paunchy, raucous men. We'd been absorbed in each other, and so I didn't even really notice until we were virtually pressed up in the corner of the pub by these oblivious men needlessly crowding the bar, occupying the centre of the room as if by right. And I turned to my girlfriend, who was called Zelda, and I said to her "I never *ever* want to be like that." And I think that was a lot of my politics – anger at the powers that be. Dr Johnson diagnosed it in Milton as "an envious hatred of greatness", and I think there's something to that. I think I've been motivated more by dislike of authority than by fellow feeling. Certainly fellow feeling alone isn't enough for me in Illeshall.'

'But you felt solidarity with Zelda.'

'Solidarity because we shared a situation in common.'

'But that's pretty much a Sartrean definition of class-consciousness. That's alright. Because some teenagers must look at those men in suits and say to themselves "I don't much like my peers. I want to get away from them, outdo them. I want some of that." Like the Oxbridge kid who accepts the authority of the teacher because he aspires one day to possess it for himself.'

'Oxford is worldly power,' interjected Martin. 'It doesn't so much distrust as scorn the abstraction that would unmask appearances. It is the reality of appearances.'

'Hmm. But the other day, I was walking down the street when I came to a crowded bus stop, with only a narrow way through. I was on one side, and there was this little black girl on the other side; and we both stopped, then stepped forward together, then stopped, then stepped forward, several times; and I realised I kept stepping forward because I was expecting her to give way to me, an adult, as though that somehow gave me more right to move around the world than she had; and in the end she gave up, and let me through. I thought to myself: I am a man in a suit.'

'Yes, perhaps; but children are a pain. They think they can do what they like. They are, precisely, in their nonage. Whereas you are of age, a locus of rational authority, and take precedence.'

'Well, I wish noblesse had obliged. I am a man in a suit. But so are they,' he gestured toward the ruck in the centre of the room. 'I am among my own kind.'

'No you're not. You're on the margins, like the rest of us on the sofa.'

Martin was discussing the semi-colon. 'Some say it's a prevaricating form of punctuation, that you should decide whether you want a comma or a full stop, but they are brutes. I say, a semi-colon's something you just gotta feel, baby. As Duke Ellington said of swing, "If I have to explain, you wouldn't understand."'

In the morning, when almost everyone had gone, Rafferty was playing her favourite bits of Roxy Music and the sound of 'Mother of Pearl' drifted into the kitchen, where Brian stood looking into the green of the garden through the opened French windows. Was the party over? He was and wasn't tired. For a moment he fancied himself, in his suit and unbuttoned shirt, a bottle of champagne and a glass in hand, something of a Bryan Ferry character, incipient decay facing a bright new day with sad resolution. Michelle came in, fatigued, smiling, and held out a glass.

'Here I am,' said Brian, 'washed up on the shore of humanity. You'd better watch out; I'll be quoting "Dover Beach" next.'

Chapter 11
'The face of a malevolent hamster'

July 2003

Brian was feeling less like Bryan Ferry than a passenger of the Ferryman as he disembarked at Illeshall. He was conscious of blithe shrieks – 'those dying generations' – as he achieved his flat and donned the leather box jacket that he had substituted for the much-remarked-upon Burberry raincoat he had purchased with his first instalment of salary. Sortieing forth with the sounds of The Fall's 'Totally Wired' in his ears to bolster his resolve, he tried to imagine himself as a type of Mark E. Smith. A somewhat diffident and complaisant Mark E. Smith, to be sure; but at one with the post-industrial grimacing pleasure centre the middle of Illeshall became of a Saturday night: one not disposed to stop and wonder what he could possibly be doing standing on this particular patch of ground. He was a cadre with a seat to hold, and he was going to make the best of it.

As he walked, unwontedly discerning middle-aged selves in the groups of young girls he passed, breasts fulsome but lines creased if not yet cut into their foreheads, he recalled how, going forth with Rafferty, it sometimes seemed they were touring their realm in disguise. He all states, all princes she. Now he but lived where motley was worn: the music had stopped. He paused in his progress to let an ageing white van trundle past, and was cheered then saddened by the squib of a thought that he could write a Beckettian drama set in such a vehicle, and call it 'Transit'.

When in Illeshall, he had come to regard Illeshall as the nature of things. His dislike of it was so complete that it made more sense to see the problem as lying with him. He had convinced a substantial fraction of himself that the reason he enjoyed his trips to London so much, why, when there, he seemed to be breathing oxygenated air and seemed blessed by the absence of some kryptonitic property inhering in the being of Illeshall, was that, essentially, they were holidays; and that this was the lot of the modern worker, to be afforded only fleeting glimpses of a fuller, more variegated, less alienated, life. More positively, he took a grim delight in reciting to himself George Herbert's 'The Collar' – 'I struck the board and cried "No more! I will abroad"' – and considering that, in the absence of a god to gently chide his childish impulse, his only recourse was a commitment to his vocation nonetheless. He convicted himself of *acedia*, that listless restlessness of soul that beset the mediaeval monk, and searched for patterns of resolution if not redemption in the existentialist literature he had scorned as a youth. But, in essence, he just wondered why Rocquentin didn't get out of Bouville and go to Paris. And, stepping off the train at Illeshall Central, he invariably felt as though he were falling off the edge of the earth to a place where he felt isolated, exposed, panoptically visible as bare, forked man and his preening gestures. And yet he hoped he might, with Empson, learn a style from despair; develop, as T. S. Eliot had it of Lafargue, an unshakeable politeness in the face of existence. He would seek to rationalise, and minimise the proportion of his time devoted to chasing windmills. And so he dressed like Mark E. Smith.

Or, more pertinently, like Rob Jenkins and Pete Grimshaw, union delegates to the GC and influential members of the EC in their respective capacities as one of the vice-chairs and Membership Secretary. Brian liked to think that his diligence in courting them and the rest of the 'Left', such as it now was – by spending whole evenings, including Saturday evenings, drinking with them and absorbing their niggles with as much blandness as he could muster – had helped forestall such whisperings about reselection as had arisen at the time of the Iraq vote; although, in truth, such was the disorientedly quiescent, because electorally victorious, state of the Labour Party throughout the country that few enough MPs had come under threat, and certainly not Peter Middleton. Jackson and Grimshaw were already sat at a table in The Red Queen. Brian could not look at Grimshaw without thinking that his mien was made for milieux amidst the nostra of which the likes of Rafferty could never flourish. With them were Ros Grimes, a Media Studies Lecturer at the local HE college with the face – and the largeness of spirit – of a malevolent hamster – of whom Brian longed to ask 'Just what *is* the secret of your intimate bond with the working class, Rosa*mund*?' – and Janice Cole, whose Cupidish youthfulness of feature was accentuated by the steel grey of her cropped hair. It was she who led off.

'This date for the fundraising dinner is the maddest thing I ever heard of. It's almost a direct clash with the Women's Forum!' Brian was by now inured to the fact that anti-authoritarianism was not always sublimated and directed in the Labour Party, at least in its Illeshallian manifestation.

'Yes, but with *ministers* we have to take them when they're available.'

'But I've already sent round the email. It's very inconvenient for women members.'

'Yes, I can see that, and I'm sorry; but in this case I don't really see what can be done about it.'

'Well, I think we should avoid this kind of thing happening in future.'

'Yes, "down with this kind of thing",' thought Brian. 'Well, I promise I'll do my best,' he said. 'I endure myself,' he said to himself, citing Martin citing Cioran.

'We were just discussing literature,' said Pete Grimshaw, eager to take on Brian on Brian's home ground. 'Don't you think this is a brilliant image for what a real writer can do: "Join the scattered dots of our minds"?' Brian thought it very apt, indeed apposite, and said so in as many words; but more words came to him – Eliot's 'as if a magic lantern threw the nerves in patterns on a screen', Yeats's remark that Eliot's poetry was the work of a man 'helpless before the contents of his own mind', some thoughts about the vagaries of modern subjectivity and whether justice was done to these in popular culture (infuriating Rosamund), a summary of the pros and cons of Fredric Jameson's commitment to 'cognitive mapping' as the practical form of contemporary radical class-consciousness – he couldn't help himself. Grimshaw, admiration vying with the clear view that young men were generally improved by being taken down a peg or two, remarked that he hadn't asked for a lecture; and Brian, who was more enthusiast than bombaster, full of the spirit more than full of himself, as any of the true Puritan strain might have allowed him in moderation, was punctured and useless.

Just then, Julian Deauville and Gerry Maguire walked in. 'Oi Gerry!' said Brian, keen to amuse the Irishman. 'What would you say if I said to you that U2 discovered irony and took themselves more seriously than ever before?'

'I'd say it was altogether the kind of thing you *would* say, so,' said Maguire, not altogether unamused.

'Oi Brian,' said Deauville, keen to test whether Brian could take the form of address he gave, and also to trump his bon mots, 'Have you heard the new joke about Oasis?' Brian, to the best of his knowledge, had made it up some weeks previously. 'They're their own tribute band,' he piped up. 'Little shit,' said Deauville, more mutteringly than was called for, and than he perhaps intended. Brian took this as a datum to be put on the side of the ledger that held all the reasons Illeshall was somewhere he could do no more than subsist in.

Deauville was lean in every aspect, but not because the fire within had burnt the excess; rather, because he lacked the energy to reach beyond what was necessary for subsistence. His limbs, his torso, his nose, all moved in a kind of angular flow, as if manipulated by a puppeteer concerned to show his skill by how slowly and steadily he could dip the head and cross the legs. A ruminant, definitely, who could chew an idea well after the last of its goodness had oozed away, and was asking, Brian thought, to be bitten in the throat. He was soon talking Iraq to death, with a slowness way past methodical, piling up disaster after disaster at the Allies' door. One thing he knew: the US would never allow a functioning democracy there.

Brian made for the bar. The peroxided young woman behind the bar was, as ever, encased in a black Lycra catsuit. She had the body for it, if anyone did, and took care, when fetching bottles from the fridge, to bend from the waist rather than crouch, allowing her customers a thoroughly gluteal view of her posterior. Brian wondered idly what she was up to. That there was a strong narcissistic aspect to her behaviour was clear. But did she merely desire to command admiration, or was she concerned to excite the desire of her throng? Probably, Brian reflected, at some level she was keen to ensure she had her pick of the men that came her way. That was certainly no longer him, if it ever had been. Sexual irrelevance was always depressing. She took his money with an abstract, photographic smile, and left him to his fate.

Brian's last amour had been verging on the inappropriate, a nice, bright, pleasant-looking brunette, with whom he had first had sex at her twentieth. Once again he had fallen prey to the hypothesis that promptings he persisted in thinking of as Lawrentian might bind him to a nice girl. In fact, after a few weeks, she had concluded their dealings with the sentiment that, unfortunately, together they lacked 'the X-factor'. Brian had been furious with himself, partly because he realised that, in sleepwalking through their sexual relations, he had neglected to make her come; but mostly because of the blow to his pride in the thought that he had allowed himself to become a part of the story of someone to whom such a reference came naturally: 'Poor Brian: we just lacked "the X-factor".' The fact of this liaison, let alone its brevity, had been further evidence for those in the constituency who held that Brian was only interested in 'the thrill of the chase', or 'scared of commitment'. The latter seemed to him one of those 'provincial miscomprehensions' of which he was becoming so acutely over-aware, desperate for affinity as he felt himself to be, but the former had prompted a degree of introspection. For he had indeed found that, beyond the initial flush of sexual charm, he found himself at a loss for conversation. He wondered whether that was what sexual predation was.

Brian's marital status seemed to have become a subject of interest while he was away. 'What do you say, Brian? I say you meet your woman by the age of twenty-one,' affirmed Grimshaw, who had met his woman at the age of twenty-one, and had once drunkenly confided to Brian his belief that what Ros Grimes needed was to be taken hard from behind with her face shoved into the pillow (Brian had had the uncomfortable feeling that this was a recommendation, and that Grimshaw was deriving a degree of vicarious pleasure from it).

'Well, obviously I'm stuffed, then.'

'Well, no, not for second marriages,' said Rob Jenkins, who was on his second marriage. 'When you're *our* age' – patting Brian on the forearm – 'it's a matter of second chances. Third, even. And then it's a matter of taking on responsibilities, like children and that.'

Brian hoped that when he was Rob Jenkins's age – surely pushing fifty – he wouldn't think he was Brian's age. 'Oh that's not for *Brian*,' interjected Ros, '*he's* not one for *responsibility*. Brian just wants to have a good time *all* the time.' Brian, who felt that he would welcome it if he could have a good time *any* of the time, was miffed; but he was distracted by the thrilling trill of 'U Sure Do', which always cheered him, both by virtue of its intrinsic merits and because his liking for it reassured him that his distaste for the commercialisation of house, so rampantly evident in Illeshall, was not evidence that his senses had been dulled by encroaching middle age.

Soon they had lapsed into community talk. Community, Brian had become given to reflect, *fixes* us; not only in the sense of limiting us, but also in giving us definition in a more positive sense, through not only mores and customs and attitudes, which, being mimetic creatures, we take on, but by simple repetition – 'Do you remember that guy who had a wife with blue hair/did Cruyff turns at the Rec/ wrote Don Juan/discovered electromagnetism?' Repetition lifts particular experiences or items of knowledge out of the flux of impressions and thoughts, or rather, builds them up, their prominence and familiarity a result of a sedimentation of reference such that they may even become landmarks of our mind. Brian, however, feared that alien landmarks might come to obscure and occlude, to dwarf and render insignificant his own. He felt an obscure violence in all these conversations about such-and-such a pub, now closed, this school, that eccentric that far exceeded mere exclusion. Had he become an Outsider?

After a few protests against plans for tuition fees for university, it was time to go. Brian picked up a chicken kebab in the miserably small pitta bread that was standard in Illeshall – no naan bread, like in Manchester: quality of food in Illeshall, even of popular food, was considered a 'bourgeois deviation' (as the Militant Tendency once had it of homosexuality). He made his way home and sat watching comedy with what he had come to know as his 'TV Smile', polite, concerned not to appear to be judging. He wondered if it had come on since he became an existential Outsider, and how he would react to the death of Diana if it happened now. After a couple of cans of Kronenbourg, he fell asleep to the sound of audience laughter.

Going into the constituency office the next day, Sunday, he encountered Eileen Watkins, the sourest of the Left and the spit, in her oddly chosen pashmina, of Robert de Niro playing Frankenstein's monster. 'Walking like you're important,' she barked, with malignant cheer. Brian noticed he was looking at her as if she were mad, which on reflection was appropriate. Inwardly sighing at the lunatic imbecile scummery which was his lot, he picked up his folder of briefings on tuition fees and made for Peter Middleton's. There, Hermione, now a notably elegant young woman of seventeen, as Brian was relieved he could frankly recognise without carnality, led him into the drawing room where the Sundays were strewn, Middleton and Cécile breaking surface in their midst as though the tutelary gods of the medium. Middleton, in a long-suffering voice, spoke his mind. 'I long for Iraq to go away. Every morning I get up and it is still there.' He put his hand over his eyes. Cécile stroked his arm. Brian gestured around the room as he spoke.

'Forget Iraq! Why does no one in the papers, or on the *Today* programme or wherever, ever point out that if graduates earn more, they will pay more in income tax anyway; and that if we need graduates for the knowledge economy, then even those who don't go to university will benefit from that.'

Middleton hadn't really thought about the issue. It had seemed quite reasonable that those who had the added benefit of university should make an added contribution. He quailed and rallied in less time than could be perceived.

'Because journalists are not only scum but useless, as you well know. They only think about things that someone has told them to think about.'

'And why has no one done that?'

'Because no one's found it to be in their interest.'

'Why isn't it in the interest of the universities, say?'

'Because they know that the parties don't think it's politically possible, so they wouldn't listen.'

'But if they said it, if they just put out a press release so politicians got asked about it, they'd have to listen.'

'Well, I suspect the universities also think they'll get more money this way. Universities are poor relations when it comes to spending priorities. Your way, the money disappears into the Treasury.'

'So even if the whole debate is a nonsense, even if policy is going to enshrine a principle which is obviously unfair, no one will point this out?'

'That's the way of the world, dear.'

'OK. But I'd like to think that the leadership was keeping its grip on certain basic values – like equality, like clear-sightedness, like rigour. It's like knowing Picasso could draw. It would be a comfort.'

'The possible is defined by the electorate and, if we're lucky, that's where we can nudge them.'

'Yes. But your starting point can't be defined by the electorate.'

'Your starting point is defined by your fundamental values. But your fundamental values are a product of your time. It seems to me Tony and Gordon have always had a very clear view about fairness. Or views.'

Brian reflexively, briefly, slightly, raised his eyebrows then pursed his lips.

'You're rather a native on Higher Education, aren't you?' prompted Middleton.

'I suppose,' Brian sighed.

'And rather LP, if it's not rude of me to say so.'

'Maybe.'

PM nodded. 'Your face is too expressive for the television age. Or, indeed, for onstage.'

'I'd better stay a backroom boy.'

'Yes, I think you probably had.' A pause. Moderately brightly: 'You going to stay for dinner? Roast pork. *Crackling*.'

'Oh yes.'

Brian had always avoided explicit mention of his lack of ease in Illeshall, fearing it would lower Middleton's estimation of his usefulness; but now, having despatched his rightful share of pig and veg, and perhaps a little piqued at Middleton's assessment of his range of options, he responded to Hermione's query about how things were going to the effect that things, while going no worse than usual, were not really going as he'd hoped.

'What do you mean? Membership's holding up, which is an awful lot more than can be said for the Party nationally. We look safe here now, thanks to your sterling efforts.'

'I think Brian means in his personal life,' interjected Cécile, placing a restraining plurality of fingers on Middleton's arm.

'What's wrong with your personal life?' piped up Hermione, a little presumptuously. 'Not got over whassername yet?'

'Hermione, don't be so, so... *interrogatory*,' scolded Cécile. Brian answered nonetheless. 'It's not so much that, it's the whole history of my involvement with the town. I don't really have any friends here, not like in London. I'm just starting to feel displaced. Not starting to *feel*. Starting to think my feelings might be right. I'm missing out on whole phases of my life! Single at my age! Me!'

'But lots of people break up. Lots of people are single.'

'Yes, but I've never met anyone in Illeshall that I've really felt was right. I'm not sure they're *here*.'

'Maybe they're not *anywhere*,' suggested Middleton. 'Maybe you're asking for too much.'

'Maybe,' conceded Brian. 'But I'd like to think I was at least finding out whether that were so. In Illeshall I feel I'm missing the chance really to become myself, whatever that is.'

'Yes, what*ever*,' giggled Hermione.

'So what are you thinking of doing?' asked Middleton, businesslike.

'Well, I'm not sure,' stuttered Brian. 'I don't suppose you'd consider me for Hatty's post when she inevitably moves on to do PR for a merchant bank, would you?' Henrietta Fortescue was Middleton's current parliamentary researcher.

'It's not nearly enough money for you, especially in London. It's really a stepping stone for the aspirational, the one-dimensional, people who need the buzz of Westminster. Star-fuckers. And you're no star-fucker. Henrietta is. I am, a bit; though mainly because it serves as an index of my standing in the government. It sometimes seems to me that politics are designed to magnify and encourage all the worst aspects of my nature...' Middleton looked away into the middle distance for a moment, then abruptly straight into Brian's eyes.

'You're not one-dimensional. You're more complex than that, more interesting. It's why you can think interestingly about politics, because you have a sense of the different and conflictual things that drive people. Which is why you probably wouldn't fit into a think tank, either, to be honest. Maybe you should think about PR, or reputation management, as I believe the smart ones are starting to call it. Or, you can find yourself a nice girl with a degree up here. In Illeshall they're called teachers.'

As Middleton suspected, Brian quailed at the prospect of both.

'Teachers always think they know about something because they've read a book about it.' What was more, as he said to Michelle later that evening, 'I didn't like teachers when I was at school; I don't see why I'd start liking them now.'

'No. Have you created any incident lately?' she asked.

'No. The sole source of narrative thrust in my life is history.'

'Oh well, always best to work on a large canvas.'

'Yes. I've got a meeting tomorrow with some computer games developers. The idea is that Illeshall de-industrialised so early it is already post-industrial and thus has a head start on the rest of the world. Sounds to me like an idea that started life on a computer screen, or rather, that will only ever have a virtual life. But that's what you get stuck with if you're not the type to break out. I know my limitations. I'm not political. I'm not political, and I've gone into sodding politics! I despise the self-promotion it requires to be a 'success', and yet I'm also strangely intimidated by it. I've got a commitment to egalitarianism that I just can't live with; and a belief in meritocracy that I just can't live with. I seem to be confronted with an unbearable tension between my life and my work that could only be resolved or dissolved by a political economy even more utopian than communism.'

'Try reading some Beckett. "I must go on. I can't go on. I'll go on." Etc.'

'Beckett moved to Paris – fled, in fact, to Paris.'

'Paris it is, then.'

Chapter 12
'Hysterical people who aren't very good at reasoning'

31 January 2004

'How dost our go-to hermeneut this bright morn?' Michelle was being especially nice to him: it was one thing being a Blairite cadre in difficult circumstances, quite another to be held a member of a crew of liars and murderers, which had been Rafferty's climactic asseveration the night before, as they discussed the Hutton report. The media furore over the suicide of Dr David Kelly had led as far, in what Brian considered almost clinically paranoid quarters, as a suspicion that 'the Blair regime' had had Kelly done away with, on account of what secrets no one could even surmise. Brian had maintained that Dr Kelly, who believed Saddam was a serious threat and was in favour of removing him from power, had been improperly speaking to journalists, and that he had lied about this to a Select Committee of the House of Commons. Exposed, humiliated and quite rightly fearing for his job, he seemed to have sought a way out of his miserable perplexities in death. Lord Hutton's moderately rigorous exoneration of the government's conduct in the affair had annoyed the media, which wanted a story, intensely, and in consequence propagated the idea it was a whitewash, which helped whip up new heights of rage among those deprived of proof of the dastardliness of Tony Blair and thus the legitimacy of a dislike that had been inchoate and diffuse until fused and focused by Iraq. Now, spin seemed to sum him up as something like The Deceiver.

Michelle returned with a cafetière and some mugs. Brian was looking at the latest Harry Potter. 'You know, when I have doubts about "The Project", it's this I think of. Adults reading children's books is almost coincident with our time in government.'

'Oh Christ, we're all doomed,' intoned Michelle.

'Intelligent people,' continued Brian, 'read novels to gain perspective on and insight into their own lives and troubles and relationships and moral quandaries. What kind of insight does Harry Potter offer? People only read Harry Potter if they're living lives that don't bear a single second's examination.'

'Gavin and Louise read Harry Potter,' prompted Michelle, who personally believed the books were extremely good, but was determined not to have an argument of any kind with Brian this morning.

'Well there you have it,' said Brian, confirmed in his righteousness. 'PR people for the banks. That's the Harry Potter audience.'

'Did I tell you about what Gavin did the other day?' continued Michelle, pleased with her own tactical astuteness.

'No,' said Brian expectantly.

'Well, he went as a helper on the school trip to Hillfield Theatre, which is where Foxe's School is. Now, Gavin would love Alastair to go to Foxe's, but he knows he's not bright enough. So what does he do? He tells this little girl, who *is* going to Foxe's, that all the gangs around there hate Foxe's kids, which is true, but he's told her in order to make himself feel better, leaving her terrified. He couldn't just think it to himself, he had to make it true by saying it.'

'Like Harry Potter,' interjected Brian.

'Hmm... People are just appalling about schools. Half the parents in Sean's school, including Gavin and Louise, are renting properties by Northgate School to get their kids in there.'

'Don't you sometimes, or somewhere, think you should be doing the same if you're going to be doing right by Sean and Jack?'

'Well, a bit of me; but basically I just think they're hysterical people who aren't very good at reasoning. Sean and Jack will go to Hartsfield, which is perfectly fine. In the end, they'll be good, happy boys. And, most importantly, they won't be scum.' They both chuckled.

'Why was everyone saying "That's hot" and "That's not" last night?' asked Brian, who hadn't wanted to seem so out of things as not to know.

'Oh, they're copying Paris.'

'Who?'

'Paris Hilton, the one in the sex video.'

'Oh yes!'

'Have you seen it?'

'No, what's it like?'

'Dunno, I've not seen it. Didn't you even look for it?'

'Oh, I looked for it a bit, out of interest, but I think I just got a few fakes and loads of other porn sites, so I lost interest. I mean, I get the picture!'

'Hmm, yes.' Brian felt the pressure of incipient anger over 'That's hot' and 'That's not'. He could not at first locate its cause.

'Didn't it piss you off?'

'What, the video? No, not really. She's just a silly spoilt girl, he's a massive wanker, but no, it doesn't really occupy my mind.'

'No, not that; or maybe partly that. The "That's hot," "That's not" thing.'

'Well, that's just people being silly.'

'But can't it be quite meaningful, *how* people are silly, what fantasies are in play?' And as he said this, he realised what it was. 'It's the whole media–celebrity complex! It's an enactment of it! It's not something they're outside and mocking, it's something they're ritually performing, a collective act of obeisance to a goddess who is their ideal ego inasmuch as she doesn't even have to give reasons for her judgements, simply deliver them, and by fiat things are so. It's what they'd really like to be able to do themselves! They identify with postmodern power!'

'Wouldn't we all like to be able to do that, though? It would guarantee a universe in which our likes and dislikes, our desires and aversions, our *identities* were valued.'

'Don't you feel you're sufficiently valued? Consultant, breadwinner, mother.'

'Well, I suppose I'm valued enough not to really mind people being a bit silly. Maybe it's you who wants to be valued sufficiently for your judgements to count.'

'Maybe,' said Brian, and wondered whether he would care to have his extolling of Henry James taken as edict. '"The vanity of others offends our taste only insofar as it offends our vanity,"' he quoted. 'That's Nietzsche, that is.'

'I thought you didn't trust people who read Nietzsche?' prodded Michelle.

'Oh, I picked it up at Rafferty's. I think it's Sebastian's. It's rather good, don't you think?'

'It's got something to it, though I can't quite see to the bottom of it. Anyway, you're not vain, or at least not especially. You've just had an overdose of meeja.'

'Oh yes?'

'Yes. Their sense that what they have to talk about is what there is to talk about. I mean, fair enough, they're talking shop. But then consider the shop. Just think if the media were personified. It would be the most insufferable, know-all, know-nothing, grabby, preening, insecure-yet-self-congratulating, under-cerebral, over-articulate, emotionally labile and morally suspect person you knew. Now consider that, inasmuch as a group of people have one feature in common, they will not only resemble each other but, as their number increases, more and more take on the aspect of an identity. In other words, a party full of media types is the closest you can get to the media personified. Knowing one person in the media is good; it keeps you sharp, and abreast of things. Two is more problematic, especially two at once. Three is impossible, even for people in the media. Perhaps especially for them. No wonder they seek refuge in ritual affirmations.'

'Whereas I'm left with *ressentiment*, and a slave morality.'

'Yes; you have virtue, which is its own reward.'

'It fucking has to be. *Media: The Second God*: that's what Tony Schwartz said. Well, lots of people seem to worship it.'

'Maybe they're right to. I mean, largely its values are their values. Martin would say that you are the priest of a dying religion. Indeed, a lay preacher rather than a hierarch, since you don't even have an academic pulpit from which to pronounce. According to Martin, the invasion of the academy by consumerism is the last phase in the disenchantment of the world, the full subjectivisation of value. That's what he was saying last night, anyway. It's his latest lament. He's been asked to speak about it *everywhere*.'

For the first time, consciously at least, Brian felt a twinge of envy for Martin. Someone who could so readily turn his plight to good use, capitalise on it culturally. Whereas he? He was just moaning. 'What a Marxist would say is that this is the basis on which we can have a proper, democratic, socialised form of value.'

'Perhaps it is.'

'Perhaps indeed. It puts me in mind of something Frank Kermode once wrote about Auden, something like "He never mistook the fact that he was good at something" – i.e. poetry – "for the fact that it was important".'

'Hmm. But what would life be without the poetry?'

'Yes, but that doesn't mean *poetry*, or poetics, or literary study. I mean, I read Henry James not because I'm so sensitive, but because other people are such a mystery to me.'

'*We're* not, though, are we?'

'I don't know!'

'We're not. You're just suffering from a common or garden case of alienation, darling.'

'Me and the workers.'

'Oh, no; not the workers. They're more and more at home in the world. Just you and the underclass; the unemployed and those seeking a liberal-minded James aficionado in Illeshall.'

'Hmm. It's true that it's in Illeshall I seem to have learnt about what bores me and what I despise. I mean, I've seen a lot of fucking stupid behaviour; whole *deserts* of *pretty* stupid behaviour. But maybe that's just misanthropy.'

'Maybe. I mean, most of the people *I* work with seem like lunatics to me.'

'So how did we end up *misanthropists*; I mean, *us*? We had such *hopes*! I feel ready for the bleedin' Charterhouse of Parma.'

'Not yet! The Charterhouse only turns up at the end, remember. And then you're done for in a year.'

'I think I might be able to find some wiggle room re the mortality bit. It's the death of hope that's the point!'

'Aha! Unrealistic expectations. That, and a lack of self-knowledge about what *we* were getting out of the whole deal. Self-righteousness, feeling better than other people, is pretty intoxicating stuff.'

'Yes, but we were never *intoxicated* by it. *You* weren't. Even *I* wasn't for long. It didn't take that many Students' Union General Meetings, demanding more money for this, more money for that, shaking my fist at the world for not being perfect and getting applauded for it, before I felt like a fraud, that it was all a bit easy.'

'That's true.'

'So why do we feel like this? Washed up on the shore of history?'

'*I* don't feel like that, or at least not terribly keenly. I'm too busy with the job and the boys and branch meetings and the odd GC.'

'Hmm. So it's just my lone egotism.'

'Well no, I just expect you're a bit more aware. I mean, we did embark on adult life with a collective sense that we were engaged in a historic struggle; and that's receded.'

'Partly because we *did* change the government. It's something not to feel under constant attack, and going without it must have caused the adrenaline to recede. But sometimes I feel as though I thought I was part of a republic of virtue-in-waiting, a roiling, rolling boil of anger and optimism, and that it's now evaporated, leaving my soul a bit of sediment or residue standing out against the smooth surfaces of global capital. A sterile gleam they give, and I exposed to the glare.'

'Oh dear. You really do need something to distract you, something to engage with. Why don't you join a book group?'

'I don't think they have those in Illeshall.'

'I bet they do. You can search on the interweb.' Steve wandered in with the Saturday *Guardian*. It thwomped on the coffee table. 'Have a look at Soulmates,' prompted Michelle. Brian did. An ad under 'Men Seeking Women' was first to catch his eye. 'Always and Forever. Caring, B'ham male, seeks single female. If you would like no more pain and suffering in your life, then call me.'

'Listen to this,' he said, and read it out. '"The Angel of Death gets lonesome." No, I don't think the personals are for me.'

'No, you're not a personal kind of guy,' said Michelle archly, meaning she knew not what.

'I'm a bit worried about this,' said Michelle, that evening, sotto voce. 'He hasn't exactly been dedicated when it comes to practice.'

'Oh, well, it'll be over soon,' said Brian.

It was the Summersfield Primary Concert, and Sean was one of the violins in the finale, the chorale section of the 'Ode to Joy'. They sat tight, murmuring the odd comment about how sweet this or that child looked, genuine apprehension starting to startle in Michelle's eyes. Steve had assumed a mien of resigned gravity. At last, the stage was cleared, seats arranged and Sean and a dozen or so violins, trumpets and other pieces took their place. Soon it started. 'Ode to Joy' was a deflation of brass: a dissonant collocation of plaintive farts, both muffled and parped, along with a frankly upsetting scratch and drear of strings.

'Oh dear,' said Michelle, looking perturbed, though whether from the assault on her ears or due to the knowledge that her son was among the perpetrators, it wasn't clear. Steve's lips were pursed as he sat, adamantine.

'Oh dear,' said Michelle, pouring out large glasses of claret. 'All those parents thinking it's a good thing for their children to play an instrument; the teacher thinking it's good to stretch them; and the children, poor things, wretchedly innocent of the upset they were causing. Well, at least I can say that though I was caught up in the dream for a while, as soon as I saw the consequences I put a stop to it.'

'Hmm,' said Steve, smiling.

'Maybe they could play something easier,' suggested Brian. 'I'm told saxophone is quite forgiving.'

'I am NOT having Sean get hold of John Coltrane!... Or Eric bleedin' Dolphy!' proclaimed Steve, and they managed a small laugh.

Next day was roast beef and Yorkshire pudding.

'I was at a meeting on Friday held by a drug company,' said Michelle, cutting chips from a parsnip.

'Oh yes?' asked Brian.

'Yes. To promote their new treatment for bipolar disorder. There was a good talk from the Chief Pharmacist at the Maudsley. He's very respected, and the figures and graphs seemed sound, but it still *feels* compromising.'

'Doesn't it just make you scrutinise the science even more carefully?' asked Brian.

'I suppose it does, yes,' said Michelle, conceding a little. 'But the market seems to be getting everywhere. I mean, when I'm training my junior doctors, they fill out questionnaires on me!'

'But Michelle, they've had *those* in universities for fifteen years! That's not the market, it's just good practice.'

'But it treats my doctors like consumers of a service!'

'But aren't they? I mean, it may not be exactly like buying a packet of gum, but isn't the role of the consumer the most powerful model of client empowerment we've got? Shouldn't we adapt from it what we can? And are you sure it doesn't help keep you up to the mark?'

'Oh darling, I make a particular point of always stepping *over* the mark, daintily. It's just our management is so thoroughly imbued with a market ethos. Anything we say is dismissed as the squealing of "producer interests".'

'Well it's difficult, isn't it? On the one hand, you need management; on the other hand, management tends to attract cunts.'

'Hmm.'

They lapsed into silence for a while, resurfacing to sing 'I'm in Love with a German Film Star' when it came up on Steve's CD (Steve was some years older than them, with the musical tastes of a cool elder sibling). But once they had filled themselves and started on a restorative glass to aid the digestion, Michelle started up again: 'Forget Hutton. What about tuition fees? Your manifesto–'

'*My* manifesto?'

'Well, your lot–'

'*My* lot? Not *yours?*'

'Well, yes, though it's getting harder to feel involved. Anyway, it was expressly stated in the manifesto that there would be no tuition fees in the next Parliament, and what do we get? Tuition fees.'

'Well, the legislation won't come into effect until the next Parliament.'

'A rather lawyerly distinction. Anyway, it's more marketisation.'

'It's more money for Higher Education, when we need Oxford and Cambridge and Imperial to keep up with Harvard, Yale, Stanford.'

'Who cares about Oxbridge?! What we need is a more democratic university system, not more money for the haves.'

'The nation needs science and technology to fund all your democratic aspirations, and that means concentrating funds. At the same time, your democratic universities will have more, too. But they will be increasingly subject to consumer pressure.'

'And management consultants, who know nothing about what they're being consulted on. Like they say in the NHS, why are the operating theatres empty on Friday afternoons? What an obvious waste of capacity! But they don't factor in the fact that people who have operations on Friday afternoons are more likely to *die* over the weekend, when there are no consultants around.'

'They can be a fresh pair of eyes. For a start, they might ask why there are no consultants around at weekends.'

'Christ, don't we work hard enough already?'

'Well, still you could reorganise *when* you do all this work, couldn't you? You're already on call some weekends. I don't see the major issue of principle here.'

'Well, it just sounds like trying to get more work for the same money.'

'Darling, *every* organisation is in *that* game, all over the world, and we've got to keep up!'

'And what about all these Indian doctors we're taking? It's imperialism!'

'How is it *imperialism*? We're not *ordering* them over here! We don't rule the world any more! It's an inevitable consequence of being a relatively wealthy country in a globalised economy. It's the same with Indian computer engineers. We've got tens of thousands of them! It's a matter for the Indian government, or their consciences.'

'How can you say computing is the same as healthcare?'

'Well, how is it different, unless you're going to maintain that something mystical and sacred inheres in being a doctor, i.e. in being you?'

Steve intervened: 'It's not a matter of sacredness, it's a matter of extreme complexity. The NHS is not a supermarket, it's a whole ecology, and what you do in one part of it is liable to have unintended consequences in other parts of it.'

'Yes,' Michelle continued, 'like involving private contractors. Private contractors will just want to do the easy, cheap stuff, like millions of hip operations. Meanwhile, who's training the doctors to do the hip operations, to assist at them, all that? The NHS! Which is more expensive in consequence, and so it loses out on contracts as a result!'

'Well, I'm no expert, but it looks to me as if that's an imbalance which could be fairly easily rationalised and remedied.'

'But you've just made a problem where there was none before.'

'One easily rectified, meanwhile saving an untold amount in efficiency.'

'Brian, I think we're going to have to stop talking about this.'

'I'd be only too happy to,' said Brian, and it was true. The constituency party he could take. But this kind of conversation seemed to eat away at something inside him. Happily, Jack came running in, dropping something as he came to a stop.

'Oh bollocks!' he exclaimed and, laughing, Michelle reproved him.

'Darling, don't say that, at least not at your age and in company.'

'But why not?'

'Because it's not polite.'

'Well, Sean said he heard *you* saying the s-word.' Michelle feigned incredulity.

'Did he? And what is the s-word?'

'I don't know... slavery?'

'Yes, that's *right* darling,' she laughed, taking him up on her knee. 'A victory for Labour educational values and citizenship classes,' affirmed Brian, and they all drank to that.

'You haven't talked about Illeshall all weekend,' prompted Michelle. 'Good boy.'

'Oh, it pinches me like Paulus Emilius's shoe,' groaned Brian.

'Paulus Emilius?' asked Steve.

'Yes, Milton references him in one of the divorce tracts, as an argument for why the right of divorce should inhere in the husband and not in the civil authority. "This shoe," said he, and held it out on his foot, "is a neat shoe, a new shoe, and yet none of you know where it wrings me; much less by the unfamiliar cognizance of a feed gamester can such a private difference be examined, neither ought it".'

'Ouch!' said Steve. 'Bit of a shame it only counts for the husband, though.'

'Well, elsewhere Milton allows the same for either partner, though it's certainly true his preoccupation is with the pangs and plight of masculine subjectivity.'

'You discuss this much in Illeshall?' asked Steve, smiling. On the TV, Jamie Oliver said, 'Change! I'm talking about changing things!'

Chapter 13
'A vast conspiracy of death'

November 2004

'Top deck on the 77.'

Brian looked to his left. Three lads were walking up the slip road curving away from the station that he was walking down. Catching his eye, the speaker repeated his phrase. At this, Brian put down the carrier bags containing his excess baggage, turned to maintain the gaze of the young man he had now engaged, and asked, in sheer bafflement, '*What?*' Friendly enough, his newfound interlocutor repeated himself again, smiling, and walked on with his mates. Brian watched them on their way for a brief spell then, shaking his head, picked up his bags, was on his way and started to muse.

The first thing that occurred to him was that he had just been subject to an angry accusation that he was treating Illeshall like a bus, and was upset because it wasn't taking him where he wanted to go. This itself he attributed to the same current of discourse that had rendered him suspicious of any and all references to the subject of 'London' since he had discussed his desire for a job there with Peter Middleton. He had been surprised and upset to find Eileen Watkins, among others, thoroughly apprised of his thoughts on the subject but had tried to count it as merely another instance of how much more discussed he was than he had ever expected to be.

But he had never seen these lads before in his life, nor – to the best of his knowledge – had they seen him. Brian told himself commonsensically that there must be some other explanation for their remark, but could find it only in the bare fact that he was holding carrier bags in his hands, which might have suggested shopping – though not typically, in all fairness, at 10.30 on a Sunday night walking down from the station concourse – and that shopping might have suggested buses. He wondered why the reference to the 'top deck' – perhaps his manner suggested either superiority or delinquency, he pondered –

before his mind refused to think about it any more. Rather, he asked himself, 'In what kind of place can carrying a carrier bag be regarded as the occasion for a joke?' Certainly, the residual literary critic in him prompted, not a realist place, a place of accepted convention and familiarised perception, but a site of excess signifiers, meaning on the loose, ready to be picked up and re-cathected, rendered significant by desire and disgust.

His sofa was strewn with books and papers, so he sank into his bed. He felt slight relief in finding he retained a distant capacity for pleasure, in the form of seeing the bitter irony in his Swedish furnishings coming to resemble the set in a deleted scene from *Fight Club*. He remembered buying from Ikea the furniture he had not inherited: all those couples who had settled for one another, all those women who had chosen all those men. 'No one's chosen me,' he thought; 'or settled for me,' he thought. Nor have I for them. Sardonic, in his head he sang to himself his own private version of Chesney Hawkes's 'The One and Only': 'I am The Beautiful Soul'. Nobody he'd rather be. The bed, constructed around a single spine that had proven brittle, had broken and tilted, with the result that the stuff he left on it slid its way toward him whenever he was in occupation. Abutted by creasing papers and splintering spines, he thought of himself, fancifully, as a sea that pounded and ground his possessions into their constituent parts. Instance his headphones, from which the 'phones had separated before detaching from the brackets that had connected them to the headband, then themselves coming apart until they lay, beached and stranded, solitary, disarticulated emitters of distant, frail voices: he had Radio 4 on permanently, a memory of sense and reason. He had told himself his sense of purpose would intervene, a deus ex machina, before the headphones disintegrated utterly, but the foam had detached altogether from the plastic shells and their lines to the main lead had become lost somewhere.

It had been a day of strain after a year of – what? Horror? The quotidian operations of fate? The inevitable? No, more than that. No sooner had his father died than Rafferty reported in with breast cancer. It had surely been happenstance that his dad's last words to him had been 'I have no idea what you are talking about' (he had fallen asleep not long after asking Brian to explain what he meant by the phrase 'strategic state'); but life was serving up a suspicious amount of aesthetic and moral shape. It didn't help that Rafferty was trying to amuse herself by, she said, seeking to improve the odds that her last words would be famous ones. 'To philosophise is to learn how to die' she was given to proclaiming, or 'Cast a cold eye on life, on death. Horseman, pass by!' Then both Martin's parents had been diagnosed with cancer at almost the same time. Brian had taken to remarking that it was as though 'a vast conspiracy of death' was stalking his acquaintance, but in truth it was a suspicion he was trying to ward off.

He had thought about commemorating the day of his father's death by ending his practice of upturning a lucky cigarette in each pack, but had decided that this would be a gesture toward self-harm, though of the mildest kind. He had not been able to avoid, however, becoming dissatisfied with the way he smoked. He found that he was no longer closing his lips after he drew on the cigarette. He tried to readjust his technique, but found himself doing the teenage thing of letting a wisp of smoke slide from his mouth then whipping it back in. It was obvious he couldn't stick with that, so he tried to go back to simply closing his mouth then breathing in; but he had become self-conscious about it: the action had lost its innocence. He persisted, hoping the action would become second nature again, but worried that second nature was not innocence at all, but an encrypting of affectation – 'but error grown old,' as Milton had it of custom. He resolved to read *The Confessions of Zeno*, but couldn't. He felt he was trapped in a lift rushing somewhere bad.

He resumed his reading of a film review. The writer seemed very sure of the characters' thoughts and feelings. Were they more intuitive and empathetic than he? Or more prone to projection? Before he had finished, he felt his phone go: a tiny shudder too small to buzz in human ears. Ami was coming round. Compassionate and opportunistic, she was showing signs of taking him on. He had met her through the book group he had joined at Michelle's urging, once he had dismissed the fleeting notion that he might advertise in Soulmates with the words to Bob Dylan's 'From a Buick 6'. She had been sufficiently attractive to persuade him to read *Chocolat*. He found her company partly annoying, mostly agreeably boring and overall strangely tolerable. Amid the unreality of his instincts being no guide, because his instinct was to withdraw absolutely, which was hardly sensible and meant everything was to some degree willed, in some way acted, he was as grateful as he could muster. She was a lecturer in Literary Studies at Illeshall College of Higher Education. She had angular cheekbones and eyes that were sharpened ovals, the pupils within a cool grey, and dressed mainly in black, which made him nostalgic. She was a specialist in chick lit – Postmodern Women's Romantic Fiction (Brian wasn't sure whether it was the women or the fiction that were postmodern, or indeed the romance; probably indeterminately all three) – and the only men she read were overt misogynists – 'they lay bare the deep structure of masculinity' – and Ian McEwan – 'defines the contemporary bourgeois norm'. Something in Brian had died when he learnt that, while she could quote excerpts from Jilly Cooper – 'mother to Jane Austen's grandmother' (the ages telescoping) – she had never read a single poem by Seamus Heaney. In her department they taught no Milton and the bare minimum of Shakespeare. He continued to fight the urge to phone Rafferty and lament, triumphantly: 'I've found the interesting people here, and they're boring!'

He buzzed Ami in. She arrived brandishing a copy of *Twelfth Night*. Pedagogic as ever, in a bid to expand her horizons Brian had seized on a Christmas visit by the Royal Shakespeare Company to the leisure centre in Warrington.

'It's literally *Blackadder*, and I don't mean it's funny. Someone literally says "You're in good fooling today, my Lord," or something like that.'

'Oh yes, I noticed that bit. Sir Andrew says to Feste, who is after all The Fool, "thou wast in very gracious fooling last night". Well, it's Elizabethan, there's no denying it.'

'Yes, but it's not funny.'

'But maybe that's interesting. What does it tell us if humour seems to be so much more historically specific than our loftier concerns? What's more, it's arguably in part at least about the *threat* that a certain way of life and the humour associated with it are becoming outmoded, historically superseded. Feste remains in touch, through his songs, with what Orsino calls "the old age" and its "innocence of love". Malvolio the Puritan, by contrast, with his "politic books", represents the coming social force, temporarily ridiculed but with his promise to be "revenged on the whole pack of you" bearing the weight of the revolution to come. Anyway, it's not all supposed to be funny. Comedy can be serious. As Shaw said, though he didn't mean it quite as I do, "there are few things as tragic as a Shakespeare comedy".'

'Hmm. I suppose all the gender stuff, the cross-dressing and that, is quite interesting. Might be able to do something queer with it.'

'Oh darling, that's been done and done and done. Not that you might not bring a fresh eye to bear.'

'So, according to you, Malvolio's the hero, is he?'

'History says so, dear. With a capital "H".'

'Well, at least it's not Orsino. He's a real tosser. Poor Viola.'

'I couldn't agree more.'

'What's this?' asked Ami, holding up a copy of Nietzsche's *Ecce Homo*.

'Just what it says on the tin,' replied Brian.

'I thought you didn't trust people who read Nietzsche?' Brian took the volume from her hand and shook it at her: 'Illeshall has shown me the error of my ways. Who can resist a man who not only calls sections of his book "Why I am a Destiny", or "Why I Write Such Good Books", but was also right to do so?'

'I hope you're not going to make me read him.'

'No; I'm just going to act on his precepts: "If you are going to see a woman, do not forget the whip!"' He failed to land the book on Ami's backside with quite the crispness he had envisioned. Her cry of protest had its quotient of seriousness, modulated to mock-seriousness as she snatched up one sheet from a messy pile of bubble wrap.

'And why haven't you popped this yet?'

'Because I am a Grandmaster of Deferred Gratification.'

'If you're not going to pop it you should throw it away.' Brian took the sheet from her and twisted it between his hands, causing a crackle, then cast it aside.

'Because I have both too much and too little interest in simple passing pleasures!' he declared, flashing his eyes at Ami.

Brian was quite himself by this point. It was as though Ami's arrival had relieved him of the thought that his flat might have become uninhabitable, unsurvivable even. He felt reassured that it had not, whether by some secret emanation of himself, or some unwitting awful error, become quietly inimical to life. At this still, small voice of hope he became almost domestically vigorous, picking up a couple of scatter cushions and taking an empty glass and a mouldy half cup of tea to the kitchen area and even watering his peace lily.

Flattered, Ami decided to 'relax' Brian, and it pleased him as she did so to imagine she was nodding in affirmation of an especially strong point he had made. Over dinner, she sought to unburden him further.

'Oh, it's nothing, really; just another argument with Kieran about Iraq. It's more what I was thinking about on the train on the way home.'

'And what was that?'

'Well, I always thought we shared a kinship inasmuch as he was political – you know, *serious*; that we had more in common in that sense than either of us had with the soft Left. But it suddenly struck me – I don't know why it didn't before – that I prefer the world we already have to the one a revolution would produce. I mean, given the dawning of *The X Factor*, I really think we've got enough popular democracy for any modernist sensibility... Maybe it's the Nietzsche, too – affirming the world as it is, not denigrating it in the name of imaginary otherworldly values. I don't know. But it suddenly seemed to me that my friendship with him was less a matter of accepting differences of emphasis among the Army of the Saints, and more predicated on his relative powerlessness; in other words, on regarding him as fundamentally deeply *un*serious. And I'm not sure where that leaves us. We'd have been on different sides of the split in the SPD in 1918: he'd have been with Karl Liebknecht and Rosa Luxemburg, and I'd have been nodding through the deployment of the Freikorps that would have been out to kill him. And that just seems like another relationship proving to be built on shifting sands.'

Ami couldn't help but feel a little quickening of excitement in her belly. Brian was a bit difficult, yes, and needed training in tidiness. But he was good-looking, with eyes you could dissolve into, and intelligent and well meaning, no common combination in her experience. Now he was feeling alone in the universe, which had to bode well for her chances. Naturally, most of what occupied her were feelings of compassion.

'It's cold when you're on your own.' Unperceived by Ami, Brian's face briefly froze then instantly thawed, as though nothing out of the ordinary had occurred. Ever since, before the last Executive Committee, two people in a row had made their first remark about it being 'cold', only for him then to sit down and see that Eileen was reading Le Carré's *The Spy Who Came in from the Cold*, he had had a suspicion, growing with each comment about the temperature, first, that something was up; and, second, that for him to let on that he was aware of this would confirm his would-be tormentors in their suspicions about him, whatever these were. (He had spent some time considering this, and decided that it was either a reference to his emotional coldness, or else to the way he carried on his life in Illeshall while secretly devoted to somewhere else, namely London.) It was a bit like when he once confused 'there' and 'their' and word went round that he was dyslexic. He found it hard to believe Ami was involved – that would take a genius in duplicity of which he could not quite believe her capable – but he could on no account tell her of his suspicions: one thing he had learnt was that the keeping of secrets was foreign to Illeshall.

One secret he had – another thing he wished he could tell Ami – was how much he was looking forward to tomorrow's visitor from Central Office, Jessica, or Decca, Carruthers. Brian thought of her coming as that of a kind of messenger-angel, like Raphael in *Paradise Lost*, and fantasised about having calm, methodical Orwellian sex with her, for the Party, combining to form little cadres. As usual, in the flesh her pristine aura was too intimidating at first to excite anything other than a kind of spiritual adoration. She wore her hair in a dark helmet of a bob that emphasised the faintly freckled paleness and elegance of her face and throat. Her green top and dark trousers were of a fine wool that draped her form, concealing and not revealing, but intimating, the subtle curves beneath. Things were 'rather difficult', she conceded, but it was evident they left her soul unspotted, because what had to be done was 'necessary' if we were to be 'serious'. She gave the impression of a genuinely unified being, one in whom sublimation in the name of the Party was complete. Brian saw himself through her eyes. In younger days he had played the worldly smoker with these types, and was occasionally flattered by a faint smile, but as the years had gone by and he had developed a slight paunch, the act had become harder for him to believe in. Rather, he reminded himself of the regional officials of his youth, portly middle-aged men in what were effectively dead-end jobs, while these envoys of the strategists discharged the electrical pulses that lit up the nerves of the body politic. He was no longer slightly scandalous, a maverick, even in his own imaginings; he was not worldly but earthbound. The word 'granular', usually so pleasing to him, fell dry from his lips as he discussed voter ID; her professed desire to 'drill down' into local psephology was testament to how deep beneath the surface of things he had sunk. He wondered if he was coming to understand the Illeshallian desire to bring him down a peg or two.

Brian thought he objected to the attempts to bring him down he encountered in Illeshall because they implied that he was the kind of person who needed bringing down. But when he pondered it further he wasn't sure he didn't feel a resentment against the very urge to bring anyone down, and wondered whether in this he was manifesting the group consciousness of the tall poppies in the field; which prompted in him the reflection that maybe he was the kind of person who needs bringing down. Brian pondered whether he was the victim of a self-scrutinising, self-condemning, self-crippling glitch in the class-consciousness Brecht admired in Shakespeare's *Coriolanus*. Reading *Twelfth Night*, however, he wondered whether he wasn't reading too much Nietzsche, whether he wasn't Malvolio. Decca, he felt sure, would be impervious to any attempt to bring her down. Impervious, but perhaps not impermeable. If people in Illeshall seemed like billiard balls with biases, ploughing a course regardless of the ricochets that randomised their destination in a way that sent his inner geometrician haywire, Decca seemed at once receptive and self-contained, tremulous yet delicately defined, like a finely attuned sensor:

instance her nose, which Brian could sense, or imagine he sensed, but could not catch, twitching. It was as though she were possessed of an immensely sophisticated force field, which did not vaporise, but rather neutralised, all that came within its ambit. She looked, Brian thought, like someone who would appreciate Henry James. Of course, she only read about politics; but maybe if she came to James on his recommendation it might serve to turn her head from her partner, Parliamentary Affairs Officer for a children's charity.

'Have you ever read Henry James?' he asked, finally, as they sat musing over Labour's electoral strategy.

'No. Why? Isn't he terribly apolitical?'

'No! But his politics are those of the fine grain of human relations, the warp and weft of our being together. In some ways, he is the most fundamentally political writer of all.'

'Really? Well maybe I should give him a go. I keep resolving to read more fiction. Help with understanding people.'

Brian's pulse quickened. 'Oh well, then; let me recommend one to start with: *The Spoils of Poynton*. It's middle period, not as simple as the early stuff, but before he gets what some people call convoluted. It's not one of his best-known, but it's quite representative.'

'Oh well, maybe.'

'I'll send you a copy,' said Brian, flushed.

'We need to keep tabs on this going forward,' said Decca, and when their discussion of the point was concluded, he picked her up on her usage.

'"Going forward" is *aspirational*,' she responded. 'It's positive, it looks to the future and it's part of the argot of our new classes. It only annoys the intellectuals, and that's what they're for.'

'Are you sure it doesn't annoy the working classes, too? Those who might say that, going *backward*, it's important to remember the miners, the Luddites, the Diggers? So it annoys the intellectuals, and it annoys the working class: in other words, the two constituencies of which the Labour Party is, as it were, constituted.'

'(a) You don't believe a word of that, and (b) the Labour Party doesn't do retrospection any more, and neither do I. Maybe it is a bit middle management, but then, I'm political middle management and proud of it.' Brian smiled. She had shared something of her self-image with him. As she nipped to the loo, Brian thought he caught the merest hint of a wobble in her backside, though he was wrought to a minor excess and might have imagined it. Still, suddenly his thought descended, or ascended: 'Easier than air with air when angels love,' he mused. He was taken with the idea that, with Decca, body and soul might be fused again at last; the prospect, going forward, of a kind of secular salvation.

His body felt less solid, more ethereal, and once Decca had taken her leave he spent a couple of hours dazed and confused, both inclined and disinclined to masturbate, until Ami picked him up for ju-jitsu, in which she was a black belt and he a beginner, and he berated himself for his diffuse visions of a greener place.

Chapter 14
'Women are so difficult to work'

Summer 2005

The Cheshire plain rolled out beneath them, green and pleasant, as it often is in such places; spacious. Unsurprising clumps of trees picked their way into the distance until stopped by the dim ridge of the Derbyshire Peaks. Brian had needed to get away from Illeshall, away, briefly, from Ami, and had not been able to face London and its arguments. What is more, he thought, maybe what he needed was a man-to-man talk, and so he had come to Alderley Edge for Sunday lunch with Matt and Tara in their cotton magnate's mansion. Matt had taken the lead in preparing lunch, so Tara was taking care of the kids for the afternoon at Teeny-Weeny Tots, the children's destination of choice, despite the fact it was a beautiful day.

'We might as well get it over with,' said Matt. 'How's Illeshall?'

'Oh God. "I was the shadow of the waxwing slain/By the false azure of the windowpane".'

'Who's that?' asked Matt.

'Nabokov. It's the opening of *Pale Fire*. Not quite sure why it came to mind. Try this: "Life, friends, is boring/We must not say so".'

'Ain't that the truth.'

'The man who wrote that killed himself.'

'Oh dear. Try this: "Man must fall in love or else fall ill". Freud didn't kill himself.'

'In a way, the moral might be, if you are diffident, if you are "biddable and unforthcoming", if you fail to be ambitious, you will find yourself among idiots; or at least among people who are not terribly interesting and dynamic.'

'You want to try Cisco. Everyone's terribly dynamic there. And terribly, terribly clever.'

'But you're terribly clever too. How many of you are allowed to get on a plane at the same time?'

'Three. A bit like the Royal Family. Doesn't mean I'm not bored, though. I think I'm not in love.'

'That's my problem, too. I think it's why I've lost interest in sex with Ami.'

'The thing about women is,' Matt embarked, 'they're so difficult to work. The only instruction manual is the noises they make, unless those noises come across as orders, in which case you fold them up and put them away, like a deckchair. It's like trying to listen to *Test Match Special* on long wave. You get closer and closer, through a confusing sea of shrieks and wails, but the moment you think you're on the point of getting there a sudden WAOOOW of pain and exasperation breaks the mood. I imagine it's how MS-DOS is for you. Men, on the other hand, are Apple: clear design, readily comprehensible, accessible even to beginners, generally easy to use.'

'Tell me about it, brother.'

'But Tara had the most fantastic breasts; I mean, truly miraculous!'

'Ain't that the truth!'

'Amen brother. And then you think, the whirligig of time's revenge has come round.' The allusion to *Twelfth Night* was enough to start Brian on a wild surmise, but he managed to say only, 'What do you mean?'

'Oh, just time passing,' said Matt. Then, after a while, 'Tara wants to get her breasts done. She's been obsessed with pectoral exercises, but now she wants to have them done.'

'Her breasts?'

'Yes. Fake breasts. Smaller than the ones she's got now. I think she's been looking at the same women we have.'

'Speak for yourself,' said Brian.

'Anyway, I'm not stopping her. Maybe I'll want to have sex with her again.'

'You don't have sex any more?'

'Well, we do; every now and again, but...' Matt drew his chin into his neck, relaxed, looked off to the Peaks.

'You know what I have to do to keep our marriage together?'

'No.'

'Prostitutes.'

'Prostitutes?!'

'Yes. To keep my erotic interest in female-kind alive. In order to fuck my wife I have to kid myself she's a prostitute. I mean, I'm not turned on by the idea of prostitution in itself. It's just you can buy yourself an hour with an attractive woman. A different woman. New. Fresh. Sex like it was when you were a teenager. Well, not exactly; I mean, you know you're kidding yourself.'

'Kidding yourself?'

'That they want it. That they want you; your cock; your humping and groaning – even your sperm, in the reproductive race. That's how I stay hard for it. Prime cuts, bent on your sperm – well, bent over a chair, literally, but you get the picture.'

'I'm not sure I want to.'

'Sorry. Anyway, I can carry some of that difference, that newness, that cheap excitement, into the marital bed, as it were; if it's within a few days.'

'Hmm.'

'You disgusted?'

'No. Well, I don't know. We're all trying to get through the day... But don't you think you've turned to a rather desperate last resort before exhausting all the options?'

'Well, I couldn't have an affair or she'd have half my money off me, and more.'

'Hmm. Did you try being nicer to her, taking an interest, rekindling the flames?'

'But I'm *not* fucking interested in her, except as mother of my kids.'

'But that's stupid. Think of yourself. Do you want to grow old like that, look back on a shared history of détente? That's mad. Are you sure you didn't just want to bang a few whores?'

'Maybe. I didn't say I was proud of it.'

'But you're not quite ashamed, either, are you?'

'Maybe not. Can we leave it now?'

'OK.'

Martin upped his tone a little. 'You remember the first time I saw her?'

'No.'

'You must do. Students' Union social. 1989. Christmas.'

'I didn't have much to do with the Students' Union, don't you remember?'

'Of course, of course. I only went in there for parties myself. Well, all the Students' Union staff were at the social, and that included the girls from the crèche. She was one of them. Blonde, attractive, petite.'

'Hm.' Brian had to concede the truth of this.

'She was so set on gaining male attention that she changed, after the meal, from jeans and a low-cut white top to a skimpy white low-cut minidress; and showed off her wares, shaking it all about. She either wanted to give every man in the place a hard-on or she was looking for a ride a few notches up the social scale. Both, probably. I thought she might be waging class war, and maybe she was; but she came up to me. I think it was because I'm tall, and I was wearing my glasses, which probably made me look intelligent. Anyway, when we parted that evening I had formed two definite impressions. One was that if I played my cards sensibly I was definitely going to get thoroughly laid. The other was that it was going to be at a time and a place of her choosing. I masturbated furiously for a week, curiously enough about anyone but her. I mean, I'd start with a general blondeness and skimpiness and her tits, but half the girls I'd ever taken a shine to helped me on my way. Then she phoned, and I instantly regretted it all, thinking my balls might have been drained too dry to take her on. No fear. It was an easy matter to get me to fall halfway in love before we had sex. And then it was really good, so that's three-quarters, or seven-eighths of the way there.'

'And the last little bit?'

'I think it was the fact she worked in the nursery. You know, good with kids, caring, maternal. That kind of thing. I was the one who broached the question of kids, though she was keen once I'd mentioned it. I think I thought, "I'll never do better, get her knocked up now good and proper, she'll never leave". Be careful what you wish for. Fucking lioness now. She's got a hard face, Brian, a *hard* face. Twenty years of living off me and she's got a hard face.'

'She hasn't been living off you; she's done all sorts.'

'She wouldn't be doing all sorts in *Alderley Edge* if she weren't with

me! And I'd be living in Chorlton, with the rest of the crew, all living their young-professional baby-buggies routine.'
'Baby buggies? Aren't we all a bit past that now?'
'Yeah. Well, it's how I'd like to have lived.'
'Regrets? You know what Nietzsche said? "You must live as though your every action will recur for all eternity." Or at least look back at your life, good and bad, as what made you what you are.'
'Yes, well I'm not sure I like what I am. In fact I'm mostly sure I don't. Anyway, Nietzsche was a fucking loony.'
'Fucking clever loony.'
'Yes. Fucking clever. Fucking clever does you no good.'
'But this is twenty years later... It's no small thing, you know. I mean, think of the alternatives.'
'I could have ended up like you: footloose, fancy-free...'
'In Illeshall.'
'Hm. Could be worse.'
'Oh, it could always be worse. "This is not the worst, as long as we can say: 'This is the worst'." That's what Edgar says, in *King Lear*, when everyone's dead; or nearly everyone.'
'That's pretty grim.'
'Hah well, they'd had a lot on their plate, see.'
Brian pondered Matt's belly which, as usual, he was sticking out. Defiantly defeated, Brian thought. Matt made a querying gesture and they began their descent.
'Don't you feel guilty about the prostitutes, though?'
'No. I've got it all quite compartmentalised. We're not unified subjects any more, are we?'
'Hmm. Maybe not.'
'So your suggestion regarding my problems with Ami is that I should visit prostitutes?'
'*No!* Start with porn. Maybe that'll be enough for you. Me? It was porn that got me started. A higher class of masturbation, your fantasies no longer merely inner and ethereal but *there, concrete*. And then I got to thinking, "What's the difference between this and a high-class prostitute? Wouldn't that be an even realer masturbatory fantasy?" Well, worked for me.'

'But don't you think that, even with the ones who aren't impelled by necessity, the ones who seem like free and rational subjects, that there must be something wrong with them, something damaged. Like pornstars, in fact. I mean, it's not within the range of normal behaviour, is it?'

'Everyone knows norms are repressive. And anyway, everywhere you turn, people are monetising their traumas, like that tiresome tart Wurtzel. Why should pert young chicks be any different?'

Brian could think of nothing to say. Suddenly he remembered a trip to Alderley Edge when they were students, for the Midsummer Solstice, he supposed.

'Do you remember talking to those old women that night we came here in summer?' he asked. 'We thought they must be witches, how they talked about how they'd come here since they were girls. That was remembrance, that was belief, that was togetherness. That was a lack of irony.'

'That was fucking barking,' said Matt, but continued, 'I could do with less irony in my life, though, more time for the Party. You don't get so much irony in the Party, and it tends to be gentle, not corrosive.'

'It's because it's a form of collectivity,' said Brian, 'even in Illeshall. A degree of earnestness, *seriousness*, depends on a project beyond the self – like Weber sees the fundamental *commitments* on which political negotiation and compromise are founded as developing out of voluntary associations, ties to other *people*. Irony, by contrast, tends to be the project *of* an individual self looking to gain status in the form of displaying that they are *in the know*, even if it's just a matter of the supposedly transcendental self looking down on the empirical self that slips on the banana skin. I sometimes wonder whether this isn't why the meeja hate Tony so much. They can only see his earnestness as a hypocritical form of self-advancement, because their only form of transcendence is an ironic self-transcendence that can only grasp belief as a convenient form of self-deception.'

'Hmm. I wonder what Alderley Edge Labour Party is like?'

'Thin on the ground, I should think. But nicer than the norm.'

'Do you know the story of the Iron Gates?' Matt asked suddenly, turning toward the rock face that abutted their path.

'No.'

'Well, there's a tradition that one day a farmer from round here was taking his horse to market in Macclesfield, when suddenly an old man in a grey cloak stopped him. The old man banged on the ground with a stick, and all of a sudden the rock face opened to reveal a pair of huge iron gates. The old man led the farmer through the gates into a cavern in which there slept countless men and white horses. The old man said these warriors were ready to awake and fight should England ever fall into danger. The farmer was then led back out, whereupon the gates slammed shut and the rock face closed up again. Some say the old man was Merlin and the sleepers King Arthur and his men.'

'Hmm. "Rise like lions after slumber/In unvanquishable number". Sounds as much of a myth as the revolutionary proletariat.'

'I wish I didn't believe that.'

Matt prevailed on Brian to stay the night and have a few drinks, and they talked about Malcolm Gladwell and *A Brief History of Time*, which Matt plausibly seemed to understand; and about how they used to get stopped by – they presumed – Special Branch every time they went to Dublin as teenagers; and about Iraq, about which they broadly agreed, which was some comfort. As indeed was the thought that he had not turned to prostitutes.

The trip had just had its intended effect of making Brian feel more contented with his lot when Seb's name, unusually, appeared on the display of his phone. Rafferty had gone missing, taking a lot of cash with her.

'I don't think it's kidnap, because I've not heard anything.'

'How much cash has she got? Enough to last how long?'

'Well, possibly a year or even two if she made it stretch. But you know her. It might not last her half an hour.'

Chapter 15
'People, you may find, are not universal sockets!'

Autumn 2005

If MI5 *was* tracking him through the security cameras that were no doubt dotted throughout town, he wondered whether they held the information that he had been a schoolboy rugby star – the kind of inside centre who was a second fly half, a true second five-eighth. His spatio-temporal sense was on heightened alert as he read the trajectories, anticipated the swerves and jinks, of the mass of people before him. He prided himself on needing to make a minimum of deviation from his speeding course by virtue of this superior apprehension.

He was stopped in his tracks by the sculpted racehorse quiver of Hermione's backside in a clingy skirt. He wasn't sure he hadn't recognised her from her backside alone, but the mane of blonde highlights confirmed his sighting. He resumed his course, picking up speed to keep her in sight: unable to bring himself to resist, he decided such a chance for unobserved voyeurism was within his margin of tolerance. She was a truly majestic sight: Brian was struck stupidly bad, sick with lust and adoration. For a while it seemed to him that he would be content forever to follow her thus. Soon, however, she turned into a shop and he was bereft: he was not so far gone as to loiter.

Sufficiently far, though, to determine to resort to pornography. Something had to be done to distract him from Hermione since her transformation. She had returned from Oxford after her finals quite unlike the girl who had left Illeshall, and very much unlike what her parents had envisioned. The demure and slender gazelle had become, in appearance at least, a sex bomb, her statuesque figure and strikingly regular features augmented by blonded hair and, most shocking and striking of all, surgically enhanced breasts. Brian could only imagine what her parents thought.

It could not in all honesty be said that, in other circumstances,

Brian would have failed to notice Hermione's physical charms. But he would not have been intoxicated by them. For them to render his senses drunken, it was necessary first, that they be either on the verge of, or already, deranged (it was equivocal whether and to what extent she was the cause of the derangement of which she was the object, but Brian was becoming convinced that she resembled his mother, that this explained her hold over him and that this meant she just might possibly be the one for him); and, second, that he should have been seized by an apprehension of her intellectual distinction. This it was, or at least this in combination with her looks, though pre-eminent above them, that caused the keening that coursed through his being. It was a keening the more affecting for being at a middle pitch, gathering and channelling the full spectrum of his being, felt in his belly as much as his heart: it seemed at once a suprasonic siren call and the answering resonance of his soul, pulling his flesh with it.

He had taken a keen interest in her Management textbooks, alighting with especial avidity on *The Seven Habits of Highly Effective People*, which he adjudged a profoundly Miltonic text. Hermione thought to herself: 'he's more interested in my books than he is in me'. But he was interested in the contents of her mind, and in how he might reform himself so as to conform to her ideal managerial type. He toyed, in idle moments, with doing an MBA, as she was planning to do; and daydreamed about their becoming a 'power couple'. He mused on how typical it had used to be that the apprentice should marry the master's daughter. It was thoughts such as this that had endowed her backside with Lawrentian import; without them, it would have been of fleeting phenomenal, almost asexual, interest.

Brian was determined not to imagine having sex with Hermione, at least not wantonly, wilfully: he would not be able to look her in the eye. His general condition of arousal had certainly invigorated his relations with Ami, but he strove, though failed, to keep images of Hermione from his mind. At least they never swam into focus. Ami was away, however; so he hurried home with his laptop. He wasn't sure what to look for, so googled the best quick description he could come up with: 'Young blonde with large breasts having sex'.

He quickly found a video of a blonde woman with very large

breasts sucking a similarly prodigious penis, and bouncing up and down on top of its possessor. It was a thrilling amazement to him that you could just see people doing this kind of thing; but, against his will, the image that brought him to climax was Hermione with her backside stuck in the air, the skirt in which he had just seen her yanked up around her waist. He would have to work harder to find the next image he employed, he resolved, then became engrossed in imagining having sex with Hermione before he remembered he had determined not to nurse that particular unacted desire. Instead, he pondered why she seemed to have joined with those who had developed a tendency to reference *Twelfth Night*. What could it mean? 'If music be the food of love,' she had said the other day, clicking on 'U Sure Do'.

Brian was almost drowning in Shakespeare's text. Only that morning, the postman had said to him 'I couldn't get in,' and he had made himself discount the notion that the man was comparing his situation with that of Viola/Cesario refused admission to Olivia's house. But 'If music be the food of love' was direct quotation, what could she mean? Was she teasing him about being Malvolio? That he had pretentions above his station? That he was a modern Puritan? After all, he did read 'politick books'. Or maybe she was implying that she was Viola to his Orsino, pining for the love of one of nature's lords and masters? Or maybe – given that she had transformed herself into his fantasy busty blonde – she was playing the role of the yellow-gartered Malvolio to his Olivia? Surely wishful thinking, he reasoned. And yet... his mind flickered with images of a naked Hermione. She seemed 'a garden escape in her unconscious solidarity with darkness'. There was no question she was paying him more attention than she had before her transformation. But surely that was a trick of the mind? She was probably just more assertive in general, had found herself, or a stance which suited her, brought her out of herself? That would make sense. It was unlikely that it had anything to do with him. Typical male vanity. And yet, enough women had wanted something to do with him that the thought was not so easily extirpated. Hermione was certainly a woman, now. He laughed at the thought that he was like Queen Elizabeth in that film. 'She's been cropped.' Well, if Hermione had not been cropped he was a Dutchman. By some young buck, he reflected, forlorn. Lucky little fucker.

Brian was by this point quite mad, but madmen, like stopped clocks, are right sometimes. Hermione's reference to the play had been an attempt to impress him: knowing that Brian had taken a group of people from the Labour Party to see it, she had opened a copy, seen its opening line, recognised it and realised she had enough for her purposes for the moment (if he picked her up on it she would, after all, have to read it). It had been a little joke among some in the party that Brian was Malvolio, since he was, as it were, chamberlain to their MP, something of a reader, and not without self-importance. On one occasion, he had even been provoked to pronounce someone 'Fool!' She hadn't been sure how else to have an effect on his consciousness beyond that made by what she thought of as the gawky teenager who had adored him from afar. Even when she had 'warned' him that she was sunbathing topless in the garden he had seemed unmoved. Such subtle provocations, she had come to suspect, would not be enough.

Hermione had had an adolescence which, while outwardly serene, had been troublesome for her, sexual desire thwarted by the fact she was the MP's daughter and everyone would know what she was up to. It had fostered a deeply pragmatic attitude toward her desires, assuaged by having sex either with men who had no idea who she was or, as in the case of certain tutors and the cutie Brian, would on no account dare divulge her secret. Brian she regarded as unfinished business. He had dominated the sexual imagination of her teenage years, cute, kind, amusing, indulgent, above all cute, with those long, long lashes and pert firm buttocks; and even now, a *little* overweight, to be sure, but looking no more than thirty with his thick hair with no trace of grey, and his failure to be disconcerted by her, his retention of his self-assurance, she relished the thought of a summer of love before she returned to her labours. If she was scheming, it was only in the most innocent sense: she was quite convinced of her capacity to show him a bloody good time.

Brian, meanwhile, having connected with her on Facebook under cover of just having made Illeshall Labour Party friends with her, had found what he assumed was her boyfriend, and discovered that he was an apprentice footballer. Typical star-to-be. They were the ones who got the glamour modelesque girlfriends, of course. Suddenly, he was seized by an anxiety that she was apprised of his doings on the internet in some newfangled techno way. Was the game not up? And, furthermore, did he not owe it to himself to confess? He was compelled by her, and it seemed both dishonest and a lack of justice to himself not to own it. 'If I had a wife, this wouldn't be happening to me,' he thought; there would be a powerful counterforce commingling the physical, even beyond the first flush, with steadfastness. And then he thought: 'What if I were married, and this was still happening?' It would be even worse. Which, by perverse logic, made his desires more acceptable to him – acceptable enough to have become Facebook friends with her without having brought the whole goal quite into view. He came to a conclusion and texted her: 'Hermione. I have a terrible crush on you. Brian x.' After enough time for him to feel relief at having unburdened himself, terrible regret at having done so, yet maintain hopes of a response, she replied: 'U bttr ask me rnd for dnnr, then.' Brian almost passed out, then texted that his place was a tip. 'After ur arse not yr plce.' Brian fought the urge to masturbate, counterproductive as this would be, and suggested she come round some time before dinner, like now, to which she responded that she was on her way.

Assured now of Brian's desire, Hermione was in her element: he was a man with a hard-on, and she knew what to do with them. Before he could grab her and kiss her, she brushed past him and strode into the flat. Brian, for a moment all at sea, felt the relative firmness of compacted sand beneath him, grew steadier with each step behind her and emerged from what seemed like gently but firmly buffeting waves as he followed her into the open air. Hermione motioned him to the sofa, recently cleared at Ami's behest.

'You've got some explaining to do,' she said. Brian looked dumbfounded, afeared.

'Where are all the pictures of you?' she continued.

'They're in London,' he floundered.

'That's no good,' she rebuked. 'And you've got something else to explain.'

'What?' asked Brian, frightened again.

'You've got to explain exactly what you want me to do. Exactly.'

Brian was in no condition to argue; indeed, it came to him with perfect clarity.

He felt the kind of awe he felt when he saw a man in rugby batter his way through opponents. This was a woman who knew what he wanted; and that clearly wasn't all she knew. Then the intensity of feeling diminished. The whole situation – Hermione's astounding breasts, the satin cushion of her posterior, her effortful panting – seemed shot through with an unreality that was not fantastical. In a short while it seemed he couldn't feel anything at all. He began to fret. Was he still hard? Hermione maintained her strenuosities for a time, then stopped.

'It seems to have gone to sleep,' she said.

'It must be nerves,' said Brian.

'Oh yes, a lot of people get nervous with me,' sighed Hermione.

'I'm not a lot of people!' responded Brian.

'Oh yes you are... Let's get drunk!' she suggested excitedly. 'Then you can make *me* come. It's quite easy.'

So they got drunk on shots, and he made her come. Pheromones flared, synapses fired, body and spirit were at one. They knew no shame. Then they talked. Brian found himself raging against the pettiness and injustices of Illeshall, bidding fiercely for understanding, sympathy, affinity, until, solemnly raising a hand, she stopped him instantly, like a maiden taming a rearing unicorn.

'If you're so unhappy here, why don't you just go? You've got to take control of your life, take responsibility. You are author to yourself. Like Milton, "authors to themselves in all," like you told me. You've read the *Seven Habits*. You've got to be proactive, effect a paradigm shift. Remember: management is effectively climbing a ladder; leadership is leaning it against the right wall.' Brian was fainting to be led by her, to know conversion into a new man, to learn to synergise. She was his ideal: the new aristocracy, the managerial class. When she told him that what she was looking for in a relationship was the opportunity to 'add value' he ached to be her raw material. And yet she seemed to believe his unhappiness was his fault.

'"It is not in vain",' he protested, quoting St Thomas Aquinas, '"that the fires of this divine discontent have been kindled within us".' It was his lot, he protested, to '"seek beyond the skyline, where the strange roads go down".' He instanced Goethe's *Faust*. 'Maybe I don't fit like a finely honed precision component into the gearings of late capitalism; and you may find that you don't either.'

'But you have to take responsibility,' she countered, again. 'You have to be adaptable.'

'People, you may find, are not universal sockets!'

'You're being absurd. You don't have to fit in everywhere; just somewhere. Anyway,' she said, her tolerance sustained, 'what do you want to eat?'

'What do I want to *eat*?'

'Yes. What have you got? I'll make you something.'

'*Make* me something?'

'*Yes!*' she barked, like a nightmare doll, 'like a *sister!*'

Brian didn't know whether this was because he was, of a sudden, radically desexualised in her eyes; or whether it was a role she liked to play, being, like him, an only child. But he tended to think the latter as she got together spaghetti on toast with apparent delight. Over their meal, they discussed aspects of their sexual histories. Hermione had tried girls but 'I want a penis!' Brian reflected that this had at least two possible meanings, and recommended to her *The Passion of New Eve*, that tale of a lecherous misogynist forcibly turned by fundamentalist feminists into an ideal woman or iconic parody of femininity. She seemed enthusiastic.

'I'm a parody and I just love it. Even better than the real thing!' Then she fled into the night, and he was dark.

In the morning, Brian was in a dreadful state, but he didn't know it; he just knew the world was agonising, strange and frightening. Desperate to legitimise what he had done, he texted Hermione and proposed marriage. Amused at first, after his third text she asked him to stop as it was freaking her out. When Brian went out to work, people talked to him in the street or muttered nearby in terms freighted with sarcasm; when there were no people, threat seemed to pulse from wherever he looked. Just in front of him, one man said to another, laughing, 'He can't get it up,' and Brian realised he knew about the night before: the feeling that he was being recorded had hardened into conviction some time since. He passed another pair of men, and when one of them remarked, 'It's his birthday,' Brian sensed an implication that he had hired a prostitute to celebrate the imputed occasion. When he finally got into work and Nicola asked, 'Good night?' his response was, he hoped, sufficiently collected to give nothing away, but he was troubled by the thought that his colleague might be laughingly hinting at her own knowledge. The rest of the day was a heaving ocean of excruciation, as he strove to keep his composure, until at last he could close his laptop and leave.

When he got home he paced and drank sauvignon blanc to calm himself down, his footsteps clattering back and forth over wooden boards, threat pulsing from the corners of the room, his agitation screwed to such a pitch that he walked and drank until he was limping, then drank some more before falling into a dead sleep. He woke suddenly, early, jackknifing upright on the sofa, and started drinking again while playing 'Red Alert' by Basement Jaxx on repeat.

He pondered what he thought of as this evocation of Hegel's notion of history as a 'slaughter-bench' – Napoleon, Kronstadt, Blair – for much of the afternoon, though he had little notion of time passing: 'Red Alert' was a track he remembered from evenings at Rafferty's. The next day was the same, except that, on impulse, he suddenly watered the now-almost-extinct peace lily Judy had given him. On Monday he phoned Peter Middleton, audibly distraught, and asked him why and how on earth he had organised such a conspiracy against him. He did not return to work. He continued drinking until he was sectioned after trying and failing to assault a stranger for, as he assumed, insulting him, and found himself in what he thought was Party HQ, but was in fact a police station.

Chapter 16
'A sort of dismally failing Son in the wilderness'

2006

Detox was hell. After some days, as he became more perceptive, he heard a woman visitor to the ward describe to her friend how another acquaintance had used henna on her hair, but what he took from what he heard was Gehenna, a place or state of torment or suffering, the abode of condemned souls, hell. He was not so deranged as to think he was in *hell*; he was sufficiently so to believe that he was being deliberately put though an experience that was its secular equivalent.

Withdrawal from alcohol is far more dangerous than in the case of most other drugs, such as heroin. In the case of the latter, cold turkey is a matter of acute physical and mental suffering, but it is not potentially fatal. Those who have drunk excessively for an extended period of time, by contrast, must on no account stop dead without medical care, for their nervous system has become literally, physiologically, dependent on alcohol and its metabolites: stroke and even death can, in some cases, result from their sudden absence. The police were familiar enough with the perils of drying out that, when they saw he could not stand up, such were the cramps and spasms afflicting his legs, they called an ambulance. One of the few things said to him on his admission to hospital that he remembered with any clarity was a remark from a doctor: 'You really need more alcohol. But this is a hospital.' The Librium that he was prescribed instead perhaps took the acutest edge off what he had to endure, though it was not a mercy he could discern.

As he lay, trembling and sweating, acutely awake, the night was worst, for the cries of the old men around him served to amplify his plight. 'Be good!' shouted one. 'Be good!' An echo of exhortation perhaps still resounding in the hollowed shell of an utterance that was nearest neighbour to mere reflex memory. Piercingly, more conscious emotion lingered in the refrain of another: 'Harry! Help me! Help me, Harry!' Whenever Brian ached so hard from tensing and trembling that he could bear it no longer, he buzzed and asked for more Librium. Nearly always he was told it was hours before his next dose, no, they would not forget, yes, they would be on time with it, please, try and get some sleep, this last a bitter prompt to realisation that not even those who spent their working hours caring for such as he had any inkling of what they were going through.

Even when the trembling had eased, after some days, and he was able to use a bedpan by himself, even after he had been moved to a ward on which psychosis was less audible, sleep was an impossibly distant land. He longed for a break from his consciousness, but was told repeatedly that sleeping pills could not be prescribed along with Librium, which was in any case a tranquilliser and should be helping him sleep, until he happened to ask at a time when a consultant was on duty and felt able to combine the two at a suitable dose. He managed an hour or two of shallow sleep, a blessed release, rocking at the lapping edge of a sea of ward talk, swishing curtains, trundling and laughter from the nurses' station.

After some time, Peter Middleton and Cécile came to visit. They brought flowers, fruit, chocolate, books, changes of clothes, toiletries. Brian could think only that they were determined not to let on that they knew what had happened between him and Hermione, and could see nothing for it but not to let on himself. They were concerned, reproached themselves for not having realised how hard he had been hit by recent events, assured him that his job was open for as long as it took him to get back on his feet, said they had called Michelle and that she and Colleen would be coming up to see him and take him to stay with Colleen. All would be well in time.

Once he was able to get to the toilet unaided, Michelle and Colleen came and took him to Colleen's flat in Belsize Park. There, he sank relieved into the fact of his collapse, which seemed largely to absolve him of responsibility for what he had got up to with Hermione. He was not a creepy middle-aged lecher, or an absurd aspirant Malvolio, but a vulnerable man who had been at his wits' end. And perhaps, after all, Peter didn't know his secret. Most important, he was sure no one in London did. He lost, without noticing its passing, the sense of being recorded. As he grew stronger, feeding on the rich bean soups the vegetarian Colleen made him for protein, he relaxed into London life – the British Library, though he was dismayed to find it now full of students; his favourite pub with its prize-winning pies; the Old Compton Street Patisserie Valerie; the Curzon for the odd foreign film and a spot of gazing at brightish young things; and, of course, old friends. These were his amenities, his pleasant places, he thought as he enjoyed the insane bustling of Oxford Street on his way to John Lewis to buy kitchenware for Colleen, or made his way along the South Bank for something at the Hayward. This was the source of his longing, the only cure for his nostalgia.

Yet still Illeshall beckoned, just beyond the horizon, like the sea we competed to glimpse first on childhood trips, but with different import. It seemed another world, with its terraces and civic grandiosity, but also a grim destiny that loomed the larger the further he meandered through brightness. He could see no acceptable means of maintaining himself in London, no way of sustaining the effort of Illeshall. It seemed he was faced with the same old dilemma: his work or his life? Yeats was no help ('The mind of man must choose/Perfection of the life, or of the work'): he lacked the means to do any such thing. A helpless sadness suffused him. He pondered Satan's speech in hell: 'For who would lose/Though full of pain, this intellectual being/Those thoughts which wander through eternity?' He must buck up, he would at length affirm, and perhaps be more buoyant for the lack of drink – something he scarcely missed at all, even in company.

And so to Illeshall he did go, full of vigour and purpose. Once he'd found himself a good woman, anything was possible. 'There's no discouragement/Shall make him once relent/His first avowed intent/To be a pilgrim,' he would sing to himself, jolly. But he had not been back in Illeshall long before the echoing song began. In truth, it may have started even before he returned. Certainly, when he took his laptop to be repaired, he found the computer guy's advice that he get a new hard drive (he still couldn't help thinking of them as hard disks) – 'if you want to start from scratch' – curiously pertinent. Then, after he remarked to Nicola in the office how pleasant it was to be back amid the slowness of Illeshall – a slowness in the very way people moved – he was suddenly transfixed by what seemed the exaggerated speed with which the cashier in the supermarket seemed to be going about her business. An elderly man, with slightly elaborate courtesy, made way for him on the escalator in Marks and Spencer and he recalled having talked to Rafferty about how people in Illeshall did not line up on one side or other of escalators, but rather disported themselves in a manner that suggested it had not occurred to them that anyone might think themselves busy enough to want to walk up them.

After a couple of weeks of this, Illeshall had once again gone from a world apparently devoid of meaning to one suffused with it, bursting from the walls and sky. Sealed as he was in a matrix of his own fears, desires and compelling preoccupations, the material world became indistinct, as though he were underwater, as though his head were in a goldfish bowl filled with the waters of his mind, its tidal pulls and waves. If he had been able to consider the matter, it would have seemed as though perception was the preserve of some higher, clearer element.

His eyes were not quite the same since his bout of illness, and so he was using a font size of twenty. 'Why's your writing so big?' asked Nicola, laughing. 'You working for Gordon on the sly?' Unlike many psychotics, Brian was not convinced of his own secret greatness, to be unleashed on an as yet unknowing world. Rather, he came to fear that the world suspected him of being secretly great. In his case, the egotism characteristic of paranoia was less a matter of an inflated sense of self than of an accelerating profusion of interpretations and connections among which, rationally, the only uniting principle there could be was himself. He did not communicate cryptically. Rather, he came to fear that everything he ordinarily said and did was liable to be read as code. When Nicola came over and scooped a baseball cap from the floor, the presence of which, in truth, baffled him, he exclaimed, 'There haven't been Americans in here' in the process of forming that very thought.

When Nicola remarked, 'The desire to be interesting is a weakness' he took it to heart, and pondered whether his belief that the world was more interested in him than the occasion warranted was in fact a desire that this be so. But then, after he had delivered a diatribe against anti-modernism, and proclaimed his commitment to the ideals behind both council estates and Ikea, the young Turkish guy in the corner shop had nodded at the bag containing his chicken kebab and fries and remarked, smiling, 'Something burning in there,' and he wondered whether the reference was to Brian's smouldering socialist passions.

Facebook was no help at all. Each time he tried to share something, usually either from the Labour Party or involving animals, he was asked to type a pair of words into a box. The first couple he encountered were 'Comrades' and 'Power', which Brian considered a little disturbingly apt. He was still more troubled, given his responsibility for getting speakers to the constituency for fundraising events, to encounter 'Burnham' and 'evening', which he wasn't sure whether to take as a suggestion he invite the Member of Parliament for Leigh, or as an implication that he was Macbeth and 'Burnham Wood' was coming his way after some putative reign of terror over Illeshall. He experimented with refusing to enter the words, and found the answer, 'Please provide a response for the security check,' less than reassuring; even less so when the next request was for 'the' and 'decanted': he had no idea whether he was meant to be the dregs, or what the opposite of 'dregs' was or, indeed, whether the accusation was that he had a puritanical manner of separating sheep and goats. The next pair he noticed were 'cosmetic' and 'runes', which he took as an admission that he was being presented with what on the face of it was a code – and, indeed, the experience he was having with the words he encountered was far from random, his faith in which was only strengthened by the duo 'stuccoes' and 'artillery', of which he could make nothing: coming so soon after he had pondered the significance of the code with which he was confronted, he construed this absence of significance as a piece of taunting, and thus an obvious confirmation of his suspicions.

By the time Nicola made reference to a couple who had come to Middleton's weekly surgery – 'the couple in shell suits' – Brian heard '*hell* suits' and was confirmed in his suspicion that, in a real sense, he was in hell. If there were a hell, for him it would be this, a bespoke hell designed by those who must be picking up on his thoughts, so finely modulated, so exactly fitted was it to provoke a suffering seemingly played out before some great, almost cosmic, audience kept abreast of, and sneering in ridicule at, his plight. 'What the hell am I doing?' he wondered to himself. 'Am I acting out the epic of *Gilgamesh*, seeking my bosom companion in the underworld, an appreciator of Henry James in Illeshall?' He began inputting literary allusions as his Facebook status – 'Brian makes nothing happen'; 'Brian is sympathising with vegetation'; 'Brian is the perfect pleasure; he is exquisite, and he leaves one unsatisfied'; 'Brian is half in love with easeful death' – and fancying that the people he passed in the street had read them.

'I am, literally, battling the devil, like a sort of failing Son in the wilderness,' he explained to Martin.

'Brian, your problem is that you think the canon of English literature is your spiritual autobiography. And I don't think Hermione would appreciate your patriarchal construction of her as an avatar of the Infernal One.'

'Not English literature per se. I mean, I turned to Milton because Baudelaire and Rimbaud always seemed a bit obvious to me. There was more mystery about the seventeenth century, religion, all that, though I think what attracted me was that my politics then were essentially religious. Still are, in a way... Oh God! I'm half aesthetic decadent, half political militant: a Milident. Sounds like something for fixing false teeth in a twenty-first-century stylee.'

'No; you are a milicadent, dancing the dance of a thousand beats, with a thousand dying falls thrown in. If I were you, I'd reread *The Passion of New Eve*.'

'Why? You think I need castrating and turning into an ideal woman?'

'No. I think what you've got on your plate is a castrated man and an ideal woman all in one, as we always are: the best things come in twos.'

Brian's thoughts crystallised. Not in terms of Martin's playfully crude Freudianism, but quasi-theologically. He suddenly realised he was exactly like Milton, filled with a 'rational burning', 'the desire and longing to put off an unkindly solitariness by uniting another soul, not without fit body'. Rafferty had been his first Eve, but she had fallen and, though loss of her would never leave his heart, was he not now beckoned by a second Eve, product of postmodern simulation and post-structuralist feminism? What might they not prove? The rational kernel of Christian doctrine on sexuality, even! Brian recalled *The City of God*: before the Fall, sex was to have been rational: 'the sexual organs would have been brought into activity by the same bidding of the will as controlled the other organs'. The thought, as expressed, was clearly absurd: Augustine himself turned to funny examples in giving postlapsarian instances of the remnants of this faculty – in those who can, perplexingly, deliberately wiggle their ears, or fart at will, even to the extent of playing tunes. And yet, like any good reader of post-structuralist feminism, he was aware of woman's allotted role as bestower upon man of his embodied being. What if this took the form of her rational control of his erection? Then the couple would be fully rational, transparent to themselves, a higher oneness: divine, even. He would have made a heaven of hell.

And yet Hermione had spurned him. No sooner had he had his epiphany than he was cast into the Slough of Despond by this recollection. Surely there could be no third Eve? That was altogether too Hegelian. And besides, the first two Eves were already syntheses of nature and artifice. Also, Brian wondered, must there not be something patriarchal about a resolution that overcame Augustine's conception of the Fall so neatly? After all, such a desire had informed Milton's conception of the marital relation and his desire for there to be only one ruling rational will within it, the husband's. For the ruling will to be the woman's was surely a mere reversal of the values attached to the different terms of the argument, a kind of shadowy seductive underside to the rule of light. And yet how wonderful to surrender, perchance to dream! Brian couldn't help it if his identity was patriarchal: after all, he was a man! And what did men do who wanted to submit to a beautiful woman, but did not have one to hand? He thought of Matt – though he had his doubts about how submissive Matt was. But Matt could surely point him in the right direction, so to speak.

And yet Brian, insane and 'elevated' as he was, hesitated. It seemed mad to substitute a cash transaction, a commodity relation, for a genuine feeling, however embarrassing. Brian was pretty sure it would require a more active fantasy life than he possessed to forget that what was at stake was not mutual recognition, the desire of the desire of the other, but consumer satisfaction. Part of Brian counselled that there was no doubt how he truly, authentically felt as an individual. Part of him, rather madly, told himself that this was how Blair had felt about Iraq. But there lurked within him some ineluctable shame he could not be rid of.

And so, as autumn turned to winter, and Saddam Hussein was sentenced to death, Brian drank. Feeling nothing but emptiness, blankness, he drank until he was unconscious, and thereafter in gouts of half a bottle of wine, finding loss of consciousness again and again until, waking after midnight to the permanent rumour of Radio 4, he would find himself without drink or people and stare from the lights of his hi-fi to the clock, to the ceiling to the clock, to the grey sky to the clock, until 7.50am, when the walk to the supermarket would take him the ten minutes until it was legal to sell alcohol, and back again, whereupon he would recommence the round. He ceased to feel hunger, and in any case the irritation of the alcohol made his stomach shun food, so he did his best with milk. His walk to the shop became slower and slower as he weakened, more unsteady, more and more the shuffle of the old and afflicted, until one day he fell down in the street and stayed there until some bystanders called an ambulance.

Chapter 17
'A lower deep still threatens'

2007

Detox was worse this time. In the lowest deep a lower deep still threatens. He was taken to an observation ward, the purpose of which was to determine who required admission for a longer stay in hospital. It was run by a doctor junior enough to be thoroughly cognisant both that she would be looked on with more favour the lower her admissions were, and that it was notionally, if variably, the hospital's policy to refuse admission to those withdrawing from alcohol (at the same time as it was the policy of the shop opposite the hospital to refuse to serve them alcohol). After a night spent pleading vainly for sleeping pills, Brian was introduced to a physiotherapist whose task it was to instruct him in how to get himself home without falling down. Brian, however, having been manoeuvred into the chair next to his bed, found himself so clamped to it by the tautening of his thighs and calves that the physiotherapist couldn't manage, and didn't dare try further, to remove him from it. Another day and night of torment and Librium intervened before the physiotherapist returned and, having got him upright, escorted him a short way along the corridor with sufficiently little assistance for the doctor in charge of the ward to convince herself he was safe to be discharged, which he was, without Librium, as was hospital policy, despite his pleas. 'What are you afraid of at home?' quizzed the physiotherapist. 'Nothing!' snarled Brian. 'But I don't think I can get there!' Brian had no option but to leave on his own two feet. He was in such a state the taxis waiting at the hospital refused to take him. In the course of an hour or so of strain and agony he inched seventy yards down the hill, juddering with the effort of not tumbling down it, and collapsing to sit on steps until each time he was moved on, almost fainting at the thought he had a mile to go but seeing nothing else for it, until the steeper slope of a pedestrian crossing pitched him in front of a car.

Fortunately, he picked up speed from this short slope and was flung headfirst, so that the car broke only his trailing left foot. The Librium luckily dulled the pain, and Brian once again felt the consolation of a small concerned huddle of people. Once again he was lifted onto a trolley, into an ambulance, and returned to the hospital. This time, after some hours on a bed in A&E, where he asked for and got some more Librium, he was admitted to the hospital proper. X-rays showed only a small tarsal bone was broken, and so his trousers were cut off him, he was given a temporary cast, hooked up to some vitamins and minerals and left in a daze, periodically interrupted by replacements to his drip feed, until night fell, whereupon his request for sleeping pills was answered with blessed zopiclone.

He was certainly not well enough to be left to his own devices on crutches, and besides, this ward was not under pressure to minimise admissions, and so the hospital set to restore him to physical health. In the morning he was urged to eat some cereal, which he managed, and a huge black male nurse came and bathed him carefully, thoroughly – he had not undressed in weeks, let alone washed, the effort of dressing again too much to contemplate. After the exertion of being washed, he lay, once again counting and recounting the curtain rails, coordinating each one with its bed, until a couple of days later Michelle and Colleen arrived.

Almost the first thing he asked them was, 'Do you feel like you're being recorded?' Colleen looked nonplussed, but Michelle froze.

'What do you mean? Here?'

'Yes, here. But elsewhere, too. In fact, I can't *quite* shake the feeling I'm being filmed.'

'Brian, that's quite worrying. You do realise that's not a normal thought to be having, don't you?'

'Well, it does seem quite odd that someone would want to record me.'

'Yes, but thinking someone is recording you isn't normal, is it?'

'Well, I suppose not.'

'Because no one is recording you.'

'If you say so. I still *feel* like I am.'

'What do you mean, you feel like you're being recorded?'

'Well, the same as when you feel there's another person in the room with you, and sometimes you're wrong.'
'You mean someone you can see?'
'No! I just mean the sense of another presence, say late at night. I'm sure it's quite normal. My dad used to feel it. I'm sure I've read about it in novels.'
'I suppose so. But you're *not* being recorded, are you?'
'Like I say, if you say so. I just feel like I am.'
'Well, you need some help with that. Probably some medication. Are you OK with that?'
'Sure, if you say so.'
'Right. I'm going to talk to the nurses.' And so Brian was prescribed first, as a precaution, two, and then, when he showed no ill effects, 3mg of risperidone (the side effects of which can include, in fairly rare cases, neuroleptic malignant syndrome, most markedly in the form of the muscles becoming entirely rigid so that, for instance, the patient cannot direct his gaze; and dyskinesia – repetitive, involuntary body movements, sometimes accompanied by a feeling of inner restlessness and torture).

Brian was released to Colleen's care, and in a few weeks, the sense of being recorded had receded; in a few months, he was only rarely preoccupied by strange coincidences, such as when he bumped into one of Rafferty's long-ago acolytes, of all people, just before seeing a man with a resemblance to Paul Foot throw a copy of the *Daily Mirror* into a bin. Considerable were the machinations in his mind that night. During this period, Brian was buoyed both by his return to London and by the feeling of regaining his health, of getting better all the time. But then he hit a plateau. As summer came he found himself watching Wimbledon all afternoon, mystified and transfixed, wondering where the players found the psychic energy to compete as they did. He felt pity and awe for those who went even one set down, who had just lost a set, and had to find somewhere the resolve to battle to win a whole other set just to get to the point at which they'd started, and so often did! If they were winners, he was no winner. Maybe the current distribution of wealth, absent some aristocratic hangovers, really was merited? Colleen, whose kindness and tolerance were almost boundless, was dismayed at this turn, and still more so when it turned out that these were good days, that on other days he complained that his brain felt like it was being squeezed and dried out like a sponge, and went out and came back lucid and serene but smelling of drink.

'Alcohol is a depressant,' she affirmed. 'It's probably what sent you psychotic, and it won't help if you're feeling down.'

'But it *does* help, and it's not like I'm drinking myself into insensibility, or into hospital; and it's not as if I behave badly.' All the same, Colleen found it too upsetting and told Brian so. The next time he felt his brain being squeezed he resolved to return to Illeshall, where he could get some relief.

But in Illeshall he no longer had present distractions from his lack of faith in the future, the absence of hope, despair, the unforgivable sin. He could see no way back to London, no way he could forsake a job that kept his mind alive for one which, he imagined, would afflict and then kill it. He started going to AA meetings, but was depressed to find that, whatever the exhortations to identify with the experiences of those who shared them, he fundamentally did not recognise them. He sat in his flat consumed by the feeling of having missed some important lesson in life – some introductory remarks, some off-the-record tip, something not in the handout. He became preoccupied with the apparent loss of an exemplary photograph of him and Rafferty, sat on the sofa at her parents' house when they were about twenty, she in a snit about something, shoulders hunched about her head, nose wrinkled in disgust at a universe that had refused to comply with her wishes, and he, smiling at her in indulgent amusement. He was sure she had given it to him quite recently; but it was nowhere to be seen, no matter how often he started up and riffled a shelf of books before falling dispirited on the sofa. When the spirit had been with him he had gone whole days on a tin of corned beef and dry bread a bit like, he fancied, Antony drinking the horses' stale on campaign; but he phoned out again and again for pizza: 15 inches, half and half 'Meaty One' and 'Jalapeno Hot'.

The final straw came when he ordered Paul McKenna's *Instant Confidence* in a bid to hypnotise himself out of his torpor. Asked to remember a time when he felt happy and in control, he found himself at a loss. He mulled it over for the best part of a day, getting more and more miserable at the thought of his misery, until the head cramps came on and he drank again until one morning his neighbour, coming round to the flat to ask about the source of the smell emanating from it, found the floor carpeted with emptied wine bottles, fermenting milk cartons and sandwich containers in which maggots writhed, and called social services.

Clare – not Clair or Claire – the social worker to whom he was assigned, found that she got lucid, coherent, composed speech from him whatever time of day she visited. Unlike the psychiatrists, who had thus far merely checked he was taking his medication, was having no severe side effects and had neither attempted nor was planning suicide, Clare realised he was profoundly depressed, and told him so.

'I think there's a fair chance you're just self-medicating with the alcohol. You didn't have problems before all this went on; and unlike most people who have a specific problem with alcohol, you're not back on the bottle as soon as you're out of hospital. I'm going to see about getting Professor Draxler onto your case. Whatever happens, I'm going to recommend you go straight on some strong antidepressants. Now, as I'm sure you've been told too many times, alcohol is a depressant. It helps in the very short term but is deleterious after that, so you should try to restrict the amount you drink. Don't make yourself suffer, but try only to drink if you're really starting to get tense or your fingers start to shake or quiver when you hold your hand out.'

Brian might even have seen a glimmer of light. Certainly, he was at once convinced of light's existence, and that it could possibly be for him. His head still cramped occasionally, and sometimes he drank it off; but Clare suggested a higher dose of venlafaxine, Professor Draxler agreed and, once at the slightly unusual dose of 300mg, Brian's psychosomatic symptoms stopped. For a few weeks all was sweetness and light. He seemed wonderfully free of an impossible burden. Until it loomed, as in a computer game or an epic quest, the tallest, most insurmountable tombstone of a challenge after a host of lesser challenges, stark as darkness at noon: Illeshall.

Brian realised he felt tense and faint. His head drifted light and at the same time was clamped as if by a vice at the back, inside his skull. He felt partly sleepy, and at the same time as though full of adrenaline. He was very anxious, tight in the shoulders and thighs. His eyes hurt. He had butterflies in his stomach and he was restless. Overcome with tiredness, he tried to lie down and close his eyes but jumped up again and paced round the flat, then lay down again, then leapt up, electric, again and again and again. The message flashed up in his head: 'It is just like it was when I heard my dad was to die.' He had to do something, anything, to be free of this feeling. Each time he leapt up he wrote down a description of his feelings, for Clare, as though it might be the saving of him. Then, panting for relief, he drank. In the morning, grey but much better, he phoned Clare. 'That sounds absolutely awful,' she said. 'We must talk to Professor Draxler about that.' Some days later, after a long talk about how he must not get dependent on it, and that if he did, the effects might even be reversed, leaving little or no recourse, he left Professor Draxler's room with a prescription for clonazepam, 500µg.

It happened that Brian's allowed period of sick leave ended that June. Peter Middleton had hired a pleasingly intellectually capable replacement, but had felt duty-bound to hold Brian's position open for him. Now there came, it seemed to him, a natural crunch-point, and it was he who raised the issue first.

'Are you going to come back? Permanently? And, excuse me for saying this, properly? You know, the old Brian, before all this awful business? You say you're feeling much better?'

'I am feeling much better, Peter. But...'

'But you don't want to be in Illeshall?'

'Well, it's more that I'm not confident that I'll *stay* well as long as I'm in Illeshall. I just don't have the support structure, or the steadying influence of a sense of an ongoing course to my life.'

'What will you do?'

'I'm not sure, but I've got a lot of money in ISAs, and from Dad's house. I could buy a flat somewhere quite nice outright. I just really need to do something that will pay my living expenses and a bit over for saving, even holidays. Maybe teaching English as a foreign language.'

'*Brian*, on *holiday*? I thought they were for civilians!'

'Oh, no more New Modelling for me, I think.'

'Oh, I'm sure you can manage a bit more. Leave it with me. I'll have a bit of a think.'

Peter's 'bit of a think' involved what to do about replacing Darcy, who was leaving at the end of August to visit Rwanda before starting a PhD in Development Economics at the LSE. And so Brian cashed in his shares when they were at their peak, not long before the run on Northern Rock, sold his flat in Illeshall likewise and found himself a spacious two-bedder in a quite-nice North London suburb.

Brian couldn't bear the thought of the local Labour Party after all he'd been through – to his friends he cited Orwell, who believed the Labour Party's membership to be the best case against socialism – but had much to occupy him nonetheless. As a junior minister, Middleton had three researchers, and Brian was given the title Office Manager. Since two of the researchers were women in their early twenties, a significant part of the managing he did was to wait at Middleton's beck during late-night sittings: the corridors of Portcullis House, where half-sodden high-flown legislators roamed, were no place for a young woman alone at night, and he didn't think it fair to make Giles, the young man among them, the sole researcher obliged to sit out the graveyard shifts.

Sophie Pleasaunce, in the next-door office, *was* thus obliged, however, and this became the basis of a fledgling friendship. Sophie was quite good company, as most women are, and Brian was better company than most men, and so they tended to have lunch together, rather than brave the loneliness of The Debate, the cafe for non-MPs in which none of the livelier denizens of Portcullis would be seen dead; and drinks together after work when they dared pretend Middleton was due to meet them in the Strangers' Bar over in the House. Once she even invited him on a trip some of them were making not, as usual, to the nearby Pascha, but to Fabric and, having heard of its 'bodysonic' vibrating dancefloor, Brian was moved by nostalgia for the Ritz to accede to playing the role of 'favoritized uncle'.

At work and in some of his free time, he so arranged things that he became moderately expert in schools, securing a quarter-hour coffee here and there with relevant peers of the realm and quango-members. He felt he should make some progress toward think tankery, though in truth he was little troubled at finding himself much older than most of his work companions, at whose exuberant charm he could smile, in whose romantic disappointments he could find moderate pathos. After all, he had his friends and his home comforts. His life was one of mild dissatisfactions tempered by the quiet joys of mutuality and the fruits of contemplation. Sophie, in particular, was food for considerable thought. She clearly enjoyed his attention and interest, as he was mildly flattered by hers; and yet he sensed nothing remotely sexual in their relationship. In large part he construed this as but one aspect of the larger waning of sexual appetite he so often pondered in himself, wondering whether it was the effects of age or a kind of chemical castration. Whichever, it was in many ways a blessed release. He recoiled at the thought of the torments this sexual irrelevance would have visited on a younger Brian. And yet, as he contemplated the sheer misery her features manifested as she sat with peers among whom the occasional one would fleetingly accord with her aspirations, before setting her down once again with Brian, it seemed to him that she would almost certainly be at least marginally happier getting knocked up by him and opting out of a race she lacked the gifts to enjoy, and was a little puzzled and even piqued that she gave no sign of exploring this avenue. This added a tiny vial of venom to the exquisite mingling of pain and pity in his apprehension, on a Friday when the MPs were away, of those broad hips emphasised by skirts that were too short.

Sent at the last moment to deputise for Middleton at a roundtable on education at the newfangled and heftily funded Institute for Socialization, he found himself just to the left of, in the chair, Juliet Neilson. He felt just the right amount of excitement to be able to shine moderately with his knowledge of what was up in Hackney, and his tact in not making too much of it.

Brian was quite used to contemporaries failing to recognise him, or affording him no more than a friendly but noncommittal raising of the eyebrows. Juliet, checking his career details, such as they were, and introducing him, had shown no more than a polite professional interest. But having drawn the session to a close she turned at once to him and, with a dazzling smile, congratulated him in warm terms. 'Well now, Brian! *That's* what you've been doing with yourself, becoming quite the intellectual! Look, I've got to dash now; but do call me, we *must* hook up! Professionally, that is,' she laughed, affording him a wink. And then, having proffered her face to be kissed, she was gone with a lick of clicks.

Brian felt too elevated for the office. He was all of a sudden in the kind of mood where he might pat Sophie on the backside, actually start thinking about bending her over one of the desks in the office, though not, at his age, actually try it. He left a message with Middleton to say that he was going for a walk, checked that the office had enough to be getting on with and made for St James's.

Urged to 'hook up' by a deputy director of the Institute for Socialization: now *that* was something. Indeed, for the first time, Brian was struck with the feeling of being Something-in-the-World and, coeval, the thought of being Something More. Himself a deputy director. Even, Lord smite him not, a director! And all at once Brian foresaw, away in the distance like a sparkling sea, its every glistening a seeming wink, television.

Chapter 18
'A name to put on flyers'

2008–9

Julia, of course, was not free until several weeks after Christmas, but when she was it was for dinner, which was a considerably better than average start. She looked no more than thirty. Brian wondered whether to be flattered she had left undone – or had expressly undone – an extra button on her blouse, so that she was suffused with an intimation of embonpoint, or whether this was her way on an evening away from the Institute. Brian had been unsurprised to learn that she was quite openly sleeping with the Director of the Institute, but had no idea what this implied about her comportment in general.

It was apparent, however, from the laughing way she recalled their 'previous negotiations' that she did not overdo reticence and that she was concerned to be friends.

'See how liberal and concerned we are on social matters now? We've even pledged to match the totals of your spending plans. I've even read John Rawls! A bit.'

'We'll see how long that lasts,' said Brian, in what to him sounded surprisingly like a growl.

'Nonsense! We're hugging photogenic huskies, harnessing the potential of hoodies; we've got an A-list of the brown and the breasted.'

'Speaking of which, are you on it?'

'Yes. But we're getting ahead of ourselves. First we've got to do something about *you*. We thought it would be nice to get you seconded, part-time – though only at first, and on the strict understanding that your work for Peter would be policy work, i.e. no more hanging round the Commons late at night taking advantage of children.'

'I can assure you they're not interested in me.'

'Not what I've heard, darling. Anyway, we set you to work writing a pamphlet or two—'

'But I don't have any new ideas as yet.'

'Oh, you have plenty of ideas, and your inimitable style, besides which, I can chuck you one or two: such as making it a condition of their charitable status that public schools set up academies, stuff like that – bit radical, but drawing on traditional virtues.'

'And you'll make me a senior researcher?'

'Senior researcher, bollocks. You've done enough researching. When I do something for a man, I like them to stay done, at least while I catch my breath. We're gonna make ya, a star-ah-ah-ah. Well, a deputy director, at least; like me. Except not quite like me.'

'No...'

'What do you mean by that "No"? Have you been earwigging?'

'I might have been, a little.'

'"Course you have. Anyway, it's no secret I'm shagging the boss and I can assure you he hasn't the time or energy or inclination for anything else. Well, he is sixty-five. A very debonair sixty-five, if I say so myself.'

'So how did this all happen?'

'To be honest, it's all sex – well, sex plus the sine qua non of my exceptionally high intelligence and organisational bravura. I was just settling into my second job with someone who was considered Cabinet material – if you really want to know who you'll have to find out for yourself – and this seemed pretty good, land of the SPADS in prospect, nice seat in the distance. But, classically, came one of those late nights. He was more than half-cut and wholly horny. If he'd just slapped me on the arse it would have been one thing. After all, any girl with my backside who stalks around in Lycra is presuming, to a degree, on the social contract: it's whence much of the frisson derives. But grabbing and rubbing my breasts as persistently as he did was something else. Well, I shouted at him loud enough to bring him to his senses, left shrouded in my sense of dignity and the next morning put it to him that I could cause him quite a lot of trouble, and certainly nix his place at the top table, if I had a mind to. I didn't have a mind to, as it happens: I've always felt some sympathy for men on heat, and there's not a few people from whom I would have regarded it as an acceptable if clumsy form of seduction. So I simply said it offended my sense of natural justice that his invasion of my boundaries should redound to my detriment, and that he should see whether he couldn't come up with a nice little replacement number. Which he did, as a senior researcher at the Institute. To be honest, I kicked my heels at that level a little too long. I could never shake the feeling that someone, somewhere, had had a word and that I was one to be watched. But then along came Cecil, and he was just lovely, a real silver fox, but genuinely charming to everybody. I thought, 'If I'm ever going to shag the boss, now's the time,' and I really worked away at clever policy lines, even got friends in marketing and advertising to brainstorm them, kept feeding them to my lovely Deputy Director, who was sufficiently enamoured of me to let me take the credit, until one day the man himself called me into his office, told me what good things he kept hearing about me and made me a Deputy Director, Schooling and Welfare. Told me how much good taking on the welfare remit would do me in Tory circles these days. And then, charmingly – and, mark you, *after* he promoted me – a little mumblingly, he asked me out to dinner. And he had such range and depth! Any little remark I made he could amplify and ramify until it seemed an aphorism of penetrating brilliance. And he did it again and again – take me out to dinner, I mean – and didn't once try it on! After a while I was getting genuinely frustrated, thinking about him all the time, worrying about how he clearly wasn't interested unless I stayed interesting, until I decided that if I wanted my knickers pulling down I was clearly going to have to slide them off myself and present them to him on a silver tray. Well, luckily I realised I'd better come up with something slightly less tacky than *my* sexual imagination was going to provide, so I got the idea of commissioning a love poem. So I asked around among friends who'd studied English, and asked who the best love poet in the country was, and they couldn't think of one. Not one! At least, not one whose work wasn't too personal and idiosyncratic to be any use to anyone else. So they suggested 'Come live with me, and be my love,' but I thought that starting with domestic arrangements might be a bit forward. Then they suggested the Cavaliers. And so there I was, flicking through a book of poems from the seventeenth century, when I came upon Carew's "A Rapture": "I will enjoy thee now, my Celia, come" – and it was just too perfect to change Celia to Cecil, some thines to mines and thys to mys. And such a piece of high-class pornography, basically, really sexy, and with a rather unmissable point. And I thought, "I'll send him this, in my best blue handwriting; and if he's interested in me in the way I'd like him to be, he'll recognise it from my signature." And he did! We've lived happily ever since.'

'Wow!' was all Brian could muster. 'Like in the old times.'

Julia found it sweet that Brian had got so het up about Hermione ('You can fuck my daughter, if you like; at least I'd know you were doing it properly. Not like these little bastards who've got it all off the internet. I've told her her backside is strictly hers to do with as she pleases, just like the rest of her'). Before long it came to seem to him that he had suddenly realised that the ceiling on his aspirations was not even glass, that he was suddenly through it without having noticed, an ethereal ascent by the favour of a fair lady, same as it ever was. All he had to do, he told himself, was float like the cloud he clearly was. It was all, no doubt, a matter of the air getting thinner and thinner until only the finer stuff remained. Released to write, and on manageable projects, most notably the philosophically flavoured *The Objective of Objectives*, he became in education and Party circles a name, if not to conjure with, then to put on flyers for events at which he spoke ably, fluently, even wittily.

At a Progress fringe event at NUT Conference, he lambasted as lazy and malformed the teachers of his youth, which made him catnip to Teachers' TV, on which he was careful to strike more amenable chords, while all the while making it his refrain that 'it's the children: first and last and always'. He even toyed with making The Sisters of Mercy his theme music, but a raised eyebrow from Julia was enough to put a stop to that. He came to feel how fortunate he had been to do his growing up out of the public eye, to have loosened the kinks and coils in his personality in the little boudoir of Illeshall. As Peter Middleton became more inclined to ask him to search out some toothpaste here, some socks there, he felt disappointed in him at first, and then gloried a little, along with the sadness, at the ease with which he left him behind.

As 2008 turned to 2009, and the fortunes of the Party worsened, Brian personally remained on a high. He knew as much as anyone about the drift of schools policy, was taken to lunch in 'The Adjournment' by MPs who had barely nodded to him before, came to be on first-name terms with journalists famous from the TV and bylines. Obviously, he was not taken in by all this. All that had happened was an upgrading of the frame through which he was perceived. And yet, having once admitted the insubstantiality of the element he now enjoyed, it was still hard not to fancy himself an artist of the floating world, moving skilfully among his own kind. But then would come, on evenings alone, what he came to think of as the Paranoid Hour, often several hours, when tiredness registered first as a flagging of the spirit, a sagging in the sails of his resilience, and the ostensible benignity of the day's transactions was replayed in a more sombre and even sinister light as a history of toddling optimism blithe to the slights and implications of a fully adult world, alive with wonder at his innocence and fatuity. The feeling was so familiar he resisted with ease the temptation to lift himself with alcohol, though he had long since resumed drinking, and instead looked forward to a sounder start, at least, to the day that would come after his senses had dulled and sleep crept up to do its work. Adding to his reassurance were the farts that came unbidden to him, farts that in their measured fullness, their easy efficacy, their unhurried brevity of emission and in seeming as good as without smell, rather than bespoke confections that savoured agreeably of his own special unique specialness, seemed avatars of a healthier life carried on in his body. He considered them a form of corporeal pastoral and dubbed them Tolstoyan. Occasionally he would muse how pleasant it would be to share this observation with an understanding woman, in the face of her good-natured, feminine disapproval. He would fart only a modest, appropriate amount, he decided, and only when egress was impossible.

He couldn't but be pleased with his new self. The world, he

reflected, defeated most people, who lose their dreams, believe they have few choices, accept their lot. He, however, had kept his dream, though it had all but broken and certainly battered him, as Donne had implored his god to do with his heart. He had been New-Modelled. To compare great things with small, he thought modestly, he was a little like Zarathustra descending from his mount. He was quite in earnest. As he explained to Juliet – after a teach-in at a squat in a disused pub near Leicester Square at which he had fancied the pair of them like Antony and Cleopatra consorting with their subjects in disguise – in his view, radical adulthood was to realise that you were part of the army of the saints in the consciousness that there is no such thing as saints, that you were a cadre *sous rature*, under erasure. Too much of the Left was stuck in adolescence: it was like being a mod, set apart from the rest, different and special. And the rest of the country was well aware of this, and on the whole quite averse to being ruled by people who think they're special. 'But don't get me wrong. I feel special too. I can hear the music! But that's just what tells me we need the exact opposite of dog-whistle politics, because the mainstream can hear the slightest strain of it. We're a spiritual aristocracy, an army of saints each marching in their own way to the same music, the music of that which is not unjustly called The Good Old Cause.'

'Are you taking your pills?' asked Juliet.

'Of course I am!' said Brian, a little cross. 'Just because I draw historical parallels, doesn't mean I've got a dopamine dysfunction.'

And, indeed, Brian didn't care if he had. What counted was what worked. If his world had once been enchanted with meaningfulness by Marxism and the folly of youth, only to fall into a universe of Blairite *fortuna* and *virtù* that had brought existential blight upon him, he now felt an access of power and purpose. He had found his own not inconsiderable current in the eddies around the tidal pull of global capital. Even the internet's offer of more string quartets, given that he had purchased string quartets in the past, seemed evidence of a world ever more dedicated to his personal flourishing. 'Death?' he thought, conscious he was being a little giddy. 'Oh *Death*! Death gets everywhere, it's in its nature. It's an overwhelming positivity, a hollowing negativity, a hauntingly liminal something in-between; it's anything that's on your mind. The best thing to do is ignore it and hope it gets bored.'

Swinging by the Groucho to hook up with Martin, who was trying to find a buyer for his PBS Show *Monoculture* – an attempt to appease the neoconservative lobby with talks on The Great Tradition – Brian found him in buoyant mood: 'Sky Arts are going for anything with the word "culture" in the title, my agent says. I'm thinking of doing a sister show called *Multiculti*. After all, what have I always said? One must do one's utmost, utmost; do anything, *anything* that will keep your mind alive, to avoid becoming a poet. If you do, on your own head be it. Anyway, if art for Hegel existed to become philosophy, and if in our day its purpose was to come to the attention of Fredric Jameson, now it exists as comment on the box. Anyway, what are you up to at the moment?'

'Oh, I've a host of interviews lined up for my latest pamphlet, *Achievement Today!* It eschews the ruminative for the peremptory, which has got the journos flushed. Another latte?'

'No, I seek to undergo a more intensive coffee challenge. Quadruple espresso, with a little warm milk on the side, please.'

'Anything unprofessional planned?'

'Oh, anything with anyone posh. Nothing like the States to give you a yen for posh birds with a snarky attitude. Snitty-witty posh totty. Which could be a drum fill. How about...?' Martin whispered in Brian's ear.

'Isn't she a bit out of your league?'

'Well, I don't think she's out of my league exactly. More like a really good away win. I'd be singing on the train home, that's for sure. Maybe that's how my desire is orientated: toward not quite surprising, but nonetheless notable, away wins. A bit at odds with supporting Arsenal, I suppose, who are generally expected to win wherever they play. Unless disappointment is the essence of football fandom. Anything less than Arsenal dominating the world in perpetuity is a quietly nursed disappointment. Whereas the occasional fling with someone too good for me can keep me going for years.'

'Good point.'

'Yes, a point gained rather than two dropped.'

Chapter 19
'The vast herd of independent minds'

June 2010

What a glassy little soul, thought Brian, a chamber made of mirrors, the lighting alternately flattering and harsh, with nothing to sustain it but its own will to find pleasing reflections of itself. How lonely he must be to act the way he does. What I wouldn't give to see him shattered! It was a long time since Brian had found time to read any James, and he was sure The Master would have considered him a 'brute', but he found some solace in the conviction that he would have thought worse of his interlocutor, the new Director of the Institute for Socialization. Perhaps not: 'Judge people as critics, however, and you'll condemn them all,' as Ralph Touchett remarks in *The Portrait of a Lady*. But then, Padraig O'Hara was almost nothing but critic, except when having loud telephone conversations, door open, legs on desk, with new Cabinet Ministers before emerging to remark, 'Honestly, he's *such* a low-grade entity!'

Brian had few illusions regarding the class of being to which he had been assigned by his new boss, who liked women – it was in part his reputation for appointing and advancing women that had secured him his position – and didn't like men, the only difference in his relations with them being whether this dislike manifested as fawning or derogation. Brian found himself once again pondering whether O'Hara's photograph in the atrium, the smile somehow both a parody of self-satisfaction and yet expressive of the strained desire to please of someone who believed themselves fundamentally unlikeable, was in fact a marvellous piece of self-deconstructive art. He had been appointed from the LSE and the principal implication of his conversation was that he was much cleverer than everyone else. To answer to him was a trial. 'So, you're off to stuff envelopes for David are you?'

'Well, making a few calls, that kind of thing. I'm no good with envelopes,' Brian smiled.

'Well, if you get in with him you may be of some use to us after all,' O'Hara smiled back, stomach-lurchingly.

In truth, Brian had some input on policy, especially on education, in respect of which he had argued that David should come out clearly in favour of free schools; although most of what he was doing was trying to place stories putting out the line on everything from Trident to tin whistles. On his way to John Smith House he wondered what Juliet was up to in the land of the SPADs. He wished they were special aides, not special advisors, he thought: then he would have been able to call a SPAide a SPAide. He had been a little hurt that she hadn't answered his congratulatory calls; but then, he supposed, she was right in the midst of the whirl of government.

Mind you, David's HQ was quite a whirl. Commercial backing meant lots of space in some of the most expensive real estate in London, dominated by photographs of The (New) Man, quotations from him, press about him. Rooms around which former SPADs could continue to strut. Brian had a niggling feeling that they should be paying more attention to the 'grass roots', like Ed; but then, a following among the grass roots and a claim to a big job were the limits of Ed's ambition and, after Illeshall, the choice between Westminster and some constituency office somewhere in North London was no choice at all.

In formulating the question thus, Brian was perhaps manifesting the fashion for insistent self-denigration characteristic of the new ruling class. Certainly his experience in Illeshall suggested to him that one was either a technocrat or one of the administered, and it was immeasurably better to be the former; and he reflected on how, paradoxically, his idealism had attached him to the world, whereas now he moved more easily. But he had given some days of thought to the choice between David and Ed. He had recalled Jesse Jackson on the choice between the coming moment of history and present power; his asseveration that 'I can dream beyond my predicament'. He had pondered Obama on the importance of 'moral imagination'. But there resounded in him the Blairite maxim that elections are won from the centre ground, along with Philip Gould's addendum that the centre ground is further to the right than Labourites are wont to believe. The line that the Labour Party had to choose between its head and its heart struck home. Plus his dad had been of the opinion that David seemed cleverer, and more like a leader. And he said to himself that the difference between someone like him and the enthusiastic devotee of present power was that he was forever pondering the social dynamics of his situation, the ways in which it might be evolving – were, for instance, the banks' power, and the wealth of bankers, testament to a polarisation of society which Marx had predicted, yet innumerable social thinkers had professed themselves unable to discern?

And what did a disciplined commitment to the centre mean, how did it ramify? Did it mean he had to listen to Andre Rieu? Perhaps not, since he didn't know anyone who didn't prefer Philip Glass. In that respect, at least, he was typical: in an age of change, the safest place to be. Like that advert for butter-like spread said, the middle is best! All the advantages of the extremes and none of the downsides! An age of Lacedaemonians, distrustful of zealots! How sensible – and that, surely, must be a virtue in middle age. As Sebastian said, only a fool tries to work things out from first principles, to wind up in crankiness: the swarm knows best! And that's why people tend to be apathetic about politics: they trust that they will be adequately represented by the aggregation of views, the same way as they find what they like in the supermarket. A new take on what the Middle Ages knew as 'virtual representation', the embodiment of the people in the form of the gentry in Parliament. They disliked 'Party' then as they dislike it now, when they say they want all the politicians of different stripes to get together and solve the country's problems. That, effectively, is what goes on these days in the contestation of the middle ground, the bid to inflect it, shape it, nudge it, but always address it, never to ignore it or think that we know best, except technically.

At David's HQ they were talking about Boris Johnson: many of those working for David were also working on Oona King's campaign for the Labour candidacy for Mayor of London. 'You see, not everyone can cut it. Johnson had a glittering career till he found himself in the House, having to deal with his peers. He was found out;

never mastered whatever brief was given him, never rose above junior minister. Whereas with London he can more or less exist just as a figurehead, a personality, which he's made for.' This kind of conversation was not, in truth, good for Brian. All the talk of the House, of seats, even peerages, for David's favourites, stimulated his still overactive imagination and capacity for making intellectual connections. Who among them had always mastered whatever brief came his way? Why, Brian! Could they be implying as much? Of course, he could expect no more than implication: no one addressed such things face to face, but there were people considerably less able than he being tipped for safe seats and long careers. And then, who knew? Baron Harper of... Muswell Hill?!

By the time he got home he knew he was in for a sleepless night, pacing his flat. He got through the next day, and the day after that; but around 5am on Sunday morning, he realised that he was missing the latest in a series of interviews with pop stars on Sky Arts 2 which for the last couple of nights, he retrospectively registered, he had been taking as if screened purposely for his benefit. Despite having caught himself, he almost turned the TV on. At midday he popped out to the shop, having left iTunes playing on his laptop, and found that the exit door was not working. Immediately, he thought of the security services, while registering that this was probably a mad thought. Returning to his flat, he was greeted by the sound of Dylan's 'Ballad of a Thin Man' which, he reflected, was the precise track he would have chosen if he were an operative charged with unnerving him. He phoned Michelle, who confirmed what he suspected: that he needed a higher dose of aripiprazole and some sleeping pills as soon as his GP opened the next morning. He spent the rest of the day alternately on the phone, keeping his mind on the straight and narrow of discourse, and lying down once thus constraining his mind became too much of an effort. He remarked to Matt, in one of his lighter moments, 'If I were God, I'd be perfectly sane. Everything *would* be related to me. I'd be pretty sane if I were ruler of the world, or failing that President of the US, or a world-famous film star.'

'That's a novel contribution to the psychiatric literature.'

'Or else if the world were a conspiracy; I would be at the centre of a gargantuan plot to make me do something. Like save the world. Like in a blockbuster movie. Maybe *The Bourne Experiment*, though I can never be bothered to watch it. Maybe I am, but I just don't know the ending yet.'

'You are joking, aren't you?'

'Mostly.'

'Some might say you went into professional politics because you had a God complex.'

'Pretty funny kind of God complex considering the way I went about it. A Hidden God? A *Deus Absconditus*? Perhaps A God of Small Things? The local deity of Illeshall, whose spirit resided in the Constituency Labour Party Offices? Actually, maybe that last one I can plead guilty to.'

'And now? Now you're dreaming of ermine.'

'Well naturally; I think it would suit me admirably. In fact, I think we should all be Lords and Ladies. Of Byzantium, for preference.'

'Yeats again.'

'Naturally, darling.'

'You are a one, aren't you?'

'I am *mei generis*, darling. Now, the being mad with my eyes open is hurting; I think I'll have a lie down.'

30 January 2011

The Thames was grey and swelling and showed no sign of stopping it. The others had been led off by Martin to the Renoir for a showing of a little-known late Fassbinder that Martin felt held the key to his oeuvre, *The Undemonstrative Life of Klara von Einekleine*. It was the day after their annual party to mark the anniversary of the execution of Charles I. One of the many things Brian wondered was how long they, a bunch of middle-aged woolly humanists, were going to celebrate the death of a man in the name of historical forces. Perhaps it would live on a half-life, an eroding monument to what they had been and what remained of it. After all, his commitment to (radical) centrism had recently been risking his coming adrift. He had wondered, to the others, whether the fuss over remarks on *Top Gear* about Mexican cuisine had not been overblown. Was there not in it something of the Puritan seeking out pornography in order to be offended by it? Was it not really a matter of boys being boys, and they should pay it no more mind than that? No, it had been pointed out. They had called Mexicans 'lazy and flatulent,' when they did much of the hard labour in the US, a combination to which those of Irish extraction should be particularly sensitive; and, even more pertinently, it wasn't hidden away in a corner but right at the centre of the culture, on one of the BBC's top-rated programmes. Courting the *Mail* had corroded his soul. Brian wasn't sure whether it was simple relief or vindication he felt on hearing the news that the BBC had defended the programme as an example of 'robust' British humour; and though being on the same side as the BBC seemed right as far as centrism went, being on the same side as it when it came to defending casual racism felt a bit pro-Establishment. He was philosophically disinclined to see political efficacy and integrity as incompatible: that would have been to imply they were simply opposed, external to each other. It was better to say that efficacy was challenged by integrity, integrity a brake on mere expediency and the moral life more effortful than he had ever supposed at university.

Certainly his dad would have despised what they had said on *Top Gear*, as he had despised *The Daily Mail*. But one simply could not pretend to be *serious* about politics and ignore the views expressed in the second biggest-selling newspaper in the land. He had been thinking a lot about his father. Indeed, he had been thinking a lot about everything, even more than usual. There had been a lot on his mind since he'd been sacked from his job by O'Hara in the wake of David's failure in the leadership contest, and Ed had neglected him when choosing whom to save among David's crew when it came to jobs coordinating the Policy Review, understandable though this was in terms of the politics of education. He thought of David on the Saturday night in the Midland Hotel, shoulders hunched almost to the waist, top lip flecked with blood, the work of a razor held too tight, facing music his whole being told him to shun. He thought of

O'Hara, primly smiling as he minutely adjusted, with one finger from each hand, the position of his wine glass.

Since his father had died, there had tended to be a new intensity to his mental processes. At first, he had slept all day, lightly yet persistently, images of his dad passing though his mind both waking and sleeping, images he did not know whether he was processing or dispelling. Then he slept a dream-riven, dream-burdened, dream-constrained sleep, waking only to find that the grossly over-heavy, tangled bedclothes of residual sleep pressed on his mind like a burden of snow. Then he ceased to sleep, and not only did the snow disappear, but the habitual coating of his nerves became attenuated and the world dug and grated at them.

He pondered Geoffrey Hill's 'September Song' throughout the North London derby and an Arsenal loss in Europe. He was making an elegy for himself, he mused. He recalled how, before he fell ill, his father had bought him Cormac McCarthy's *The Road* and clearly would have welcomed a discussion of it, but he had failed to find the time to read it.

Eventually, Brian had recognised within himself what it pleased him to dub 'mixed feelings' – both grief and joy, a honeyed sourness he couldn't help but relish like a dish of Chinese food. It was a comfort that he knew feeling, knew it in his body, in the strange heaviness of his legs; that he was confronted by irreducible loss and yet was consoled that he was who he was because of his parents, and had reason to hope that they knew that, and that he was glad of it. Both heavy exhaustion and light elation were his. He found himself in tears over a performance of Beethoven's Ninth in the small hours of the morning on Sky Arts; he found himself, weirdly, playing air guitar to The Who's 'Love Reign O'er Me' and 'Won't Get Fooled Again'. He fancied that he might become the kind of person who took the latter's blanket, easy scepticism as a code to live by, with its apparent mastery by default of the complexities of life and world.

Perhaps he would live as Nick Hornby man: grow feckless, obsessive, itemise his top five metaphors, or the greatest mots justes in Proust; then find himself and grow up by the mediation of an appropriately desirable woman? Presumably, however, he found himself thinking, such a creature would believe they despised Blair, and in this respect he had to recognise in himself an immunity to what produced in others something akin to an allergic reaction. Just what was it people had against Tony? Of course the Right hated him, since he kept them from power and made the country more equal and tolerant than it would otherwise have been, but why did the Left swallow so gratefully, so unthinkingly, the critique of the Right and of lazy, superficial harrumphers? (The Left even repeated the Tory line that inequality had grown under Blair, a statistical effect of the rich having grown much richer, as they had everywhere, when in truth both the worst off and the majority were better off than they had been.) Why was such nonsense invariably found wherever houmous was near?

Well, in part the answer was in that question. Most people didn't particularly hate Blair. At most, dislike for him was a function of an accumulation of particular and largely unrelated grievances, such as was inevitable in the case of a leader of such longevity, and was in any case subsumed in a general distrust of politicians per se. This was probably healthy. No, it was the middle classes, and above all the 'cultural classes', whose relation to Blair tended to be pathological. Tony personified modern Britain – more informal, more tolerant, a bit brash, a bit sincere, a bit 'American', and in part a product of the celebrity culture that had come to preoccupy the country of which he was leader, a culture despised by the 'cultural classes' in the same proportion that it broke with their value system, even as Tony's government radically increased spending on 'culture' and the number employed in its dissemination. Tony's own relation to elite culture was, Brian reflected, encapsulated in his programmatically unliterary memoir, about which he could not decide whether it held language in the grip of mummified metaphor or was admirably efficient in its recourse to readily digested images.

Ally these classes with the (often overlapping) Old Left 'political' people (i.e. those who worshipped ideological totems), and you had a politically thwarted and thus vicious, and yet culturally privileged and thus vociferous, minority. A small minority, which subjectively grasped the complexity and unmanageability of the world by means of hatred of it, and found comfort in clustering around this emotional core. They hated Tony because they hated the world he understood, and loved each other for comfort: 'Bliar', borrowed from the Right, was a cry of mob hate. And then of course there were those, mainly journalists, who would say they hated his 'sincerity', hated the way he seemed to believe what it suited him to believe (suited him, of course, as a man determined to believe the right, effective things, which is to say, more or less true things). 'Hypocrite', they called him, as the Cavaliers called Cromwell The Seeker, as the skewed call those who strive, those who are 'serious', 'earnest', *in* earnest. 'US lapdog' they said, jingoistically implying Britain should behave as a Great Power, and he said 'It's worse than that: I really believe in what we're doing'. Not that there wasn't hubris, and nemesis. Iraq provided a cause for all those who hated the way he had proven their politics failed, but could not muster a sustained assault for the very reason that he had succeeded. More damaging was the way it encapsulated, for the nation at large, the way New Labour had been not liars, but fly with the truth, convinced of their own ability to persuade. Few like to be thought too persuadable; it is too near to being a dupe.

No. It was impossible that he should join the vast herd of independent minds; those who couldn't now see that Bill Hicks was really a big fat overgrown adolescent, and that the day it had ceased to be uncool for comedians to do voiceovers was now lost in the mists of time, somewhere around the fall of the Berlin Wall. That much political judgement he possessed. But what to do? *'Il faut cultiver son jardin.'* Juliet still wasn't returning his calls. He'd put word around leftish and centrist think tanks he was looking for a new position, but no one had got back yet, not even Policy Network, for which he personally felt he was ideal. He could lodge his CV with a public affairs agency, but that really was scraping the barrel; and besides, it might queer his pitch should he decide to set about getting himself a seat.

At last Juliet called. 'What was it Stendahl used to say? That women will be your fortune because stupid old men will resent you?'

Chapter 20
'A quiet inglorious Milton'

March 2011

Brian admitted to himself at once that his head was turned by the silver Lexus. The sound system was playing cerebral drum 'n' bass at an acceptable volume, just high enough for the bass to resound, the snare to snap, the hi-hat to hiss. Nodding and swaying away on the dashboard was a miniature version of the dancing yellow flower he remembered from the *Mancunion* office of the late '80s. 'I thought we'd get right away from Westminster,' said its owner, John Quinn, and they nodded away and chatted about old vinyl until they arrived at an Italian place in Twickenham. 'I love the food here,' said Quinn, 'and it's *very reasonable*, considering.'

'Nice,' said Brian. 'Nice car, too,' he decided to profess.

'Thanks. It's a hybrid – well, you never know who *that's* going to impress... I thought about getting the... Nice glasses, by the way. Make you look like a cross between a professor and an assassin.' Brian had only noticed that his eyes had flickered away from Quinn when Quinn had changed the subject almost seamlessly, and he worried a little that an instant's private thought had been taken as a sign of lack of interest. He wasn't sure he hadn't been about to daydream of Lexuses – Lexi? – but smiled and said 'They're supposed to be correcting an eye that's halfway to lazy.'

'Oh, well I'm sure nothing about you has even got that far,' said Quinn, smiling back. 'Not that that your idiot director ever noticed, I'm sure.'

'Well, you can't expect to strike the right chord with everyone, I suppose,' said Brian, worrying that this would be exactly what Quinn was looking for.

'Absolutely not. Some people will take against you just for being personable. What can you do?' Brian signalled his assent with a sideways tilt of his head.

'The question is, do you really want to be an MP? Do you want to be on television that much? Because otherwise, I don't really see what's in it for you. Dreadful workload, awful, stupid, *tiresome* constituents, the feelings of futility as you walk in circles round the House, waiting to vote and voting and, worse, sitting in the House listening to the lesser talented of your generation. All for 65,000 quid a year? *Really?* When you have to bow and scrape to everyone from the members to the moaners of Pisshole-in-Arse-end? I *really* don't think that's *you*. The only reason for doing it, more or less, is to become a Minister; and at *your* age, even if you're lucky, even if we get in again next time, you'll be a junior minister at fifty, signing letters all night, never seeing a piece of paper that isn't for information only. By the time you're ready to be promoted we'll be out of government, or they'll say you're too old.

'Well, you know what I think. You did good work at the Institute, you've got more friends than you probably realise, plus which you are an in to the Opposition, which is how most of our ideas get aired. We're more or less a default civil service for them, aren't we, we lobbyists? Plus which we want someone leftish who knows their way around education. For us, it's a no-brainer: a directorship, and talking definitely six figures.'

'Well, naturally I'm very flattered,' said Brian, flushed, 'and everything you say makes sense. But, without wanting to seem too precious, what is the, as it were, *existential* value of what you do? I mean, do you enjoy it?'

'God, yes!' affirmed Quinn. 'I'm glad you didn't ask me what the point of it was. Then I'd have had to truck out all the obvious stuff about how there needs to be a nexus between politicians and interest groups in society, and lobbyists *are* that nexus. But enjoy it as well as see the point of it? Yes! I mean, like you, I've always been obsessed with politics, with making a difference. Like you, I toyed with academia. But academia was so impersonal, in a way. It seemed to me that any personal qualities one had apart from the ability to argue – looks, charm, friendliness, whatever – were regarded with deep suspicion, and certainly didn't get you very far. Whereas the political life, well, it's very intellectual, certainly; but it's about the *whole person*, deploying – exploiting – *all* their resources. Plus which you have the luxury of a kind of semi-detached view of the whole process: you don't have to answer questions in the House, the press aren't judging your performance, your life isn't in the balance. There's always another day. In a way, it's power without responsibility.'

'It's very tempting,' admitted Brian.

'It's a no-brainer. And if, like me, you feel the need to do a bit of charity work, then you can run for the Council.'

And so Brian set about promoting, in Labour ranks, the extension of private universities. With his new salary he was able to afford a nice flat with a view across London to the South Downs, on a clear day. 'I think I've recently developed a taste for the luxury I could have had,' he thought to himself, relishing his first properly solid and crafted – though impeccably modern – furniture.

Perhaps the most noted feature of the new flat, pointed out as it invariably was to first-time visitors, was a pair of flowers set upon the mantelpiece. Brian would invariably quote Wilde, roughly accurately: 'If I had the choice, I should be something utterly beautiful and entirely without soul, like a flower.' On the one hand, there would bop, a token that their younger selves persisted yet, the yellow, smiling sunflower, briefly turned on to jiggle mindlessly; on the other, the persistent peace lily, blind patient life occasionally emanatory of elegance in the form of white blooms. And Brian? Brian, writing anonymous barbs for a Labour website, smiles to think of himself as a quiet inglorious Milton. We might think with George Eliot of his 'unhistoric acts'; with Wordsworth of 'his little nameless, unremembered acts'; with Milton that 'They also serve who only stand and wait'.

Chapter 21
'The futility of all human endeavour, especially his'

November 2015

Brian trudged toward his front door with a head in which foreboding, aggravation and suspicion, along with a sense of the futility of all human endeavour, especially his, contended sluggishly for pre-eminence. For a considerable portion of one evening he had been excited by the unexpected, if vague, offer with which he had been presented – a very large salary from an as yet unnamed Russian businessman, in exchange for coordinating and, most importantly, calibrating, said businessman's efforts to foster, carefully, the rudiments of a civic and even weakly liberal culture in his homeland: 'Brian, let me tell you this,' had said the intermediary. 'Brian, I know you think your mastery is politics. But I think... I think your mastery... may be... mastery. Some people? They think their mastery is politics, but their mastery is actually whatever they put their mind to. Think about it, Brian!'

Bollocks of course, but even so he had been flattered by the approach, rather odd and probably not inconsiderably dangerous though it was. Not something everyone in his position would have leapt at – there must have been others who had been asked and had refused – but intriguing and no job for a fool. Unless that was exactly what it was.

Not the least of the attractions was a chance to get away from a Labour Party that was apparently in the process of righteously self-immolating. In the view of the appallingly innocent young, and fractionally informed and grossly indignant older malcontents, the country had elected a right-wing government because the alternative had not been sufficiently left wing, and the answer was to hand the party over to Marxist-Leninists. Evidence and logic suggested very, very strongly that this was a course verging on the suicidal, but desire had comprehensively trumped reality, and any attempt at rational discussion was met with an insistence that #JezWeCan, even though they really, really fucking couldn't and never would.

No sooner had the idea of getting away from this morass of self-righteous, irrational and ignorant nonsense fully formed in Brian's mind, however, than he seemed suddenly to be plagued by chance encounters with such loons. Sophie had started seeing one of the less prominent of the child journalists who had lately been sullying the reputations of broadsheet newspapers now more concerned to 'resonate' with demographics than to provide informed and adult analysis and comment. Brian had been able to cope with this for a couple of hours, choosing to reflect with wonder as production of discursive effluent soared.

But then he had bumped into Sebastian quite by chance in a pop-up bar somewhere on Dalston High Road, to find not only that Sebastian was quite caught up in this political pop-up – this was rather satisfying, in a grim and disgusted way – but that his German gallery-owning acquaintance, Bruno, was remarkably aggressive about his avowed pacifism. Brian had been asked what he made of the Corbyn phenomenon: 'It's totally absurd. They've gifted the country to the Tories for the next fifteen years.'

'But the Labour membership has more than doubled in size!' exclaimed the German.

'Yes. But a couple of hundred thousand nutters won't hold much sway in an electorate of 45 million. It just goes to show: a little knowledge is a dangerous thing.'

'So you think we should just choose the lesser evil?'

'Well, I wouldn't describe the Labour Party as evil.'

'But under Blair, and Brown...'

'We had a government that was more redistributive than Attlee's, that doubled spending on education, trebled it on health.'

'But Blair was a warmonger: all those wars!!'

'What? Sierra Leone? Bosnia?'

'Ah. But the attack on Serbia was just geopolitics. Restrict Russian influence.'

'Well it certainly wasn't *just* about geopolitics–'

'Yes it was.'

'No, even if there *were* geopolitical considerations, it wasn't just about them–'

'Yes it was.'

Brian didn't want to be talking about this while he was eating, and certainly not in this manner with someone he'd barely met. Fucking cultural-class ignorantly assured groupthink about politics.

'If you talk over me again, to say Bosnia was just about geopolitics, I'm going to hit you.'

Brian relished observing Bruno adjust his discursive expectations, and protest: 'I'm not being talked to like this! I'm not staying here!'

'Well I'm sorry, *Jurgen Habermas,* but I find superciliousness and plain bloody rudeness just as much a violation of the ideal speech situation as a good plain punch in the snout. Especially when I'm having my flaming dinner. So: I am in complete agreement with you. I think you should go. Now.'

Satisfying for a while. But that was the second incident in as many days, and once he had got on the Tube he had started to wonder: was he somehow being nudged into accepting the Russian offer as a means of getting away from this kind of nonsense? For the most part, Brian now regarded such intimations as due to something like scar tissue remaining from his episodes of acute psychosis: having developed a propensity for such a mental dynamic, a kind of emotional 'muscle memory' meant that sometimes paranoia came as something like a reflex. Mostly he could avoid taking such spasms too seriously. Even so, as he fished out his keys and unlocked his door he decided he should try to lie low and minimise human interaction for a few days, lest over-interpretation begin again to take hold.

He shucked off his coat, walked through to the kitchen, and froze. For a short while his visual field, too, fixed still as though he were a digital camera taking a snap. It was definitely Rafferty. Cropped, dark hair but definitely, definitely Rafferty. Was *she* involved in this Russia thing? Was the Russia thing part of something larger? She wasn't *dressed* as though she were part of a high-level conspiracy. Even medium-level. Medium-level *anything*. She reminded him, if anything, of *Swampy*. But better-looking.

'What the fuck is this? *L'Avventura 2? The Unexplained Reappearance?*' The glare from this flash of wit kept from view whatever was happening to him emotionally.

'Ha! Watching that was why I left! They look for her for a bit then they just get on with their lives! Ha!'

Brian's stomach relaxed a little, and he reached for a chair, at first only managing to push it away before getting a grip and sitting down.

'Where the bloody hell have you been?'

'Away.'

'You don't say.'

Brian puffed out and tried to get a handle on his thoughts, but he hadn't quite located any before Rafferty spoke again.

'I dropped out.'

Brian waited.

'I was sick of it all, sick of it. But I didn't really realise until I got ill.'

'Sick of it?'

'Of *everything*. Sebastian, the children, stupid fucking journalism, North London, *everyone and everything I knew.*'

'A comprehensive assessment, then.'

'Oh, and sick of myself too, of course. Though I may have realised that last. Can't really remember now. Not that it matters.'

'So where did you go? Where have you been? Did you know I went mad?'

'No! Because of me?!'

'Well, no, not quite. Because of *everything*. It seemed like everyone was dying, and I couldn't see what to live for, and then I got ill and kind of exaggerated everything...'

'You better now?'

'Mostly. I'm not as good as new.'

'Who is?'

'True.'

'So what do you live for now?'

'It's better than the alternative. Small pleasures.'

'Not as good as having a *purpose* though, is it?'

'Probably not. I mean, I'm not *entirely* pointless you know.'

Rafferty gave a brief, loud cackle, head back.

'I'm sure there are people who can think of a thing or two to do with you. Put you to good use.'

Brian started. Had his suspicions been founded? 'What do you mean?'

'Oh, nothing serious. Breeding. A man about the house. That sort of thing.'

Brian relaxed. Then Rafferty spoke again. 'Actually, *I* can think of a thing or two to do with you.'

Brian looked at her interrogatively. 'That's what I'm doing here,' she continued.

'Oh yes?'

'Well, for a start, I've missed you.' Emotional disclosure on a need-to-know basis.

'I've missed you too... You haven't told me where you were.'

'Well I was here and there. Lying low. Among renegades. The details would be dull. More to the point is where I've ended up.'

'Oh yes?'

'Yes. I've been engaged in politics. Kinda underground politics. I mean, I got so sick of the whole London political scene. Metropolitan liberals make me sick. On the whole, I mean. Rank egotists. The kind of people who think that, because they *think* the right things, they don't have to actually *do* anything about it. I mean, they'll go to meetings and *say* the right things; they'll manoeuvre themselves into positions of authority in which they *stand* for the right things. But are they good-hearted? Do they chip in for the sake of it? Do they actually get their finger out and *help* someone because they need help? No! They think they've got that covered because their *politics* say the *government* – i.e. *someone else* – should be doing the right thing. So they stand in the right in their ordered mental universe. They've, as it were, *legislated*. Ooh! I'll get myself worked up if I don't watch out.'

'I know what you mean. London is just chock-full of fucking egotists. Everyone's engaged in their own little Sartrean project, and that's all they really care about. That and their children. They're *consumed* by their children, because their children think they're wonderful, while nobody else thinks they're wonderful at all.'

'Ha! Sartrean projects. Speaking of which, I'm kind of formulating a project which might involve you...'

Once again, Brian gave Rafferty a questioning look. 'Oh yes?'

'Well... you know about the upturn?'

'The what?'

'The *upturn*. In the fortunes of the Left. You know, what comes around every now and again depending on economic conditions, etcetera?'

'Oh the *upturn*. Well, I've noticed Corbyn.'

'You're not enthused, then?'

'Well, not really! You know I kind of like having Labour governments, disappointing though they inevitably are. Apart from anything else, it sorts the sheep out from the goats. You know what my dad used to say.'

'Yes. But we need an opposition that will oppose.'

'We can't look like a protest movement; we have to look like an alternative government.'

'But we weren't opposing austerity!'

'Our programme was three times less cuts than theirs.'

'But it's the principle.'

'No! You have to gain a place in the conversation. You have to say something people will listen to. It's no use piling up extra votes in our own areas, like every other Social Democratic party in Europe. You need to show you're addressing voters' concerns if you're going to get into government, and getting into government, doing real things people can see, succeeding, is the only way to convince them we know what we're doing. Not taking a long march into the wilderness.'

'But what about inequality? We let inequality rise!'

'Only because the wages of people like footballers and bankers got so high. That skewed the sums. In real terms, every decile – *every* decile, even the poorest – got better off. Blair didn't just double spending on education and treble it on health, he was *more redistributive than Attlee*.'

'But what about Iraq?'

'Iraq was a mess. But that was the bloody neocons. The State

Department had a document planning for the stabilisation of Iraq that was 10,000 pages long. But the neocons, who thought democracy and free markets would spontaneously emerge, threw it out of the window. And what about the consequences of *not* intervening in Syria? Far, far worse.'

'A majority of the public agree with nationalising the railways.'

'But *that's* not a red dividing line between Corbyn and everyone else! Besides, the popularity of individual policies can be misleading. It ignores the signals they send. Bringing back hanging would be popular, but if the Tories put it in their manifesto, the signal it would send would be disastrous.'

'It's all calculation with you, isn't it? What about being "a force for change in the world, a force for humanity in the world"?'

'Corbyn's speech? But that could have been Blair, or any Labour leader! But without being clever about what you're doing, you don't get to do anything at all. I've thought for years that really you're not very political. You're more a moralist, or even religious. What you call socialism is just a doctrinaire anti-worldism that gives you a position from which to denounce anything at all you don't like, from daytime TV to Dalston, and you're prepared to sacrifice everything a Labour government can do in the name of Rafferty's Righteousness... You're like the zealots who thought the Church of England was popish and fucked off to America!'

'How could you imagine I'd be enthused by Corbyn? *Jeremy fucking Corbyn!* Have you not noticed anything I've said or done this last quarter-century?'

Rafferty said nothing. Brian softened his tone. 'The essence of thinking politically is having the humility and imagination to understand how most of those you wish to persuade think and feel about things, and to produce policy and present it in a way which doesn't just make a kind of theoretical sense to you, with what you think is your enlarged and better informed perspective, but chimes with their fundamental convictions. Anything else is just proselytising in the wilderness among a small minority of purists.

'Politics aren't about approximating or incarnating an ideal of reason. It's something like turning an agglomeration of human animals into, maybe, a conglomeration. Human animals, with all their flaws and some of their virtues, open to a limited extent to being ameliorated by the force of the better argument. It's entirely pathological to take a set of working norms about, broadly, fairness and, far more than clarify or extrapolate from them, rather to refine and abstract them until they're unearthly ideals, descending from which you can then find everything wanting, and proceed to blame it on a hypostatisation like "capitalism".

'I read someone the other day saying the blame for fat people feeling bad about themselves lay with "capitalism". No it fucking doesn't! It lies with people and their propensities, with fashion, with status, whatever. All of which existed before capitalism. Sure, capitalism picks up on human nature, probably magnifies it. You can even say seizes on it with entirely amoral – *a*moral – delight. Sure, you need to mitigate and properly regulate it. But capitalism is as likely as not to invent something that makes everybody thin. And then keep rolling along.

'Anyway, I've got better things to do than preach to the unconvertible.' Brian felt both the easing of a burden and a presentiment of loss.

'Coo. That was emphatic!'

'I've been brooding about these things for a while.'

'You've always been a brooder, haven't you? You could still come with me and be a brooder.'

'Come with you where?'

'Manchester, of course. Maybe lovely Chorlton.'

'Ugh. I should think it's a Corbynista stronghold. Loads of people who like to hear their own voice being radical in meetings, and have no real need of a Labour government.'

'It might be good for you. Keep out of arguments. Just agree that the Tories are scum.'

'Hmm. So: I can have a life in which the appropriate use of hessian features prominently, both as matter for earnest contemplation and as occasion for ethical one-upmanship, or I can hang out in Moscow and gorge myself on legions of soft-as-satin women with minds as hard and sharp as the diamonds they accumulate. Well, either would be a change.'

'Ah! The days when slinky women wore skimpy dresses with nothing underneath, and got royally filled with champagne, cocaine and cock!... you *are* after a change, then?'

'Well, I'm pretty sick of my present world. The stupid grabbing for status, which ends up infecting you because, you know, *that's* the only game around. I need a spot of transcendence. Or at least a new holiday destination.'

'I just needed *out*. Everyone around me seemed a model of enlightened self-interest, everything seemed so predictable it was as though only something horrific could derail things, until I almost longed for something horrific. And then something horrific, or at least moderately horrific, did happen.'

'What about the kids?'

'Oh God, they *weren't* reasonable, of course, and that bored me shitless! Which made me feel grotesque, of course. I mean, it wasn't as though I had no maternal feelings at all, or as if I never delighted in their childish ways. Just not enough. And nowhere near as much as Sebastian did. Quite possibly better off without me, I thought. So off I went.'

'A revolutionary rupture, rather than incremental reform.'

'Ha, yes! That's why I've come for you. I need a source of self-thwarting hyper-cerebrality in my life.'

'I'm not sure that's me. It took me a decade to decide what I thought about *South Park*. Part of the appeal of this Russia thing is I suspect it calls for despairing bravery rather than cunning. And it's something I can get roused about. It would put some wind in my sails. A halfway properly organised political or civic culture is a fairly boring thing, mostly logrolling and compromise between social forces and interest groups. Which is just how it should be, mostly. But it's not very noble or heroic. Not *romantic*.'

'Oh, you're all mouthful of trousers. You wouldn't like those Slavic ice queens! You wouldn't even be breakfast for them. Come to Chorlton. Bonhomie and sodomy. I'll get you a minion. "Come live with me and be my mate/We can sleep all day and stay up late/I'll fix you up with a radical sweetie/And I can't think of a rhyme, except

'Treaty'"... *or:* "We could be each other's toad/To help our way down cemetery road."'

'Very enticing.'

'*Or:* "Let's go find an obscure hovel/And one of us can write a novel."'

'I regard most novels as acts of gross moral turpitude.'

'Quite right! We'll do one that isn't! Just contains a load of such acts.'

'Charterhouse of Parma!'

'Yes! Let's both just fuck off to the Charterhouse! It's all we're good for.'

New Thanks

Huge thanks to all those who helped me in the writing of this book, especially the following (nothing of any political or, indeed, any other kind of significance should be inferred from my gratitude): Vera Baird, Tim Bewes, Matthew Downie, Cressida Downing, Ade Jackson, David Llewellyn (Lew), Tom Sheahan, Charles Wright.

Patrons

Stacey Alexander
Jake Allen
Emily Almond
David Bald
Elisabeth Beckerle
Megan Bell
Alexandra Belzley
Nick Belzley
Robert Bennet
Charlotte Bennett
John Benson
Susann Bladwell
Cha Boi
John Bonham
Esther Boyer
Chris Brooms
Amelia Brown
Sofia Brown
Edward Bryans
Victoria Bukina
Hamilton Burroughs
Benjamin Carter
Lily Chapman
Duncan Chapple
Suwen Chen
Nick Churras
John Conley
Eleanor Cooper
Nick Cooper
Jackson Cummings
Stephen Dawson
Stephen Diller

Greg Disario
John Don
Nick Drake
Ian Dudley
Richard East
Mathilda Evans
Katie Fortney
Tim Gallagher
Bob Garland
Lucas Goes
Justus Gräf
Joseph Green
Jack Griffin
Jackson Griffin
Olly Gruner
Ethan Holmes
Hillary Holmes
Nick Hunt
Joseph Hunter
John Husband
Ben Hutchinson
Ade Jackson
Chandler Johnson
Nathan Jones
Jackson Juman
John Kiston
Samuel Knight
Claire Kober
Daniel Labell
Arthur Lewis
Thomas Lewis
Ines Litke
Sven Litke
Amalia Lloyd
Stephen Loudermilk
Vladimir Makarov

Efrem Mallach
Emma Meyer
George Miller
Rosie Miller
Stephen Miller
Josh Mitchell
Diego Montoyer
Amanda Moore
Collin Moore
David Moore
Craig Morgan
Logan Murray
Annelieke Nagel
Carlo Navato
John Nichols
Ashley Norris
Benjamin Oliver
Lee Oswold
George Palmer
Elisabeth Parker
Oscar Perez
John Plant
Roger Pooley
Steven Potter
Sam Price
Drake Ramoray
Charlotte Ravean
Joad Raymond
Charlotte Redmon
Adam Reed
Olivia Reid
Richard Reed
Ruth Reid
Grace Richardson
Peter Rickarby
James Robertson

Edward Ross
Margaret Ross
William Russell
Robin Sachsenröder
Oliver Saunders
Paul Schofield
Leon Schultze
Samarth Shekhar
Nicholas Sherwood
Nick Sherwood
Gavin Sibthorpe
Emma Steele
Donna Stein
Duncan Stewart
John Stinson
Lily Stinson
Matt Streuber
Lewis Tanner
David Taylor
Caroline Thompson
Mia Thompson
Adam Turner
Anne Turner
Grace Turner
Joseph Turner
Robert Turner
Oliver Twist
Oliver van Ophoven
Anne Walker
Keith Walker
Diane Walsh
Joseph Walsh
Tyler Walsh
Zoe Walsh
Duncan Weldon
Andrew Western

Margreth White
Michele Wilkerson
Cath Winston
James Wolley
Charlie Wood
Drake Wood
Jack Wood
Jacob Wood
Margaret Wood
Megan Wood